I0575760

BURN RATE

KIM SERRANO

S+S

SWITCH + STERN

Burn Rate

© 2025 Kim Serrano

First edition, published May 2025

Published by Switch + Stern

switchandstern.com

All rights reserved. No part of this book may be reproduced, stored in a retrieval system, or transmitted in any form or by any means—electronic, mechanical, photocopying, recording, or otherwise—without prior written permission of the publisher, except for brief quotations used in reviews or scholarly works.

This is a work of fiction. Names, characters, businesses, organizations, places, events, and incidents are either the product of the author's imagination or used fictitiously. Any resemblance to actual persons, living or dead, is entirely coincidental.

Cover design by Kim Serrano

ISBN: 979-8-9997264-1-4

Printed in the United States of America

CONTENT WARNING

This novel contains depictions of explicit sexual content and strong language. Reader discretion is advised.

1

Morgan had logged over a million miles in the air. She'd made peace with every common jetliner in the fleet. But this one? The CRJ-700. She hated this thing.

A regional jet with seats too narrow, overhead bins that mocked tall passengers, and a nose that rattled her skull on final descent. The CRJ's short wingspan made it hypersensitive to turbulence—just unstable enough in crosswinds to make every landing feel like a dice roll.

It was the only aircraft that ever made her slightly motion sick. But only on landings. And only when the wind played dirty.

Which was why what had just happened shouldn't have been possible.

She knew the route. She knew the weather—gusty headwinds from the north, just strong enough to throw most regional pilots off their axis. But this descent? It was poetry.

The flare was textbook. The alignment was surgical.

The touchdown— It wasn't a touchdown.

It was a benediction.

That floating sensation right before the wheels kissed the ground. It lingered like a prayer. A brief, impossible pause between flight and arrival. The pilot hadn't just managed the ground effect—they'd embraced it, letting the lift cradle the jet like it had permission to linger.

Precision. Finesse. Deep, embodied control.

No. This landing—it unspooled her.

The second the wheels met the tarmac—no, kissed it— something in her chest gave way. Like a ribbon loosening from the inside out.

Her body knew before her brain did. It lifted— suspended in that hush between sky and earth, held tenderly by nothing but skill and air. Something quiet and animal in her recognized it: the feel of being fully handled, but never forced. Not taken—guided. Not rushed—claimed. The kind of control that asked permission. She didn't know what it was yet. Only that it made something old and sharp inside her go quiet.

The plane didn't thud or jerk. It just arrived. Like it had always known where to land. Like it had always known the way.

Her fingers curled around the armrest—not in fear, but reverence.

Whoever flew this bird...

She wanted to shake their hand. Or write them a love letter. Or just ask—how? Who taught you how to bring something this heavy down so softly?.

She shifted in her seat remembering she had seen the pilot. She was late—last-minute security delay. She'd barely made it to Row Eight before the doors hissed shut. The flight attendant had waved her through, annoyed but resigned. And then—

Right before the latch locked—she glanced forward.

And saw the arm.

One hand resting on the center-mounted control stick. Lightly freckled skin, marked with a full sleeve tattoo—not trendy, not abstract. Old-school ink. Coils of flight lines, faded compass roses, storm clouds, wings. It moved when he moved. And he had that unmistakable posture of long-haul captains: relaxed but alert, spine straight, neck loose. Like he could land this thing in a thunderstorm with a blindfold and one hand tied behind his back.

And then—as if he felt her stare—

He turned. He was older than she expected. Not grizzled —refined.

Dark auburn hair, silver threading through at the temples. A clean-shaven jaw, laugh lines etched deep— earned, not inherited.

Hazel eyes, amber at the edges. The kind that turn gold in cockpit sunlight. Kind. Intense. Vulnerable—if you knew where to look.

He looked...private. Like a man who'd spent too long at thirty-five-thousand feet and had learned to prefer silence over small talk.

Then his gaze caught hers.

And for a breathless second, she swore she heard it—a warning.

That yes, he was the kind of man who'd walk your grandma to church without missing a Sunday...and then ruin you in the back of a pickup after Mass.

The door clicked shut between them.

The world lurched into motion.

And then—much later—he landed her.

～

SHE WAS STILL THINKING about it when she realized she'd left her work tablet in the seatback pocket.

A cardinal sin. She could already feel her deputy's judgment radiating from four hundred miles away.

She stood, smoothing the sharp crease of her black trousers—tailored, always.

She made a beeline from Arrivals to Heritage's navy-blue check-in counters, hoping to arrange a return to the gate.

The station manager spotted her immediately and took care of it. Now, nodding into the phone, the manager hung up and reassured her: someone was already on their way to hand it over.

She looked up at the sound of footsteps.

And then—him.

No blazer. No hat. Just a well-worn zip hoodie, dark gray, unzipped halfway down his chest. His pilot shirt was still visible underneath, collar slightly rumpled, tie nowhere in sight. The kind of low-effort, high-competence look that made her want to reevaluate every man she'd ever dated.

A pilot bag hung over one shoulder, slung like an afterthought. Then he saw her. His head tilted slightly, eyes narrowing as he registered her.

Before she could stop herself— "You were the forearm." Dear God. No. The words were out, floating between them like a blooper reel.

He raised one dark eyebrow. "Was I?"

She flushed. "No—I mean—yes. In the cockpit. I saw the sleeve. Your tattoo. From my seat. Row Eight. You had a... grip."

His mouth twitched.

Not quite a smirk. Not yet. Just the ghost of amusement. "I see."

She exhaled, mortified. "I didn't mean it in a weird way. It's just—you landed so smooth. Like offensively smooth. For a CRJ, that's rare."

That finally got him.

He smiled. A real one—small, crooked, warm. It curled up gently, like he wasn't used to smiling but still remembered how. "Well." He extended his tattooed arm, offering a small black case. Her tablet—of course.

"Glad I could be of service, from the elbow down," he said dryly.

She wished she could rewind time—back to the second she'd leaned into the aisle for a better look at him before takeoff. That was it. That might have been the point of no return.

"Thanks," she murmured, eyes dropping to the floor.

He nodded and handed it to her so calmly—like he hadn't just surgically landed a flying tin can in crosswinds like it was a luxury glider. Like he wasn't standing there in a hoodie that should not be allowed to fit that well.

"You really didn't have to play errand boy."

He shrugged. "The gate attendant who was gonna bring it down had to clock out early—family emergency."

A pause. Then, like it was nothing: "I was headed this way anyway."

"Of course," she said. They both turned, awkward in that way only strangers with too much unspoken tension can be.

"Good night, Gina," she called over her shoulder.

"Night, Morgan," the station manager replied brightly.

"See you bright and early tomorrow?"

"Yep. Crack of dawn." The pilot gave Gina a nod too. "Take care."

"Will do," Gina said, far too amused. Her gaze bounced between them, unmistakably twinkling.

Morgan felt her face heat. He did not help by doing absolutely nothing. Just walking beside her at a perfectly measured pace across the terminal that seemed larger than before. Silence. Footsteps. More silence.

Then—

"I'm not following you," he said. Morgan blinked, mid-step. He gestured toward the sliding doors ahead. "My truck's in the garage past the shuttle stop. I'm not—we're just headed the same way."

She bit back a laugh.

"You're clarifying that like a man who's been accused before." He gave a small shrug. "I've learned to narrate my movements."

They kept walking. The sliding doors hissed open, releasing them into the night. Cool breeze. The sharp tang of jet fuel. Overwatered landscaping. At the curb, the hotel shuttle waited—lights on, engine low and steady.

Her room was booked. She was supposed to raid the vending machine and pass out with a backlog of emails and a single keycard.

But instead—

She turned to him. Still in that hoodie. Still infuriatingly competent. One foot already on the crosswalk.

"You know," she said slowly, pulse kicking up, "if you followed me right now, I wouldn't stop you."

He paused. The curb hummed beneath them.

"I've got a room. Sleep tank. Just overnight. I'm here till morning." She looked at him. "That's not an invitation if you don't want it. But if you do—yeah. I mean it."

Something passed behind his eyes then. Something cooler. Older. Like he knew the exact weight of a moment like this. Not surprise. Just the quiet recognition of a door opening without a sound. She held her breath. Don't retract.

Don't soften it. Just stand in it. The hotel shuttle engine stuttered. He took his time answering. She wasn't used to this kind of silence after making a move. She knew she was hot —objectively, unapologetically. When she invited, men said yes. Always. But now, standing at the curb while he parsed her offer, she felt something rare flicker in her chest— uncertainty.

Then: "I hadn't planned—"

"Oh," she said quickly, mortified. "I'm so sorry, I misread—"

He tilted his head slightly, and she stopped. Realized he wasn't done. "—but plans can change," he finished.

Her pulse stuttered.

His voice was soft. Measured. Like re-routing a flight path. *There's weather over the Rockies—we'll adjust accordingly.* He looked at her. At her. Not through, not past. Then down at the case in her hand. "You gonna need that tonight?" She blinked, thrown.

"What—my tablet?"

"Yeah." A twitch at the corner of his mouth. "Or are you offline until morning?"

Her mouth went dry.

"I can be offline," she said. He nodded once. Unhurried. Like he'd already done the math and found it viable.

"Alright then," he said. "Lead the way."

2

The shuttle ride was awkward. Not tense, exactly. Just...unspoken. Two adults sitting side by side, pretending not to think about what they'd just agreed to.

He stared out the window. She stared at her phone. Neither said much.

At the hotel, he lingered near the front desk while she checked in, hands tucked into his hoodie pocket, gaze fixed on the lobby carpet like it had secrets to tell.

When the clerk asked, "How many keys?" she hesitated.

Then: "Two, please."

She felt the blush rise before she could stop it. Didn't look over to see if he noticed.

In the elevator, they stood side by side again. Close, but not touching.

The soft, tinny notes of the Carpenters filled the small space.

"Why do birds suddenly appear..."

She almost laughed.

And then—softly, without warning—he hummed along.

It was nothing. Just a few quiet bars, perfectly in tune. But it cracked something. His serious facade, all that calm precision—gone for a second. And there it was again, the flutter in her chest she couldn't shake.

Morgan shut the hotel room door behind him with a quiet click. They didn't speak. For a moment, they stood frozen, the space between them wide and strange. The room was quiet, dim, washed in the glow of the blue runway lights outside the window. It had a perfect view—planes idling, lifting, landing in slow motion, everything silver and navy against the night. Pretty, in a sterile kind of way.

He looked around like he was trying to catalog the furniture. She crossed her arms and stared at the wall behind him.

This was the part no one warned you about—the moment after yes, when you were still two people with clothes on, not quite ready to undo the hours of adrenaline and decision-making that had led here.

He offered to shower first. She nodded, grateful.

The door shut behind him and she exhaled like she'd been holding her breath since takeoff.

She sat on the edge of the bed and stared at her reflection in the dark TV screen, still trying to get her face to relax.

When he came out, towel around his waist, she nodded again and grabbed her things.

The shower was too hot. Her pulse thudded in her throat even as she tried to slow it down under the spray.

By the time she came back into the room, her face was calm again. Her stomach was not.

He was in his boxers, sitting at the edge of the bed now,

sipping a ginger ale he'd found in the mini fridge. The lamplight didn't do him justice, but it tried. The clean, lean lines of his body were the kind that didn't come from vanity —just years of moving with purpose. Muscle where it counted. Definition that didn't ask for attention but held it anyway. His posture was straight, strong, almost annoyingly confident. Both arms were sleeved in ink—full coverage from biceps to wrists. Not flashy. Not for show. Old school linework and bold color, worn-in like everything else about him.

Morgan let her eyes trace the shapes without letting her expression give her away.

The tattoos sharpened the impression that he had lived more life than he let on. His skin was ruddy, freckled in patches.

His hair—dark, with silver threading through the sides —looked like it had been tugged at one too many times today.

He wasn't particularly hairy, which felt like its own quiet surprise. Just heat and muscle and ink, sitting quietly in a hotel room like it was the most natural thing in the world. He was the kind of pretty that crept up on you—sharp lines, a soft mouth, and a face that made no damn sense all together.

She caught his eye and moved to the small table. She set down the condoms, deliberate. No commentary. Just logistics.

He nodded, didn't say a word. His gaze held steady.

"I've been tested," she said. Her voice came out steady. "You?"

He nodded once. "Yeah."

She cracked open the tiny hotel whiskey bottle, tossed it back, then chased it with a Diet Coke. It burned just enough. She offered another whiskey bottle to him without meeting his eye.

"I'm good," he said, same even tone.

Now they were here. Prepped. Responsible. Half-naked.

She sat next to him on the bed in a black La Perla slip—minimal, deliberate. She didn't speak. Neither did he.

The room felt too still, like even the air was holding its breath. They watched the runway. The last flight of the evening revved, barreled forward, lifted into the dark. She let herself exhale.

She hated this part. The stilted, silent calculus of two adults pretending they weren't strangers. But she wasn't afraid. Not of him. Not of what would come next.

She felt the shift before she saw it—him moving toward her. And then his hand was under her chin, gentle, warm. She looked up just in time to meet his eyes.

He kissed her. Not rushed. Not claiming. Just a long, unhurried kiss—like he was making sure she had time to change her mind.

She pulled him into bed and on top of her, fingers curled tight on the back of his neck like she couldn't stand the distance one more second. He landed solid against her, warm and broad, and kissed her like he meant to memorize the shape of her mouth.

It didn't stop. It went on and on—slow, open-mouthed, aching kisses. Every time she tried to deepen it, he pulled back just enough to make her chase him.

He wasn't rushing anything. He was drawing it out like he had nowhere else to be. Like he was savoring her. Like he was trying to be gentle. It made her dizzy. It also made her want to scream.

She broke from the kiss just enough to ask, a little

breathless, a little annoyed, "You always this polite when you fuck someone?"

His head turned slowly. Eyes sweeping over her face like she was a problem he'd already solved. Calm. Unimpressed. Not a single flicker of surprise.

It hit her harder than any touch. Quiet, exacting. Like he was waiting for her to check herself. He didn't say a word. Just stared her down, steady and patient.

It pissed her off. It also made her thighs clench. And there it was. That spark at the center of her. Low and hot and hungry.

Morgan barely had time to breathe before he shifted—just a slight move, deliberate, unapologetic. His hips slid between her thighs like it was always meant to happen this way. There was no rush. No hesitation. Just the quiet certainty of a man who didn't need to posture.

She felt him—hard, thick, and pressing right where she was already aching. Her body answered before her mind caught up, thighs tightening around his sides. The contact was maddening. Not enough. Nowhere near enough. But it promised everything.

He leaned in close as he spoke—low, quiet, a command dressed as a dare.

"If you're going to act out," he murmured, voice edged with amusement and warning, "make it worth my time."

Before she could come up with something sharp enough to answer, his hand closed around her wrists. Firm. Unyielding. Not cruel. Just final. He raised them above her head and pinned them there with a single hand like it was nothing, like he had all night.

His other hand didn't move. His hips didn't grind. He didn't need to. That stillness was the show. He wasn't trying to impress her.

His mouth brushed the shell of her ear, voice low enough it barely counted as sound.

"This what you want?"

She nodded, breath caught in her throat. He didn't move.

"Use your words."

"Yes," she said, the word slipping out more raw than she'd intended.

That was all it took. He pressed into her, the full length of him dragging against the slick heat between her legs, the silk slip a useless barrier. She gasped, hips twitching up, but he didn't let her set the rhythm.

He stripped her. Fingers at the hem of her slip, he didn't rush. He peeled it up her body inch by inch, his eyes locked on hers like the real reveal wasn't her skin—it was her reaction. Control shifted with every inch exposed. She tried not to squirm. Tried not to give him the satisfaction. Failed.

The slip cleared her head and he tossed it aside. His gaze dropped. Heat flared—undeniable, hungry. Then he exhaled, barely, like the sight of her knocked something loose in him. But it passed in a blink. That self-control snapped back into place like it never left.

She broke from his grasp and reached for the waistband of his boxers. He caught her wrist mid-motion.

"Hands stay where I put them."

It wasn't a suggestion. It was law. And he meant every word.

Her brain was static. Thoughts fractured, scattered. There was no plan now, no strategy—just heat, just need, just the way her body kept tightening under his. He moved like he knew every inch of her already, like he'd memorized her without needing to ask.

His hand came to her throat—not squeezing. Just there.

Holding. Claiming. Grounding her like she might fly apart if he didn't anchor her. She moaned without meaning to.

He didn't say much. He didn't need to. Every word he'd chosen so far landed like a command. Clean. Precise. No softness. No over-explaining. Just enough to make her want more.

His mouth found the spot just under her jaw that made her legs shake. Teeth dragging. Tongue chasing the sting. Her hips arched—he didn't react. He was too busy. Sinking lower. Sucking bruises into her skin. Biting the swell of her breast, licking over the hurt, then doing it again.

By the time his mouth closed around her nipple, she couldn't think. Couldn't breathe. Just sounds.

Then he was gone from her chest, moving down, spreading her open like it was his right. And then—

Then he tasted her.

And there was no thought left at all.

Every nerve was lit. Every breath came out like a moan she couldn't swallow. Her hips moved without permission, chasing friction, chasing him, chasing anything that might break the edge holding her there. Still, he hadn't fucked her. And still, she was already gone.

Her hands moved. Not wildly—just enough to test him. One slid down to trace his chest, nails light, teasing, hungry.

He caught her wrist again. No warning this time. Just a firm grip.

"I said stay still."

She should have pulled away. Should have cursed him out, rolled her eyes, something. But her pulse only jumped harder under his fingers. She tried again—subtle, a shift of her thigh, an arch of her back meant to throw him off rhythm. He didn't move. Didn't even blink. He flipped her over without a word. Her knees hit the bed, thighs parted, her palms pressing into the mattress out of instinct.

Then his arm wrapped around her waist. Tight. Solid. A vice. He held her there, chest hovering just behind her, body braced like he was anchoring her in place.

There was no room to move. No angle she controlled.

His hand slipped between her legs. The pressure was immediate. Direct. No circling, no guessing—he found her clit and touched her like he already knew her body better than she did.

She came so fast she didn't believe it was happening. Her hands clenched the sheets. Her vision blurred. Her mind blanked out, just a string of moans and the impossible feel of him pushing her over the edge before he'd even fucked her.

Some part of her, far away, was shocked. She'd never come like that. Not from fingers. Not that fast. Not from anyone.

But then she heard the sound of the condom wrapper tearing and he was inside her. One thrust, deep and rough, punched the air from her lungs. It hurt. And it didn't. Her body jolted with the force of it. It hit too deep, and she still wanted more.

The rhythm was brutal. Skilled, yes—but not showy. He didn't care about being impressive. What ruined her was the way he handled her—like she was nothing to manage, nothing to fear, just something he could hold.

At some point, she stopped keeping track. Her mouth was open but she couldn't hear herself anymore. Only the sound of his body hitting hers, the slap of skin, the way the bed creaked under the force of it.

He fucked her hard. No hesitation. No softness. Every thrust shook her, knocked sound out of her throat that she didn't recognize. Her face burned. Her back arched. She felt it in her teeth.

He held her down like she had nowhere else to go, and he was right. She didn't want to go anywhere. His hand came back to her throat, steady pressure, not too much. Just enough to remind her who had her. Her breasts were crushed against his arm where he held her tight to his chest.

Then he shifted her, still inside her, until they were both kneeling. She leaned back against him, body straining, open and trembling. He fucked up into her without slowing, without saying a word. His other hand reached around and touched her again, precise, relentless. Her vision went white. The orgasm hit fast and hard, her thighs already wet, her legs shaking under the weight of it.

He didn't stop.

He let her taste herself on his fingers and she sucked greedily, tongue swirling, even as his rhythm remained unchanged. He kept going, violent, steady. She lost the thread of time. Couldn't tell if it had been minutes or hours. Then he moved again, pushing her down flat against the mattress, pinning her face-first into the sheets. One hand gripped her tricep, the other braced between her sternum. He drove into her with everything he had.

When he came, it tore out of him. Low, rough, raw. A sound pulled from somewhere deep. She whimpered when she heard it. She couldn't help it. It landed in her spine. He stayed like that for a moment. Heavy. Breathing hard. When he pulled out of her, she couldn't move. Her body was spent, her breath caught somewhere in her chest. She felt the mattress under her, the air cooling her skin, her pulse still loud in her ears.

He reached over and brushed her hair back from her

face. Not tender. Just practical. Like she was a person he didn't want to see suffocate in her own sweat.

"You should sleep," he said.

She didn't respond. Couldn't. Her face was still pressed to the sheets, her mouth dry, her limbs heavy and uncooperative.

He pulled the blanket halfway over her before getting up and tossing the condom. She stayed where she was, blinking slowly at the bedside table, confused and raw, trying to remember what day it was.

Then her eyes closed, and she was out.

3

Morgan woke to warmth—real warmth, not hotel HVAC or the buzz of adrenaline she usually ran on. Her body was sore in the best possible way. Muscles in her back stretched as she rolled onto her side, and the dull ache in her thighs reminded her, vividly, of the night before.

Oh. Right.

She took a slow breath, like it might reset something. God, he still smelled like something she wasn't supposed to want—like soap and jet fuel and sweat and sleep. His arm was draped across her waist, heavy and possessive, like they hadn't just met twelve hours ago.

Not even met, technically. No names

She hadn't wanted names. It had been safer that way.

He'd looked at her from the cockpit like he already knew her anyways One glance that said, *Watch me land this lumbering, overworked metal like it's a damn glider.* Or maybe: *Go ahead, try not to be impressed.*

That kind of landing didn't just happen. It was the work

of a man who'd spent years in the left seat, someone who knew his aircraft like it was a second skin. Precision like that didn't come from training manuals—it came from obsession. Control bordering on pathological.

And she had been impressed.

And now here she was. Covered in his fingerprints—literally. Faint purple marks bloomed along her hips and thighs, matching the ones on the inside of her biceps. Souvenirs from where he'd pinned her in place. Fucked her through the mattress. Made her forget every rule she usually kept etched behind her eyelids.

She shifted carefully, trying not to wake him, but his arm tightened around her.

"You ghosting me already?" he murmured, voice sleep-rough and soaked in smug.

Her breath hitched before she could help it. God. That voice had been in her ear all night. Growling her name—no. Not her name. He never said her name. He didn't know it. She didn't tell him. Because she didn't fuck nameless pilots the night before FAA meetings. But here she was.

"I have to go," she said. Her voice came out calmer than she felt. Her throat was dry, lips swollen from where he'd kissed her like he was starving. "Early meeting."

"Same," he mumbled into the pillow.

Her stomach turned.

No. No, the universe wouldn't be that cruel. There was no way he was—

Except she didn't know his name. And she had skimmed the meeting details late last night on the airport shuttle, already dizzy from lust, thinking she could slide through this city undetected.

Her logic brain—usually so steady, so ruthlessly efficient

it made other people nervous—had simply blinked out the second he walked up to her on the Arrivals floor. Like her brain had short-circuited, or worse—stepped out and left her body to fend for itself. She'd thought she was being careful. Thought she was still ten steps ahead. But clearly, the universe had other plans. Cruel, humiliating plans.

She slid out of bed, ignoring the protest in her legs. She caught a glimpse of herself in the mirror—bruised, glowing, a little bit ruined—and hated how good she looked.

He watched her move, head tilted, still naked under the covers.

"Hey," he said, voice gravelly in a way that made her knees consider betrayal. "Last night was—"

"Good," she cut in. "Yeah. It was."

That was the most he was getting. He raised his eyebrows but didn't stop her. Just watched as she showered, dressed, and emerged in a fresh suit—sharp, dark, deliberate—like slipping back into armor. She walked to the door, hand on the handle, and finally glanced back.

"Goodbye." Soft. Final. Polite, because she was raised right. And gone before he could answer.

IN THE ELEVATOR, she pulled out her phone—habit, muscle memory, something to do with her hands while the rest of her tried not to implode. The numbers on the screen blurred for a second. She blinked hard.

Something was wrong.

Not big, not yet. But a tension coiled low in her, whispering *you forgot something* in a voice that sounded too much like her mother's.

She checked her calendar. There was that meeting. Nothing else.

And still—her stomach had that telltale twist, like the ground was about to shift beneath her and she was too proud to reach for the handrail.

9:30 a.m. - FAA coordination meeting.

Something about conflicting incident reports, cross-checks that didn't match, and a flight crew filing directly with the feds.

It was the kind of thing that pulled in a fleet director, station leadership, and—unfortunately—the union.

She scrolled down, skimming—her brain still half-fogged from lack of sleep and multiple orgasms.

Then stopped.

Oh. *Oh no.*

Like a throwaway line at the bottom of the agenda—

Union representation: pilot rep to be present.

Her chest went tight. Like a vice clamped around her lungs. She reread the line, then again, waiting for it to say anything else. It didn't. Pilot union rep. Just that.

Her stomach dropped so fast she had to grip the edge of her phone like it might steady her.

What if he was in that room? Who else would the pilot be?

It had to be him. Of course it was him.

Because who else would the universe dig up to humiliate her today, of all days?

She'd finally let her guard down—for one night, one mistake, one man with a voice that didn't flinch and hands that moved like they were used to being obeyed—and now she was going to pay for it in front of her subordinates and FAA suits.

It wasn't confirmed. There was no name. It could be anyone.

Maybe it was just the union brass, some retired pilot turned lobbyist, someone she could handle. But her gut already knew. Her gut always knew.

And this? This felt like a setup.

Like punishment. Like karma in a pilot's uniform.

4

Kieran O'Hara showed up fifteen minutes early, because showing up early was just good manners.

His Air Force pilot father used to say if you weren't early, you were already late, and even now, decades into a career that had taken him from puddle jumpers to widebodies, he still operated like he had something to prove.

He was hoping this meeting would be quick and painless—just another dull FAA briefing with some middle manager reading bullet points off a PowerPoint like they were trying to sedate the room. He was flying tonight and had a vet appointment for Scout and Daisy this afternoon, and he'd really rather not spend the in-between being lectured on compliance like he hadn't been flying for twenty-seven goddamn years.

He stirred his coffee, black and burned, out of habit more than necessity. Nothing fancy. Just hot enough to remind him he was still alive.

He didn't know how he kept ending up in these rooms. He thought he was done with union politics—done being the guy who stood up and made noise while everyone else ducked their heads. But Chuck had called in a favor, again, with that familiar "buddy, I need you" tone, and Kieran, like an idiot, had said yes.

He just wanted to fly. That was it. Fly, go home, walk the dogs, check in on Ren, fake like he knew the difference between a "dip" and a "death drop," and fall asleep halfway through whatever new Drag Race season they were texting him about.

But no. Here he was, reviewing meeting notes in the corner of a gray conference room, thinking about compliance regs and hoping nobody made eye contact.

Kieran followed the FAA guy into the conference room, a few steps behind, coffee in hand, not expecting anything worth remembering.

The woman at the head of the table made him stop dead.

She was already seated, tablet balanced in one hand, flipping through briefing notes like she wrote them. She didn't look up when they entered. She didn't have to. The room already belonged to her.

Gina, the airport station manager, glanced up and smiled politely as they walked in.

"This is A. Morgan Delgado," she said. "Fleet Director of U.S. Operations for Heritage Airlines."

Kieran's stomach dropped so fast he thought he might actually have to sit down.

Fleet Director.

Heritage.

Her.

From last night. From the hotel. From his hands.

He managed to keep his face neutral—he had nearly three decades of cockpit training to thank for that—but it cost him. Every nerve in his body lit up at once, short-circuiting under his skin.

The FAA Guy, oblivious, laughed like he was already halfway through a bad joke.

"Huh. You're Morgan Delgado? All these years, I thought you were a man."

Kieran had to resist the urge to bounce the man's head off the nearest wall.

Jesus Christ. Read the goddamn room.

Morgan didn't flinch. She didn't even shift in her chair.

She just looked up at the FAA guy, expression blank, and said,

"I'm sure you'll adjust."

Sharp. Clean. Deadly.

Kieran felt it cut through the room like a pressure drop. No raised voice. No drama. Just precision. Authority without apology.

And it hit him hard—this wasn't a woman who argued.

Gina kept rolling like nothing happened. She waved a hand toward Kieran.

"And this is Captain Kieran O'Hara. Representing the pilots' union. Filling in for Chuck Meyers today."

Kieran nodded once, professional, quiet, trying not to betray that he knew how the woman at the head of the table tasted.

Morgan didn't react. Not visibly.

But her eyes lingered on him just a second longer than necessary. A slow, deliberate pass.

He wondered if anyone else could feel it—the tension stretching between them, thin and taut like a live wire.

The FAA guy, either too stupid to read the room or too stubborn to care, chuckled again.

"You know," he said, waving his coffee cup like a drunk

uncle at a barbecue, "you remind me of that other ball-breaker—Ava Thompkins. Ran Heritage through 9/11. Real firecracker. Just like you."

Kieran kept his face neutral, but inside he was rolling his eyes so hard he was about to pull a muscle.

Sure. Let's just lump every woman who scares you into the same category. Real original.

Morgan Delgado set her tablet down with a soft clack that somehow sounded like a gunshot.

She didn't even glance at him. Just started speaking, cool and unbothered, addressing the room without missing a beat—and leaving him right where he belonged: ignored.

Her voice was calm. Direct. No filler words. No hesitation.

She laid out the fleet projections, the upcoming regulatory changes, and operational priorities with the kind of authority Kieran usually only heard from captains with twenty thousand hours and zero patience for bullshit.

She didn't just push numbers around, either. She brought up crew reports without being asked, cited maintenance feedback from last month's field audit, and pointed out a policy change already signed into effect—one that cut turnaround time pressure and gave flight crews more discretion without management breathing down their necks.

She was doing the thing half the room had been begging for.

The FAA guy snorted, half under his breath but loud enough for everyone to hear.

"Wow. Caved fast, didn't you? That's not what your predecessor would've done."

The silence that followed was ugly.

Morgan didn't even look up from her notes.

She just said, steady as a blade,

"No, it's not. That's why I have his job now."

The FAA guy didn't say another word.

Kieran wasn't sure if he wanted to stand up and applaud or drop to one knee.

He glanced back down at the briefing notes, willing himself to look normal. Professional. Unbothered.

He tried—really tried—to focus on the packet in front of him. The words. The charts. The action items.

One of the charts flashed by mentioning the 7X rollout schedules. Kieran flagged it automatically in his head— there were already murmurs in the union chatter about those planes. Too many quirks for brand-new metal. Crews weren't thrilled.

But it was like trying to ignore a thunderstorm from the middle of a cornfield.

All he could hear was her voice from last night, wrecked and low in his ear.

All he could see was the way her mouth looked this morning when she was still asleep against his shoulder.

All he could feel was the steady, rising certainty that he was well and truly fucked.

And all he could think about—over and over, like a heartbeat—was whether she regretted it.

And how badly he wanted her to look at him again like she had when she unraveled in his hands.

Morgan didn't look at him until she needed to.

Which somehow made it worse.

She finished a point about regional fleet allocations, tapped a note on her tablet, and then finally—finally— lifted her gaze.

"Captain O'Hara," she said, like his name was just another item on her checklist. Nothing special. Nothing personal.

"You've flown the 700 series routes out of Midway this quarter. Are the fatigue reports consistent with what your crews are experiencing?"

Her tone was polite. Neutral. Professional.

But to him?

It sounded exactly like *you're up, hotshot—let's see if you're useful or just pretty.*

Kieran cleared his throat, just once.

Sat up straighter.

He did the thing they taught him in therapy—took the thought, the memory of her voice in his ear and her mouth on his neck, and shoved it into the mental box. Closed the lid. Took a breath. Focused.

"Yeah," he said, steady. "Midway crews flagged the turn-around pressure during shift briefings. Not just fatigue— comp issues are spiking too. We're burning time chasing paper trails because maintenance isn't getting access windows. Your update should buy us twenty extra minutes per leg. That's going to fix more than the FAA realizes."

He kept his voice even. Kept it clipped.

Made it sound like he hadn't been naked in her hotel bed six hours ago.

Morgan's eyes flicked up from her tablet. Just for a second.

There was a glint—sharp, almost amused. Not surprised, not patronizing.

Noted.

Then she nodded.

"Good. We'll fold that into the final draft."

And just like that, she moved on.

The rest of the meeting was standard cleanup—brief questions, bureaucratic nodding.

Even the FAA guy, still nursing whatever was left of his pride, grudgingly accepted the terms Morgan laid out.

When the final point was wrapped, she dismissed them with a crisp, "That's all. Thank you for your time," and the room moved.

The others had filed out with their binders and laptops, trailing half-finished conversations and bad coffee breath.

The door clicked shut behind the last one, and for a moment, there was nothing but the quiet hum of the overhead lights.

They were the last two in the room.

Kieran stood there, half-turned, not quite ready to leave.

He hadn't said anything yet, but the impulse was rising —something between an apology and a question he had no business asking.

Maybe just *thank you*. Maybe *was it real*. Maybe *do you regret it*.

Morgan didn't let him speak. She didn't raise her voice. Didn't even look up from the tablet she was closing.

"They already think I don't belong here," she said, even, final. "I'm not giving them a reason to say it out loud."

Then she looked at him. Direct. No anger. No shame. Just clarity.

"I can't afford mistakes. I'm trusting you to understand that."

It wasn't a warning. It wasn't a request.

She wasn't asking him to be discreet—she was assuming he already would be.

And the way she said it, cool and practiced, told him exactly what she'd learned from experience: Men disappointed her. Enough that she'd stopped waiting for them to do the right thing without a reminder.

He took it like a gut punch. Not because she was wrong. Because she shouldn't have had to say it at all.

Kieran nodded, jaw tight. "You have my word."

That was all. That was enough.

He turned toward the door. Forced himself to leave without another look back. Almost. As he reached the threshold, something made him glance over his shoulder.

Morgan stood at the head of the empty room, tablet clutched tight in one hand. For a second—barely long enough to trust it—he saw it: devastation, raw and unguarded, flashing across her face before the mask snapped back into place.

She didn't move. She didn't call after him. She just looked down again, sealing herself away.

He left. Not because he was ashamed. Not because he regretted it. But because he felt the loss settle under his ribs, quiet and heavy, like something he'd barely had the chance to want before it was already gone. And mostly because he respected her too much to make it any harder than it already was.

5

The air at O'Hare hit her first.

Jet fuel, stale coffee, the low growl of taxiing planes pressing against the heat. The pavement steamed under the weight of July.

Nothing had changed.

The terminal windows glared against the sun. Trucks beeped in the distance, half-hearted, already losing the battle to the late afternoon.

Morgan stepped out of the Heritage Airline building and into the employee lot, her shoes clicking against the concrete with the kind of authority that didn't ask for permission.

Her honey-brown skin had deepened to a richer shade, the sun working into her the way time did—slow, relentless. She walked like someone who had survived something ugly and won something real.

Around her, the lot buzzed with half-second glances. Some curious, some cautious. She clocked them without slowing. They knew who she was. They knew what she had done. She had cut the rot out of corporate offices all across the Midwest and left it bleeding at their feet. No apology, no warning.

The scent of burnt sugar drifted behind her.

Morgan didn't have to look to know who it was.

Vee trailed a few steps back, dragging on a vape like it owed her money. She wore the mandatory orange jacket unzipped over a black vest that clung to lean muscle. Her hair, dead straight and brushing her shoulders, caught the sun in bronze streaks that should have looked tragic but didn't.

She made it work the same way she made grease-stained coveralls look good—and none of it was for anyone but herself.

Up close, she had a face that stopped people mid-sentence. Heart-shaped, sharp eyes lined with black, like she could kill you with one look and enjoy it. She wore a red lipstick that should have melted under the July heat but stayed flawless, just like the rest of her. No frills. No apologies.

At forty, the hangar belonged to her. Senior mechanic. Shop steward. The person you sent when you needed something fixed right or when you needed a manager scared into shutting the hell up. She had built her authority one overhaul, one contract negotiation at a time. It lived in the way people stepped aside without thinking when they saw her coming.

And because she looked twenty-six at most, thanks to her Vietnamese genes, sometimes she had to verbally lay somebody out just to remind them who they were dealing with.

Morgan caught a few more glances, this time sticking longer. Not just for her.

Vee exhaled a plume of sweet smoke and grinned, slow

and wide, like she knew exactly what kind of scene they were making just by walking across the lot together.

"Hey, Delgado," she said a little too loudly and easy. "Heard you cleaned house. Everybody's shook."

Morgan didn't break stride. *Let them look.* They moved the way people do when they know the night is theirs, slipping off across the tarmac until the buildings and bodies behind them disappeared. Their shoes hit the concrete in an easy rhythm, the runway lights humming faint and low.

When they were finally out of sight and sound, Morgan spoke first. Her voice was steady, casual, like she was stating a fact and not tearing open a wound.

"I pissed off a lot of people," she said. "But they weren't good people. Corrupt. Sitting around, doing nothing. Running stations like it was a damn temp job."

"I heard," Vee said.

Morgan kept going.

"I ran the numbers. Our safety rating has already improved because they're gone."

Vee cackled.

"Undercover Boss has got nothing on you, babe."

Morgan dropped into the rusted lawn chair they kept hidden on 8L like she'd been dragging herself across a war zone.

Vee followed suit, kicking back like she had a mortgage on the end of the runway, cracking open a LaCroix and handing Morgan a can of something aggressively citrus.

"The board thought I was just gonna sit pretty and send emails. Some are mad I've been out here, instead, talking to rampers, ops managers, agents. Fixing shit they've ignored for years."

They didn't say much after that. They didn't have to. They knew what it was.

Above them, a plane roared overhead barely thirty feet from the top of their heads, low and heavy, the whole sky humming. The vibration hit their chests hard enough to make them both sit there for a second, looking half-stupid and glassy-eyed. Two full-grown adults, absolutely wrecked by the sound of a jet engine like it was the first time they ever heard one. No shame. This was who they were.

Vee was the first to break the silence. She smirked like she already knew the answer.

"I heard some shit went down in Traverse."

"Nothing went down in Traverse," Morgan said, snapping the tab on her can.

Vee just leaned back further.

"You know the union steward there, Steve? He's married to Gina. Station manager."

Morgan groaned, dragging her hand down her face.

"Goddamn the union gossip network."

They didn't have to say it. Gina had that job because Morgan gave it to her. Gina wouldn't betray Morgan, but she and Steve were loyal to each other first. If Gina knew, Steve knew. And if Steve knew, Vee could drag it out of him. It was half her job description as regional steward anyway.

Vee stretched, lazy and dangerous.

"I told Steve he'd die if he so much as breathed a word to anyone else."

Morgan smiled.

"Joking," she added. "Mostly."

Another plane rumbled overhead. The railings shook from the engine's roar.

"You wanna talk about it?"

Morgan let out a breath that hurt on the way out. For a second, it cracked through—the sadness, clean and brutal.

"What do you want me to say?" she said, voice low, like if she spoke any louder it might break something open.

"I met a man who's older, hot, smart, knows what he's doing, and actually seems like a good person. The kind you don't meet in this job unless you get real lucky or real stupid."

She shook her head once, sharp, trying to pull herself back.

"But I'm in the middle of restructuring a company on the edge of collapse. My shit needs to be airtight. I don't have room to be reckless. And I really can't afford to be the woman who dates another goddamn pilot."

She kept her eyes on the terminal in the distance.

She didn't say it, but it sat there anyway: *and he might have been really, really good for me.*

"Damn," Vee said and took another drag, leaving it at that.

She shifted the conversation without warning, like flipping channels. Told Morgan she saw a picture of her ex on Instagram. Some new girl. She laughed about it, not because it was funny, but because their mutuals are apparently more pissed about it than she was. Vee shrugged like it was whatever.

They traded a few tired gripes about the staffing situation. Ramps were still short. Ops was still a mess. Management still thought speed tape counted as a maintenance strategy.

Vee insisted Morgan come out and see the new Marvel movie with her this weekend. Sneak in something terrible and cheap.

Morgan didn't commit. She did not say no either.

Then Vee's radio blinked.

Morgan's phone lit up.

Everything hit the fan at once.

THE FIRST CLIP hit TikTok at 7:42 p.m.

A shaky, vertical phone video, barely twenty seconds long, filmed by a teenager who should've had their phone on Airplane Mode but clearly didn't.

Morgan could hear the screaming before she even saw the cabin: a jagged wail of terror ripping straight through the cheap speaker on her phone.

The video shook so badly it was like watching through an earthquake. Oxygen masks dangled like dead vines from the overhead panels. Somewhere, a baby shrieked—a raw, piercing sound that cut through the chaos like a knife. A flight attendant tried to crawl down the aisle on her hands and knees, desperate to get to a woman slumped over her tray table.

Then came the jolt—the moment that made this clip the clip.

The plane bucked, a brutal vertical snap, and the camera caught a man without a seatbelt mid-stride. He lifted into the air like a rag doll, slammed the ceiling hard enough to crack a panel, and crumpled into a heap in the aisle.

Morgan didn't have to be a doctor to know he wasn't getting up.

In the captions and comments, people were already saying the words no airline exec ever wanted trending next to their brand:

"coma"

"brain damage"

"Heritage death trap"

"never flying again."

By 8:03 p.m., the video had spread to Twitter.

Viral doesn't even cover it—this thing detonated. Millions of views before anyone at Heritage could even get a statement out. News outlets snatched it up like seagulls on a french fry: CNN, BBC, Good Morning America.

By midnight, *Rolling Stone* had a thinkpiece out about "America's Turbulence Crisis" like they'd been sitting on that article draft just waiting for the right body count.

The hashtags started stacking:

#HeritageHorror

#TurbulenceTrauma

#Another7X

#PrayBeforeYouBoard

People dug out old turbulence stories. Others posted "never again" videos while dramatically canceling their flights. People made memes about airlines handing out rosaries with boarding passes.

It wasn't just a viral moment. It was a brand funeral.

6

The war room was gray in every sense of the word.

A long table ran the length of it, crowded with laptops, files, half-empty water bottles. A wide wall screen dominated the far end, splitting its feed between the 360-degree camera in the room and the remote faces blinking in from elsewhere.

People called in from homes, offices, hotel lobbies. The FAA was on the line.

It was early. Too early. The kind of early where the only real certainty was that things would get worse before they got better.

Even the CEO had docked his yacht somewhere in the Maldives, unshaven and defensive. He made a quick statement—something about Heritage's "unwavering commitment to safety"—then retreated.

Morgan stayed where she was at the head of the table, posture straight, voice measured.

When she spoke, it was only to her Deputy, Tim. She asked him to check on the passenger who had gone into a coma. Quietly, humanly.

General Counsel cut in almost immediately. No admissions of guilt, no record of concern.

"Noted," was all she said.

The screen above them flashed again: raw footage, trending hashtags, cable news tickers. Heritage's stock was cratering in real time, minute by minute.

There were eighteen faces on the Zoom call—board members, division heads, the Chief Marketing Officer, and the pilot who had flown the aircraft in question.

Morgan picked up the briefing notes without rushing.

The report was grim but straightforward: four serious hospitalizations, twenty-seven minor injuries, and a cardiac arrest midair that—by luck or intervention—had survived.

She delivered the numbers with no color, no commentary. Just facts.

Then the arguments started.

She didn't flinch. She didn't engage. She let them talk until the air burned itself out. One hand around her coffee mug. The other flipping through the file like her own name wasn't printed on the final page.

Ava Thompkins would've been proud.

First Black deputy director Heritage ever had. First woman, too. She'd run the nerve center through the post-9/11 freefall with nothing but a voice that could cut steel and a Rolodex full of people too scared to say no.

Ava had taught Morgan early:

Never flinch first.

Never explain.

Never bleed where they can see it.

Morgan kept her hand steady on the mug, and waited.

The Zoom window blinked.

A young man appeared, sitting too straight, lit too carefully.

His nameplate: **HAYES**.

"I'm just saying," he started, arms crossed, "no one I trained with would've greenlit that route. We had visual on the cells. Dispatch should've caught it before we were locked in."

The room quieted.

PR was pacing in the hall.

Legal hovered.

Everyone waited.

Morgan turned one page in the file. She took a sip of coffee. She didn't look up until the moment passed, then set her gaze squarely at the camera.

"The routing was cleared under standard procedures and validated across three systems," she said, voice even. "If anything felt unstable mid-flight, it may have been a matter of inexperience, not instruction."

Silence.

Someone coughed.

Tim shifted.

Hayes blinked, realizing too late he was out of his depth.

Morgan didn't wait for a rebuttal and closed the file.

There would be no resolution here—not in a room full of lawyers and public relations staff worried more about headlines than operational truth.

"If we want answers, it won't come from arguing. It will come from reconstructing the flight, piece by piece, minute by minute," she announced.

"I'll prepare my team for the sim."

Meaning: her team would rebuild the conditions exactly. Weather, routing, payload, turbulence. No speculation. No politics. Just facts.

Her boss, David Enright, Chief Operations Officer of Heritage, stirred for the first time since joining the call late.

He rubbed his temples, latched onto her words without even understanding the full conversation.

"Let's run a full flight sim. Exact conditions. We need a senior pilot with hours on that model."

Morgan didn't correct him. Let him pretend it was his idea.

The conference phone crackled.

"Pilot's union is requesting Kieran O'Hara."

Morgan's hand jerked slightly on her coffee mug.

She caught herself, wiped her palm on her slacks, and kept her face still.

Her boss waved a hand like it didn't matter.

"Fine, fine. I don't care who. Just get someone out here ASAP."

SHE DIDN'T SLEEP that night. Not really. Around 1:00 a.m., she opened her laptop. She wasn't supposed to be working. This was meant to be a night off. But her brain didn't know how to power down, and there was something comforting about clicking through personnel logs—clean data, clean edges. No surprises. Just a routine audit.

She typed his name into the crew manifest system.

O'Hara, Kieran T.

The search result popped up faster than she expected.

She skimmed it at first.

Then stopped.

Then stared.

Role: Captain, International Line – Boeing 777
Tenure: 12 years
Locations: ORD, JFK, LAX, NRT, CDG
Aircraft Certified: 737, 757, 767, 777, A330

Commendations: FAA Professionalism Award (2), Emergency Response Citation

Voluntary Transfer to Regional Line – Reason: Family Proximity Request

Her eyes moved back up.

Widebody routes. Atlantic crossings. Tokyo. Paris. Frankfurt.

Every heavy metal route she'd ever dreamed of commanding.

Twelve years. Senior captain. Spotless record.

Total years in commercial aviation: 27.

She did the math. He'd been flying since she was in middle school.

And then, one line—tucked in at the bottom, almost like an afterthought:

Voluntary Transfer | Pay Grade Adjustment – Tier 1 → Tier 4

She leaned back slowly, hand rising to cover her mouth. Her heart thudded once, low and hard.

Oh my God. She hadn't known. Or rather, she hadn't looked—not until now. Not really. Not when it might've mattered. She silently dismissed him as just another horribly underpaid regional pilot. He never corrected her.

And now here it was, in plain text.

He'd walked away from a top-tier career. He'd given up international prestige and six-figure bonuses. He'd grounded himself. For someone. Who? A wife? A kid?

She swallowed hard.

Her chair creaked as she leaned forward, elbows on the desk, hands braced on either side of the screen. Something inside her chest went tight. Her face burned with shame.

She stayed there for a long time. Not fixing. Not saving. Just sitting with the goddamn truth.

7

Kieran was sweating through his T-shirt before they even made it past the first row of stalls.

The market sprawled over a few cracked city blocks on Detroit's east side—blacktop, chain-link, and chalk-painted signs, stitched together by stubborn hope.

"Hydrate, old man," his kid said, pressing a mason jar of cucumber water into his hand like they were the one parenting him.

"I'm hydrating," he said, taking a sip and immediately coughing, and handing it back to the kid.

"There's—ginger in this?"

"Yup," they grinned. "Anti-inflammatory. Also, don't act surprised. You drink hot jet fuel for a living."

They swapped the mason jar to their other hand, careful not to tangle the double leash wrapped around their wrist. Daisy and Scout trotted ahead, tongues lolling, sniffing every crate of produce like they were on official business.

The kid kept a lazy eye on them, steering with a practiced tug whenever Scout tried to pee on somebody's compost bin.

They weaved through the farmers market slowly, stopping at stalls where everyone seemed to know his kid's name. The folding tables were covered in fresh collards, heirloom tomatoes, homemade tamarind jam. No cash registers—just chalk signs and donation jars. Sliding scale, honor system.

Kieran kept a step behind, trying not to hover. His shirt stuck to his back. His heart wouldn't slow down.

This was the first time they'd invited him here—not just to the market, but to their world. Their people. Their work.

He was one of a few white guys in sight, and he felt it in his skin, in his stance, in the way folks squinted at him first —rightfully cautious—before glancing back to the kid. And seeing it.

The resemblance.

His peppery straight hair next to their cloud of tied-back curls. His weathered face and their fresh one, both marked by the same sharp hazel eyes, the same skeptical tilt of the mouth. The same quiet perimeter around their joy.

People nodded after that. Some even smiled. But Kieran didn't miss what it meant, that flicker of recognition: He's with them.

And God, what a thing it was, to be seen that way.

"This one's Eileen's," they said, pointing at a table stacked with sweet corn and rainbow chard. "She runs the free fridge on Oakwood. We've been swapping compost for her chickens."

Kieran blinked, squinting against the sun.

"You've been what?"

"I'm bartering, Dad. Don't worry, I've got the municipal regs printed out in a binder."

Of course they did.

They tugged his sleeve and led him down the block,

away from the crowd, toward the chain-link fence of a corner lot half-hidden behind a mural of sunflowers and flying geese.

It looked like nothing at first—just dirt and bent rebar and a few sad starter plants. But once they pushed the gate open, he saw it:

Rows of seedlings. Raised beds made from salvaged pallets. A sign that read *Eastside Growers Collective*, painted by hand.

It wasn't much yet—just dirt and hope stitched together —but God, it was alive.

He didn't know if he deserved to stand in it, but he wanted to.

"We're trying to get it certified this year."

Kieran didn't say anything right away. He just looked around, watched them crouch next to a plot of mustard greens and tuck a little sign in the dirt that read, *Grown with joy.*

"How'd you even start this?" he asked, voice low.

They shrugged.

"Same way we do anything. Mutual aid, group chat, and grandmas who don't mess around."

Kieran smiled, a tight ache blooming in his chest.

He'd spent the last ten years trying to be better—chasing sobriety, chasing time. Missed milestones stacked up like flight delays: prom, graduation, first heartbreaks he should've known about but didn't.

And still, somehow, this person in front of him—kind, loud, stubborn, radically good—chose to call him "Dad."

His phone buzzed. The screen lit up: *Heritage Routing Desk.*

He stared at it a moment. Then let it ring out.

They settled at a shaded table near the edge of the

market—one of those reclaimed-wood setups made from old church pews and scaffolding planks.

Kieran's knees cracked as he sat. His kid didn't comment. Much.

On the table between them: two mason jars of beet-citrus juice and a thick slice of heirloom rye bread, still warm from the wood-fired oven.

The bakery stand had a little chalkboard that read:

Halfway Rising – Baked by Detroit's Formerly Incarcerated.

"Try this," they said, tearing off a chunk and handing it to him. "It's ridiculous."

Kieran took a bite. Chewed. Swallowed.

"Jesus."

"Told you."

They sat in easy silence for a moment, watching the kids run between stalls, the old men playing dominos on upturned crates, the women at picnic tables arguing over city council drama.

Detroit was alive like that—chaotic, soulful, held together with community glue.

His kid sipped their juice and leaned back against the sun-warmed bench.

"You've been quiet today."

Kieran shrugged.

"It's hot."

"Yeah, and you've been depressed since like May."

He blinked.

"Okay. Wow."

"I'm just saying. You think I don't notice, but I do. You've just been off."

Kieran looked down at his hands. They still looked capable—just not of the things that mattered most.

"I just didn't want to dump that on you," he said finally. "It's not your problem."

The kid nodded as if to say, *True.*

"But," they said. "I'm twenty-three. I pay rent. I organize boycotts and push legislation. I'm not twelve. You can tell me things."

He laughed a little, breath catching on it.

"You make it sound so simple."

"It kind of is."

He nodded slowly. Looked out over the stalls again.

"I missed a lot," he said. "Back when you were a kid. I drank too much. Was always flying or gone or angry. And you still turned into this...person. This incredible person. And I don't know if I earned that. You talking to me like this."

They looked at him, so much older than he remembered, and said,

"You didn't for a long time. But for now? You do."

Then came the grin—the one that always meant trouble.

"Even if you still wear that crusty-ass Michigan State cap like it's not offensive to me."

Kieran raised an eyebrow.

"Better than walking around in that smug Wolverine tote bag like you invented higher education."

"I earned that smug. You failed econ twice."

"The lectures were at 8 AM. I was at the bar until 2. It's called time management—I just managed it badly."

"I heard you were hungover for two semesters straight."

He huffed out a laugh, shaking his head.

"You gonna roast me or thank me for just buying you a month's worth of artisanal carbs?"

"I can multitask."

They grinned, and he smiled back.

That was how they worked now—jokes layered over history, care disguised as sass.

And somehow, even after everything, they still chose to be here.

Kieran pressed his thumb to the condensation on his glass. Said nothing for a long time.

Then his phone buzzed again.

This time, he answered.

"O'Hara," he said, voice steady. "Yeah. I'll take it."

8

The morning sun was brutal, bouncing off the concrete, flashing against every slab of metal and heating the air like a convection oven.

Morgan stood with a half-circle of mechanics outside the sim annex, sleeves rolled, pen tucked behind one ear, scrawling notes across the latest input printout.

They were mid-discussion about the crosswind profile when someone shifted beside her. She glanced up—

And there he was. Walking across the tarmac like it wasn't a battlefield. Heritage windbreaker half-zipped, flight bag slung loose over one shoulder, aviators throwing back the sun like a fucking action shot. The years hadn't worn him down—they'd sharpened him. All edges and authority, like the air bent around him.

Her brain fizzed out like a busted circuit.

The easy, cocky swing of his stride, the barest gray at his temples, the kind of unbothered masculinity that made her molars ache.

Pretty. But not soft. The kind of pretty that got sharper with age, like a blade honed down to something lethal.

He didn't walk like he owned the place—he walked like he knew he could, and had decided to be merciful about it.

He looked good enough to make a nun rethink her vows. Good enough that for one savage second, Morgan wanted to shove him into the nearest maintenance bay—and cause a scandal that would live in FAA infamy.

Her mouth went dry.

He reached the edge of the group, nodded politely to the technicians, then met her eyes—briefly. Steady. Civil. Just Kieran O'Hara, alive and breathing and cocky as hell, like the universe was kicking her in the teeth for sport.

"Ma'am," he said, like he meant it.

In her head, Morgan recoiled. *Ma'am?* Really? She was thirty-six-years old. He was thirteen years older than her, with a face that could probably convince half of O'Hare to commit federal crimes, and he was standing there *ma'aming* her like they were about to reenact the Battle of Gettysburg.

But that wasn't what bothered her the most.

It was the *way* he looked at her. Just for a breath—just long enough. The sun caught his aviators, flaring twin stars of white-hot light, but she still saw herself in them. A distorted twin reflection: sleeves rolled, jaw set, pen like a dagger behind her ear.

And for that one second, he wasn't seeing Fleet Director Delgado. He was seeing *her*. No smirk. No softness. Just history. Heavy as jet fuel.

He blinked, and the spell snapped. His gaze shifted—businesslike, measured, nothing to see here.

Morgan's stomach pulled tight. She dragged her eyes back to the printout, her pen moving without thinking, every line just noise now.

Her mouth still tasted like static.

"All right," she said, mercifully steady, "let's pivot to the simulator."

But her pulse was slamming against her ribs, hard and loud enough she was half-sure the whole damn airfield could hear it.

THE HANGAR FELT COLDER than it should have—wide, cavernous, the hum of machinery vibrating under her boots like a second heartbeat. Footsteps followed behind her: the sim crew, a cluster of engineers and techs. The air clung to the tension between them. Vee flanked her left, grinning like she knew a secret and was daring Morgan to acknowledge it.

She didn't. She couldn't.

Kieran moved ahead of them, loose and easy, shedding years with every step through the hatch. The simulator bay swallowed him whole. The door hissed shut behind him like a held breath finally exhaled.

"Captain O'Hara," Morgan said, clipboard firm in her hands, voice sharp enough to slice through the chill. "You'll be flying the June 29th scenario. Sim conditions match the original incident."

A nod. Crisp. Deferential. Hot.

"Walk us through your decisions aloud."

"Yes, ma'am."

There it was again—that razor-edged *ma'am* slipping under her skin, making her blood low and molten. She clamped down hard, moving toward the observation bay without giving it an inch.

From behind the glass, she could see everything: the ghost terrain rolling across the sim screen, the gleam of instruments, and Kieran—dropping into the pilot's seat like he owned it, like it had been waiting empty just for him.

He moved with the kind of economy that only came from thousands of hours in the air: no wasted motion, no second-guessing. Every flex and adjustment a quiet, brutal reminder of how well he knew his own body—and what he could do with it.

The windbreaker slid off in a careless shrug, and for a moment, Morgan forgot how to breathe.

The tattoo sleeve—sharp blackwork, compass points, wing cuts and storm breaks—caught the dim light. Her fingers twitched against the clipboard, a muscle memory that remembered too much.

And then she saw it.

Near his wrist, tucked against the stark monochrome, a small splash of color. A green chard leaf. Soft. Unassuming. Human.

It didn't match the rest of the ink. It didn't *try* to. Which made it impossible to ignore.

Morgan felt a strange, traitorous pang. She *hated* how badly she wanted to know the story behind it. Hated even more that part of her already knew exactly what kind of man would carry a thing like that on his skin without apology.

The sim rumbled to life around them. Wind shear. Early turbulence. The scenario flexed its muscles—and so did he.

"Crosswind on approach," he said, voice even, hands steady. "Lateral drift increasing."

He adjusted manually—no computers, no autopilot cheats. Just instinct and control, tight enough to make her nails bite into the clipboard.

Trim. Throttle. Inputs so subtle they looked lazy if you didn't know better. But she knew. She *knew*.

He wasn't just flying the sim—he was *showing off*. Not for the techs. Not for the clipboard. For *her*.

And God help her, it was working.

"I stayed under two-twenty," he said, fingers brushing the throttle with obscene gentleness. "Adjusted vector at twelve thousand. If I'd trusted the nav computer, we'd have bounced hard on final. Your alternate routing fixed it."

He said it plain. Direct. A blade slipped between her ribs.

"I'd follow her vector any day."

It wasn't flirtation. It wasn't regret. It was worse. It was obedience wrapped in admiration, wrapped in a threat she could feel blooming low in her gut.

The pen slipped from her hand.

She barely heard Vee's soft snort as she ghosted away, leaving Morgan standing there alone, caught between authority and something far more dangerous. Morgan forced her gaze back to the screen, clipboard forgotten, heart pounding.

Kieran didn't look back at her once. He didn't have to.

THE BREAKROOM WAS loud in the way only crews could be— familiar voices crashing like carts in a terminal hallway. Someone had jammed a phone into a Styrofoam cup, blasting classic rock too loud, the guitars hissing under the snap of soda cans and the staccato rhythm of shit talk.

Folding tables shoved together without elegance. Boxed lunches sweating on dented trays.

Morgan had sat early. Just tired. Just hungry. She didn't notice the trap until the last empty chair was across from her.

Of course it was.

Kieran stood beside it a second too long. Long enough that if he didn't sit, someone might notice. The moment stretched, pulled tight like a rubber band, then snapped when he finally lowered himself into the chair—calm, efficient, pretending nothing lived in the silence between them.

No greeting. No glance. Just the dry sound of wax paper peeled back with clinical precision, his knuckles flexing, the tendons shifting in his hand like she hadn't mapped them with her tongue once.

She bit into her sandwich with enough force to split the bread. Mechanical. Punishing.

Her knee brushed his. Once. Twice. Static flared against her skin, the ghost of a touch that wasn't nearly enough.

Kieran didn't move. Didn't react. Just took a slow sip of ginger ale, the aluminum can hissing under his grip. A line of condensation slid down the side and caught the curve of his wristbone, disappearing under his cuff.

She hated herself for remembering. Remembering how steady his hands had stayed that night three months ago. How hers hadn't.

The noise of the room dimmed to a smear of background static. Around them, the crew roared with laughter —Vee halfway through a story about a maintenance guy who'd trapped himself in a wheel well—but the air between her and Kieran stayed razorwire taut.

He finished his sandwich. Stood. No scrape of the chair. No wasted motion.

As he turned, the cuff of his sleeve caught briefly on the edge of the table—exposing the barest flash of ink. A black wing slicing through cloudbreak. And there—just for a second—the green of a chard leaf.

Morgan blinked too fast. Don't flinch. Don't move.

Their eyes met. Sharp. Unforgiving. Like gunfire across no-man's-land.

"Ma'am," he said—cool, unreadable, as if the word didn't already belong to something far more private between them.

Then he was gone.

Morgan forced herself to stand, feeling the echo of his knee against hers like a bruise. She dumped her trash harder than necessary, the thud swallowed by Fleetwood Mac spinning up on the speaker.

Bootsteps swaggered toward her, telegraphing chaos before the first word even dropped.

"Delgado!" Vee crowed, loud enough to turn heads. "You inhaled that sandwich like you're trying to win a contract extension."

Morgan leveled her with a look so deadpan it could have filed HR paperwork.

Vee passed with a shit-eating grin and a parting shot, low and whispered.

"Y'all gonna pretend that wasn't the horniest sandwich standoff I've ever seen, or should I call it in?"

Morgan didn't answer. Didn't have to.

Her pulse had already answered for her, pounding between her ribs loud enough to drown out the rest.

9

The post-simulator-run mixer had not been her idea.

Tim, her deputy, had pitched it during the morning standup—something about "boosting morale" after the last round of ugly Heritage headlines. Morgan, operating on roughly four hours of sleep and two hours of patience, had nodded, made a vague noise of approval, and immediately outsourced every shred of emotional labor back onto him.

Now, standing in the fluorescent hellscape of folding tables and warm cheese cubes, she regretted not shutting it down harder.

Classic rock blared tinny and distorted from a portable speaker. Someone had gone overboard with corporate-issue banners about "Excellence in Innovation." Half the room hovered near the beer coolers like survivors picking through the ruins. Somewhere near the catering tables, a junior sim tech was butchering "Sweet Child O' Mine" into the world's longest hostage situation, microphone feedback screaming through the hangar rafters. Someone whooped half-heartedly when he hit the high notes and missed by a country mile.

Morgan closed her eyes for a moment, took a slow breath through her nose, and reminded herself that this, technically, counted as leadership.

She was just starting to think she could survive this when the front doors creaked open.

And there he was.

She turned without thinking.

Kieran stepped into the room like the air shifted to make space for him. Flight jacket over his shoulder, sleeves rolled back to his forearms, freshly-shined shoes scuffing lightly on the concrete.

He didn't walk in with the rest of the pilots—the young ones clustering near the beer cooler, trading loud jokes and elbow nudges. He cut through the room at his own pace, ignoring them without even trying.

Two steps behind him was Callie Harper—a junior pilot Morgan recognized from the training pool, twenty-something, bright-eyed, absurdly competent for her age, with a sleek bob of copper-red hair that caught the light every time she laughed.

Morgan caught the flash of Callie's laugh as she said something to Kieran. Saw the way he smiled back—easy, natural, soft in a way he rarely showed anyone.

It landed like a punch.

Morgan looked away so fast she nearly dropped her beer bottle.

Of course he was laughing with someone like Callie. Not wrecked and battle-scarred like Morgan.

She shoved the thought down deep, and turned toward the catering tables.

It was none of her goddamn business. None.

Somewhere near the catering tables, the next victim had taken the mic—wailing off-key like he was trying to summon a second, even crueler hostage crisis.

Morgan tried not to flinch.

Tried not to look toward the tables where Kieran had drifted, ginger ale in hand, a low conversation pulling his mouth into something close to a smile.

Next to him, Callie stood easy in her flight jacket, her head tipped toward him like she was used to his attention. Like it was *hers* to claim.

Morgan dug her nails into the hard glass.

"Delgado!"

Vee's voice cracked through her spiraling like a whip.

"Your time to shine, babe. Come on."

Before she could bolt, Vee shoved the mic into her hand and punched in a song—some low, slow classic that left Morgan nowhere to hide.

Morgan stepped up to the karaoke set on instinct—learned young, sharpened at every birthday, baptism, and backyard party whether you wanted it or not.

She didn't dare look at the crowd.

Didn't dare look at *him*.

Except she did.

One flicker, one tiny, fatal glance—and there he was. Standing too close to Callie. His head bent toward her. Listening. Focused. That small, rare smile tucked into the corner of his mouth.

Morgan's throat burned.

It was supposed to be a joke. Supposed to be awful, like everyone else.

Instead, when she opened her mouth, the room shifted.

A soft, husky alto cut clean through the ugly lighting

and stale beer smell—low, effortless, the kind of voice that wrapped itself around lyrics like it had been waiting.

Conversations stuttered. Heads turned.

Across the room, Kieran froze with a Canada Dry halfway to his mouth.

Morgan saw it. Of course she did.

She kept singing anyway, refusing to let it show. Refusing to let anything show.

When the last note slid out of her throat and the half-drunk clapping and whooping broke out, she shoved the mic back at Vee with a flat, murderous smile.

"Happy now?"

Vee just smirked and took a bow like *she* had been the one singing.

Morgan turned on her heel before anyone else could say anything, cutting through the mixer without looking back.

The wave of night air outside hit her like a wall—thick, heavy, the kind of wet heat that clung to your skin and made every breath feel like work.

She made it to her car on muscle memory alone, hands trembling just slightly as she yanked the door open and collapsed into the driver's seat.

The silence slammed into her.

She gripped the steering wheel with both hands, hard enough that the leather creaked. The pressure behind her eyes built, sharp and stupid.

Morgan closed them.

Took a breath that shook on the way out.

Told herself it didn't matter. That it wasn't her business. That it never had been.

The ache stayed anyway, lodged under her ribs like a knife she was too tired to pull out.

It served her right, she thought.

She'd been stupid enough to hope.

10

Morgan looked fine. Kieran somehow knew she wasn't.

Tight hands. Clean lines. Nothing bleeding where anyone could see it. The hum of the overhead fluorescents grated at the base of his skull, a cheap kind of tinnitus that made the already-tense conference room feel airless. The walls were that corporate gray that always made him think of worn tarmac and blown tires.

She sat at the far end of the table, clipboard perched on one knee, pen tapping a tempo that didn't match her heartbeat.

He'd flown with enough tight crews to know—she looked calm, but it was a trained calm. A cockpit calm. The kind that came after too much—too many close calls, too many eyes looking for a reason to doubt you.

Kieran kept his arms crossed, posture easy but not relaxed.

This wasn't his first call with Enright. He knew the tone already, even before the speakerphone lit green.

"Alright, alright. Morning, team."

David Enright, Chief Operating Officer of Heritage.
Morgan's boss. Folksy in a way that always made you feel
like you owed him something.

Kieran didn't smile.

Morgan did what she always did—straight spine, clean
tone.

"Delgado here. Captain O'Hara's with me."

"Delgado," Enright echoed, like tasting it. Then the
laugh—gravelly, casual. Too casual.

"All that field work's got you real tan, huh? You're barely
recognizable these days. Looks like you've been deployed."

Kieran didn't look at her.

But something in him bristled.

He knew that tone. Heard it used on people he cared
about—the kind that made skin color sound like a disguise.
Like she was trespassing in her own damn skin. Like the
room had already decided she didn't belong.

Morgan didn't flinch.

"We work outside. It's July."

He admired that tone—knife-clean, unsmiling, utterly
unbothered.

And yet, Kieran could feel the microcut of it. That was
the thing about remarks like that. They always came with
plausible deniability and a smile.

"Just saying. Y'all been cooking out there."

She didn't need Kieran to react. But his jaw ticked
anyway.

Morgan redirected, cool and professional.

"We have updated vectors for the sim rerun, if you'd like
to start there."

"Yeah, yeah, we'll get to that. First—uh, the board's
golden boy. Nick Hayes? You know, the one who ran that
rough final? He's raising hell over the sim numbers. Still

insisting your override routing torpedoed his landing profile."

Kieran didn't blink.

Oh, he knew the name. Nick Hayes—aviation dynastic royalty. Same bloodlines. Same backroom handshakes Kieran had been born into.

He wasn't stupid enough to pretend he was different. Not really. He had the same old ghosts hanging off his name.

The difference was, he could still land a plane by hand if he had to.

Morgan's pen paused mid-air.

"Our data shows he overrode two advisories and flew into a destabilized pocket. The reroute minimized damage. If you could check your inbox, I emailed you—"

"I'm not arguing the numbers," Enright said. "He's pissed. Says there's a pattern in your routing logic that keeps screwing his vectoring. Keeps saying it's all 'subjective.'"

Kieran wanted to laugh.

Subjective. Same old song.

Morgan didn't rise to it.

"That's called judgment," she said. "It's my job."

"You pissed him off," Enright replied, voice slippery with something that wasn't quite disdain, but close. "And he's board-adjacent, so now we've got pressure for a full PAWG review."

PAWG—Pilot and Aircrew Working Group. A review panel dressed up like peer feedback, but everybody knew it was just a quiet way to stick a target on your back.

Kieran saw it in the way Morgan stilled—shoulders not tensed, but quiet. Braced.

"You're assigning a review panel because a board member's nephew got his ego bruised?"

"Look, don't make it personal. It's just protocol when

people escalate. He asked for someone else on future routings, too—says it's a trust issue. So yeah. The PAWG's going to dig through your calls, shadow a few flights, see if there's a pattern."

And that was enough.

"She doesn't need a babysitter," Kieran said, low. Measured.

A pause crackled.

"Come again?"

"I already ran the sim. You're not questioning her judgment—you're questioning the outcome you didn't like."

There it was.

That split second of silence that always came after he opened his mouth in a room like this—not because of what he'd said, but because he wasn't supposed to say it that directly.

"I mean—Jesus, Captain, it's not like she's being fired. This is a standard review."

"It's overreach," Kieran said. "And if someone lets it slide, it sets a shit precedent."

Enright narrowed his eyes, voice cooling like a blade left too long in open air.

"Why do you care so much, Captain? She's not your crew. She's not even in your chain. Technically, she's your boss's boss's boss."

A pause, pointed.

"Shouldn't you be closing ranks with your fellow pilot instead of...whatever this is?"

But Kieran stayed still. Careful.

"If there's a panel..." he said, glancing toward her. "You want me in, I'm in. I'll fly. You call the routing. We close it clean."

Another pause. Longer this time. Swallowed by the hum

of the fluorescent lights and the mechanical breathing of the HVAC overhead.

Morgan was silent.

Not still—silent. Pen slack in her fingers, clipboard steady on her lap, but the air around her shifted.

She was running numbers in her head, not flight vectors this time, but calculus just as precise: optics, power, liability, trust.

The speakerphone pulsed green, waiting. Enright's breath still audible on the other end.

"One moment," she said.

She pressed mute. The glow dimmed.

Then she looked at Kieran—really looked at him, for the first time since the call started. No executive veneer. No corporate armor. Just eyes: dark, sharp, and full of the kind of pressure that didn't show on paper.

He didn't move. Didn't speak. He didn't need to.

She trusted his skillset. That was obvious.

But that wasn't the problem.

She had one second, maybe two, before the pause would start to feel like a story. The COO was still on the call. Watching. Listening.

So she kept it clinical. Almost.

"You'll follow my routing," she said, voice low. "No commentary unless asked."

His nod was small. Barely there.

She unmuted the line.

"I'll participate," she said.

"Great," Enright said sarcastically. "Panel meets in a week. Be ready."

The line clicked off.

The room felt too quiet after. The kind of quiet that didn't land gently.

Morgan didn't speak. Didn't move.

She just stared at the dead speakerphone like it might come back to life and demand more of her.

The pen in her hand was still. Her clipboard a battlefield of notes—half legible, half adrenaline.

Kieran leaned back slowly, letting out a breath he hadn't realized he'd held.

Morgan's shoulders dropped an inch—no more. The first exhale of someone who hadn't let herself breathe in forty minutes.

She gathered her clipboard like it owed her an explanation, smoothed a page that didn't need smoothing.

Kieran stayed where he was, hands folded. Not pushing. Not reaching. Just waiting, like turbulence might still roll back in.

She stood first. Walked to the door, then stopped—halfway there, like her body didn't get the memo from her brain.

She looked back at him, just once. Not angry. Not grateful, either.

Something harder to name.

Kieran met her eyes. Not sharp. Not smug. Just steady.

No words. No fake grace notes.

She nodded once, the way you do when there's nothing else to say.

Then she left.

11

Morgan hadn't planned to be on a flight today.

She was in Gary, Indiana for a maintenance routing audit, her schedule packed with back-end compliance checks and an early evening drive back to Chicago. But just past eleven in the morning, dispatch had flagged an urgent repositioning leg—one of Heritage's regionals needed to be moved east before the storm rolling in off the lake shut everything down.

The system didn't flag it, but the vector? It was one she'd run simulations on for weeks. Dense wind shear at three thousand feet. Tight climb corridor. Tail drift. It was textbook.

She'd routed him there. Quietly. Cleanly.

Gary was short a captain for a repositioning leg. Kieran O'Hara, already finishing an assignment out west, got a new flight order—east to Indiana, quick turnaround.

Nobody questioned it. They shouldn't. She made sure it looked like it came straight from dispatch.

The tarmac shimmered like scorched metal, the late afternoon sun clinging low and mean over the lake. Wind peeled across the concrete, sharp with ozone, tugging at her blazer as she crossed toward the aircraft. Storm cells had begun stacking along the western edge—ugly gray walls of pressure thickening by the minute.

Not enough to ground flights. Not yet. But enough to make dispatch nervous.

She climbed into the cockpit jumpseat, strapping herself in with clean, practiced efficiency.

"Just me?"

Kieran glanced up from the panel. Calm, like always. No visible surprise at her arrival.

"No one else left in the hangar," he said. "You good with that?"

She gave a tight nod and flipped her notes open, pen clicking once.

"I'll stay out of your way."

He gave the faintest lift of one brow.

"Appreciated."

Then, eyes back on the instrument cluster:

"But you can lean in if you need a better view."

He said it offhand, like it didn't mean anything. Like he didn't know her attention had already locked on the movement of his hands.

The weather mirrored her flagged vector almost exactly —dense wind shear at three thousand feet, slight tail drift, tight climb window. A textbook challenge.

She'd written this scenario in three separate reports. Run the sim dozens of times. Broken it down from every angle.

But this time, there was no sim buffer. No second chance. Just real air and real metal and a seasoned captain who looked like he could fly through a typhoon with one hand on the throttle and the other checking his watch.

Kieran began working through the checklist aloud, his voice low and steady in her headset. His movements were methodical—no wasted energy, no flash. The kind of confidence that didn't need attention.

There was something in the way he flicked through the startup sequence that felt unhurried, but precise. That old-dog competence she couldn't quite look away from.

Then his hand curled over the yoke.

It wasn't a particularly charged motion. Not deliberately, anyway. But the way his wrist flexed, the way his thumb settled near the throttle guard, casual and certain—something about it made her breath hitch in a way she didn't appreciate.

She caught herself licking her bottom lip without thinking, then immediately looked down at her clipboard, scribbling half-legible notes just to give her eyes somewhere else to go.

"Weather window's narrow," he murmured, fingers skimming over the autopilot interface. "Gonna thread the cell before it thickens."

She nodded even though he couldn't see her from his angle. It wasn't like he needed the confirmation.

The jet rumbled onto the taxiway, wheels rolling smooth underfoot.

Morgan shifted slightly in the harness. The Balmain blazer suddenly felt like a betrayal—too rigid, too heavy, trapping the heat slick against her arms like a punishment for trusting it in the first place.

Her headset pressed firm against her ears, sealing in the low hum of cockpit systems and the unmistakable timbre of his voice. It buzzed softly through the foam, close and private. Like something meant just for her.

They lifted off smooth—nose high, clean thrust, no hesitation. Kieran's touch on the controls was firm but unhurried, like he trusted the jet to rise under him.

Morgan felt it in her spine, the kind of low hum that stayed with you long after the seatbelt light went off.

She made a note. Then another. Then had to stop writing, because her fingers were trembling slightly.

"Nice," she muttered, voice too dry.

"You write 'nice' in your audit?" he asked, not bothering to hide the amusement.

"Shorthand. I'll translate later."

She caught the edge of his smirk and looked away, jaw tight.

God, he was annoying. And smooth. And flying like the weather was something he'd invited just to show off.

Turbulence clipped them at thirty-one-hundred feet, a quick jolt that bumped her shoulder into the side of the jumpseat.

Her breath caught, even though she knew the profile. Knew it on paper, in simulation. Knew what came next. But knowing it wasn't the same as feeling it. Not like this.

Kieran's hand didn't even twitch.

He steadied the yoke like it was a dance partner he'd done this with a hundred times—fingertip pressure, small adjustments, complete control.

His fingers flexed once, and the jet responded immediately, as if listening only to him.

"You always this smooth under review?" she asked, trying to keep her tone neutral.

"You always this quiet when you're impressed?" he replied, voice low in her headset.

The words landed with a kind of quiet weight, like heat dropped straight into her bloodstream. Not sharp. Just warm. Lingering.

She shifted in her seat, blazer sticking to the backs of her arms. The headset suddenly felt too tight, the air in the cockpit too heavy.

She focused on her clipboard, forcing herself to write something down.

-Maintained ideal vector through wind shift.

-No overcorrection.

-Calm demeanor under pressure.

A second note followed before she could stop herself, smaller, tucked in the corner of the margin:

Shouldn't matter if his voice sounds like that.

They began their descent.

Crosswinds picked up, sharp and fast across the nose of the aircraft. She knew what this approach looked like on paper—high difficulty, high risk, the kind that cracked lesser reputations wide open.

But Kieran didn't hesitate.

He adjusted angle and throttle in one seamless motion, landed the plane like he'd been waiting all day for the chance.

Smooth. Silent. Clean enough to pour whiskey over.

Her body exhaled before her mind did.

She hadn't even realized she'd been holding her breath.

They taxied in silence, the weight of it settling over her like humidity.

He moved through shutdown procedures with lazy precision, flipping switches like muscle memory had been fused into his bones.

His headset hung loose around his neck, hair mussed from the strap, forearms still tensed under his rolled sleeves.

He looked over his shoulder, eyes soft.

"You good?"

Morgan unbuckled faster than necessary.

"Fine," she said, collecting her clipboard like it could explain the heat she could still feel beneath her skin.

"I figured."

He didn't push. Didn't try to fill the space with small talk. Just sat there, watching her with that quiet curiosity that always made her feel like she was missing something.

"I have to head back," she added quickly.

He nodded once.

"Thanks for riding along."

She paused at the top of the stairs, halfway gone, then turned back just enough to say,

"Thanks for not screwing up."

"You staying in Detroit tonight?" he asked, perfectly neutral.

"No." She shook her head. "Flying back tonight."

"That's a lot of air time in one day."

She glanced at her watch.

"It's fine. Reports to file. People to see."

There was a pause. A longer breath.

"And I'd rather not linger."

She didn't wait for a response.

Just walked off the tarmac, heels tapping against hot pavement, clipboard held tight to her chest—trying not to think about the way her pulse still hadn't slowed.

Not from the storm. Not from the flight.

And definitely not from him.

12

Kieran had been assigned to fly under her observation for the next few segments—a "logistical decision," the PAWG panel claimed, like they hadn't gleefully weaponized neutrality into punishment.

Just a hop from Chicago to Des Moines. Blue skies, light traffic, textbook routing.

Morgan boarded expecting nothing more than a smooth ascent and a clipboard full of data—the kind of flight that barely left a trace.

Kieran was already in the cockpit when she stepped inside, thumbing through his notes like he'd never left.

In the right seat sat Callie Harper—wide-eyed, restless, and already mid-sentence—the same young woman who'd shown up with him at the company mixer, laughing together like they belonged to each other.

A first officer—young, eager, and too quick to follow his lead.

"Morgan, right?" she said during pre-flight checks, twisting around to catch Morgan's eye like they were already friends. "I remember reading about you in *Air & Space* when I was still in flight school. First woman fleet director! So cool."

Morgan blinked. Compliments usually felt transactional up here—professional, rehearsed. But Callie's grin was full-throttle genuine. Dangerous.

"Uh...yeah," Morgan said.

"Hope you don't mind me asking, but how'd you end up doing this kind of work?"

Morgan caught the quick, familiar glance Callie threw at Kieran. Easy. Familiar. Like there were inside jokes she wasn't invited to.

Morgan schooled her face into something neutral.

"I grew up around planes," she said. "My dad was a mechanic with Heritage. Back when it was still PanContinental Heritage."

Callie let out a low whistle. "No kidding. A legacy."

"Sort of." Morgan shrugged. "I built dioramas next to engine parts. Flying came later."

"It said in the article you have your pilot's license," Callie said, practically sparkling. "Third-gen here. Second-gen woman. My mom flew Cessnas for fifteen years. Told me I wasn't allowed near a cockpit unless I could outfly her."

Morgan smiled despite herself. "Sounds like a good mom."

"The best," Callie said. Then, in the same breath, pivoting: "You, Captain?"

It wasn't just the question—it was the way she said it. *Captain.* A little softer. A little lighter.

Morgan caught it immediately.

Kieran, still adjusting a panel, answered without looking up. "Fourth gen. Dad was Air Force. Korean War. Grandfather and Great Grandfather, World War Two."

Short. Clipped. Uninterested in elaborating.

Callie whistled, impressed. "Damn!"

Morgan logged it away—but her stomach still twisted, irrational and stupid.

The rest of the flight was insultingly smooth. Tailwind. Pristine checkmarks.

And every time she tried to focus, her brain shoved up images of Callie's too-easy smile, the way Kieran's mouth curved—barely—when she joked.

Morgan hated herself a little for noticing. For caring.

They landed in Des Moines.

As Callie shut down her instruments, she grinned over her shoulder. "Alright, drinks. First round's on me."

Morgan opened her mouth, ready to decline.

Kieran beat her to it. "I've got early logs tomorrow."

Callie cocked her head, teasing. "Okay, I see you trying to wriggle out of it. Did y'all have plans already I didn't know about?"

Morgan's chest tightened like a pressure drop.

"No," she said, too quickly.

Kieran, almost overlapping, added: "Absolutely not."

The words thudded inside her like a missed approach.

Absolutely not. Like it didn't even occur to him.

Morgan pasted on a smile. Watched Callie beam. Watched Kieran stay carefully, infuriatingly blank.

"Then let's grab a drink," Callie said. "Relax, I'm off tomorrow. I checked. I'm not a total idiot."

Morgan's laugh felt brittle in her throat.

THE HOLDING PATTERN looked like every airport bar designed by someone who thought nostalgia was a business plan. Exposed brick. Vintage airline posters. Bourbon bottles lit like holy relics.

Morgan changed into high-waisted jeans and a tucked-in cream camisole; her hair fell into wind-mussed waves she didn't bother taming.

Kieran, unfairly, looked effortless: sleeves rolled, dark slacks, that faint scent of something expensive but under-stated. Like he didn't even try and still hit it out of the park.

Callie showed up in a floral midi dress and white sneakers, jean jacket still proudly pinned with her wing badge.

Adorable. Of course she was adorable.

They grabbed a booth. Ordered drinks and fries.

Callie, unsurprisingly, held court like she'd been born under a disco ball.

"Dating apps are a nightmare," she said. "Half the time they think I'm a flight attendant, the other half, they ask if I'm wearing the little scarf. Sir, I have two bars and a type rating."

Morgan snorted despite herself.

"I hope you correct them," she said.

"Oh, immediately. With violence, if needed."

Morgan laughed—short, sharp, a little too much.

And before she could stop herself, the words jumped out of her mouth: "Wait—you're single?"

Callie blinked, then tilted her head like a confused golden retriever.

"What, like, you know someone? Or are you—" she squinted playfully, "—hitting on me? Because I'm flattered, but I'm tragically straight."

Morgan's soul tried to climb out of her body.

"No! No, I just—" she stammered, waving her hand like she could physically erase the moment.

"I thought you two—"

She jerked her thumb between Callie and Kieran, mortified.

Both Callie and Kieran recoiled so fast you'd think someone pulled a fire alarm.

They turned and looked at each other—one of those visceral, full-body winces, the kind usually reserved for biting into bad airport sushi.

"Ew," Callie said immediately, face contorting. "No offense, Captain."

"None taken," Kieran said, grimacing like he needed mouthwash.

Morgan wanted to melt straight through the sticky bar floor and die.

She buried her face in her drink, mumbling something that might have been, "Oh my god, I'll just see myself out."

Callie, bless her, just laughed and shoved the ketchup bottle toward her.

"Here. Drown your shame in fries. It's what I do."

Morgan accepted the bottle with grim dignity.

And Kieran—damn him—had the audacity to smile at her over the rim of his glass.

A real one this time. Small. Private. Like he knew exactly what she'd been thinking, and didn't mind at all. Which somehow made it worse.

"Anyways," Callie leaned in. "What about you two? Anyone waiting back home?"

Morgan shook her head.

Kieran answered slower. "Divorced."

Before anyone could ask more, Kieran pulled out his phone, thumbed to a photo, and passed it across the table.

It was someone barely in their twenties, smiling wide, holding up two dirt-covered beets with both hands like trophies. Curly hair pulled back. Deep brown skin. Overalls. The sun hitting them just right.

They had Kieran's mouth and eyes and a kind of joy Morgan hadn't seen on his face until now.

"My kid," he said simply.

Morgan felt her heart ache sideways.

She didn't realize she was smiling until she caught Callie watching her—some little knowing thing behind her eyes that made Morgan feel suddenly, stupidly exposed.

Two drinks, that was the rule.

Callie stuck to it. Still clear-eyed, still bright.

She leaned back in the booth, stretched her arms overhead like a cat, and said, "I went to Arizona State. Number one party school in the nation. This?"—she gestured at her glass—"This is water."

They laughed. Not a polite chuckle, but real, shared laughter. Easy and warm.

Callie checked the time and stood with a groan. "Alright. I'm turning in. Thanks for entertaining me. You two are way cooler than most of the crews I get stuck with."

"Want us to walk back with you?" Kieran asked.

"I'm good. You two go ahead and finish your night."

Morgan nearly choked on her drink.

Kieran just blinked.

Callie winked.

"Kidding! Relax. Y'all are so serious."

Callie tossed them a wave and disappeared into the night.

The door shut behind her with a soft jingle.

Morgan and Kieran moved like they might leave too—grabbing jackets, emptying glasses—but neither one stood up.

"You always this good at making exits awkward?" he asked, mouth twitching.

Morgan huffed a laugh, staring at the condensation on her glass.

"Only when I'm spectacularly humiliating myself in public."

"You were fine."

He paused, let the moment hang a little too long.

"Kind of cute, actually."

Her eyes snapped up to his, heart lurching traitorously.

"Hey, it could've been worse," he added, with a shrug.

"Yeah? How?"

"You could've asked if I was dating my actual copilot. Mid-flight. Over the intercom."

Morgan groaned, dropping her forehead onto the sticky table with a *thunk*.

Kieran chuckled again, low and warm.

A moment passed.

Something shifted in the space between them—lighter, but still...charged.

Kieran took a slow sip, then asked, "You still get up in the air much?"

Morgan tilted her head, considering.

"Enough to stay legal. Nothing fancy."

"You ever think about doing it more?" he asked. Not pushing. Just curious.

She shrugged, tracing a fingertip around the rim of her glass.

"I never wanted to do it full-time. Not the way you do."

She glanced up at him.

"It was always about understanding the machine for me. Knowing it from the inside out."

Kieran nodded slowly, like he got it in a way most people didn't bother trying to.

"You miss it, though," he said, softer now.

Morgan hesitated.

"Not the flying itself," she admitted. "I miss feeling like I belonged in it."

The words slipped out before she could cage them. She regretted it instantly—hated how raw they sounded in the open air.

But Kieran just nodded again, no judgment. Like he knew exactly what she meant.

Outside, the wind picked up, rattling the old windows.

Inside, neither of them moved to leave.

They ended up staying until the bar closed at one in the morning—Des Moines didn't exactly believe in late nights —but somehow, the hours slipped past like minutes.

They talked about everything and nothing: how Morgan was named after the priest who baptized her—Father Morgan—even though her real first name was Aurelia, a fact she admitted like a confession.

That was the "A." in *A. Morgan Delgado*, she said, with a shrug that didn't quite hide how personal it felt to say it out loud.

They discovered they had both gone to Catholic school, both learned to sit too still and say too little.

There was a moment—just a flicker—where they looked at each other and very clearly *did not* say what they were both thinking about how that might've shaped their adult...interests.

They compared family trees like a contest, each trying to outdo the other in sheer numbers of first cousins. (Morgan edged him out, but just barely.)

By the time the bartender called out, "Last call!" across

the room, Morgan was laughing at something Kieran had just said—head thrown back, the kind of laugh she didn't even realize she'd been holding in.

She caught her breath and realized how close they were sitting now. How easy it had become to stay.

When she looked around, they were the only ones left.

The bartender was stacking stools onto tables with the kind of aggressive efficiency that screamed get the fuck out.

They kept talking as they walked out, their conversation spilling into the parking lot, where they lingered another thirty minutes without even realizing it.

Outside, the wind had picked up, tugging at her hair.

She tucked it behind her ear, but a strand whipped across her cheek again.

Kieran reached out without thinking, brushing the hair back—his fingers warm against her skin, lingering just a second longer than necessary.

They both went still. The moment settled between them —soft, not heavy. Something unspoken but mutual.

She glanced up. He was already looking at her.

"It's warmer than I expected," she said, her voice barely above the breeze.

"Wind's shifting," he replied. "Could mean storms by morning."

"Yeah."

They stood like that for a short while—close, comfortable, unguarded.

"I'm glad we did this," she said quietly. "Tonight."

"So am I," he said.

It wasn't a confession. Not quite. But it was something.

And for now, that was enough.

13

Two days later, Morgan stepped onto the aircraft with her usual purpose—tablet in hand, hair tucked cleanly behind her ears, ready to continue the PAWG audit.

For once, she didn't dread it.

The terminal had been quiet, her coffee was still hot, and for once, she was feeling—light.

She'd even rehearsed a few topics in her head. Something casual. Maybe she'd ask Kieran more about his kid.

The picture had stuck with her. So had the way his face lit up when he talked about them. She hadn't expected that softness from him—not then. But now she wanted to see it again.

She stepped into the cockpit. And stopped cold.

The man in the left seat turned, smiled, and said her name like it tasted good in his mouth.

"Morgan."

Her stomach dropped.

"Drew," she said—flat. Automatic.

He smiled like it was sweet.

"Technically it's Captain Svensson," he said, light as air. "But hey—whatever you're comfortable with."

He said it like a joke. Like a man who wanted her to know he'd moved on—and would never let her forget it.

He looked exactly the same.

Tall. Clean-cut. Devastatingly handsome in that Nordic, unthreatening-on-the-surface way that made people instinctively trust him.

The kind of face that got called "composed" in performance reviews, when what they really meant was cold.

Green eyes. Long limbs. That quiet confidence he wore like a tailored suit. Even now, perched in the captain's seat, posture relaxed, uniform crisp—he looked like someone who belonged there. Like someone you'd want flying your plane.

And that was the worst part.

Her hands clenched around the tablet.

She hadn't heard. No one had told her.

And Kieran—

"Hey," he said behind her, his usual easy tone warm. "Didn't know you were already onboard."

Morgan stepped aside to let him in, her heart in her throat.

"O'Hara," Drew called out, offering a hand. "Thanks for letting me take the leg. Bit of a last-minute switch—union signed off, all above board."

Morgan turned, confused.

Kieran's face didn't change. Not really. Just a blink. A pause. Then he stepped forward and shook Drew's hand.

"Sure," he said smoothly. "I'll observe from the right seat."

Morgan felt it—something shift in the air. Not anger. Not even surprise. Just the same calculation she'd seen in him during high turbulence: calm, quiet triage.

And maybe—just maybe—a flicker of something colder behind his eyes.

Morgan didn't sit in the jumpseat. She didn't breathe. She watched Kieran's face settle into neutrality, the way it seemed to do with most pilots.

Drew played the part perfectly.

As they prepped for pushback, the two men slipped into low, casual conversation. Drew brought up the union—like it was small talk. Kieran didn't bristle. Just answered with that steady, unhurried tone he used in crew briefings. They talked flight hours, fatigue policy, the latest proposed tiers for regional contracts.

They were still running checklists when Drew said it—casual, like he was mentioning the weather.

"Honestly, if the union didn't make it so easy to be lazy, maybe we wouldn't have half these problems."

Kieran's voice didn't spike. Didn't even lift.

"Right," he said, dry enough to scratch paint. "Because asking for a real night's sleep is just reckless behavior."

Morgan didn't turn. Didn't breathe. But she caught it—the edge beneath the calm. Kieran didn't raise his voice. He didn't need to.

Morgan said nothing.

Drew just laughed.

Once they hit cruising altitude—twenty-eight-thousand feet and level—Kieran was running through checklist confirmations when Drew leaned back in his seat, voice just a little lower now. Almost intimate.

"You know," Drew said, eyes forward, voice even. "I've been reading your audit reports."

Kieran glanced over.

"Yeah?"

"Yeah. Good work. Morgan has always been thorough."

She stiffened.

"But I do wonder sometimes," Drew continued, tapping the autopilot panel with a slow, rhythmic finger, "if maybe she moved up a little too fast. You know how it is."

A quiet click from the overhead panel. Nothing out of place. Just another hand gesture from a man in charge of one-hundred-and-eighty souls. Twenty-eight thousand feet above the ground, controlling a machine the size of a building.

And here he was—coolly dissecting her. With her sitting right there.

Kieran didn't respond.

His hand, halfway through adjusting a knob.

Drew smiled, almost to himself.

"Morgan, you're sharp. I've never doubted that, believe me. But sometimes...you're a little too good at getting what you want."

Morgan's pulse slammed into her throat. Her hands were suddenly slick with sweat. She focused on a single rivet in the jumpseat door. She couldn't move. Couldn't breathe right. Her ears rang.

"O'Hara, did Morgan ever tell you we dated?" Drew asked, conversational, as if they were talking about an ex-colleague who'd moved cities.

"Back in the day."

Morgan gripped the armrest. Hard. She needed something to anchor her to the present, something not made of words. Her lungs were stuttering. A dull, hot pressure filled her chest.

"Didn't end great," Drew said, sighing like it was just one

of those things. "She's very focused. Career-first, always. That kind of drive—it's impressive. Until it turns cold."

He said it like a fact. Like something already agreed upon. Like she was a machine that had stopped working once it stopped serving him.

Morgan felt it land, sick and slick under her ribs. Not just humiliation. Not just anger. Something worse.

He was telling a story where *he* had been generous and *she* had been cold. Where what he took from her was supposed to be freely given, forever, without limits. And anyone listening—anyone who didn't know better—would hear it and believe him.

She blinked rapidly, trying to focus on the sound of the aircraft systems—anything. But even the soft hum of the pressurized cabin seemed too loud now.

Familiar panic threaded up her spine in a pattern her body remembered all too well. The cabin was sealed. The doors were locked. And she was stuck twenty-eight thousand feet in the air with the man who had spent years isolating her, undermining her, and rewriting her sense of reality—now in charge of the flight deck, and everyone on it.

Kieran said nothing. But Morgan could see the shift in his body. Subtle, but there. The muscle in his jaw clenched. Hyper-aware. Controlled.

And for the first time in their partnership, she saw him frozen. Not from fear. But from the quiet, agonizing calculation of a man who knew exactly how much was at stake—and how little he could do about it right now.

Drew kept going.

"She's not wrong about the numbers," he said. "But her vectors? Honestly? I've been spotting a few flaws. I'm gonna have to report it to the PAWG. You all understand, right?"

The words landed like a punch to the chest.

Morgan's vision tunneled. She knew this tactic. Knew it in her marrow. It wasn't rage. It was precision. Casual cruelty wielded with the confidence of a man who never faced consequences.

Outside the windshield, the sky was blindingly clear. Inside, the air was sharp with silence.

Kieran didn't speak. Didn't blink. Just stared ahead—steady hands, tight mouth, eyes hard. His posture said everything: *Not now. Not here. But I'm listening.*

And Drew?

Drew smiled. Because he knew. He still had the yoke.

And they couldn't stop him.

THEY FINISHED the flight in icy quiet. When they landed, Drew smiled again. Thanked Kieran for the smooth descent. Told Morgan, with perfect civility, that it was good to see her again. And then he was gone.

Morgan stood in the aisle, back to the cockpit door, heart hammering like it wanted out of her chest.

Kieran stayed behind a moment longer, silent, before stepping out to stand beside her.

"Was that—"

She didn't answer. She didn't have to.

He looked at her. Really looked.

Then he reached out, gently—like he had that night outside the bar—and put a hand on her shoulder.

Not to pull, or to comfort, just to remind her she was still here. Still solid.

"I'm sorry," he said, voice low.

Morgan blinked fast. Swallowed. Nodded once. She didn't speak as they walked down the jet bridge. Her shoulders were squared, head high—but he could feel the tension radiating off her.

When they reached the quiet hallway past the gate, she slowed. Just enough to stop. Just enough to let the silence fall between them.

Kieran paused beside her. He didn't rush it. He never did.

"I didn't say anything in the cockpit," he said finally, voice low but steady. "Because I couldn't. Not without risking the flight."

Morgan nodded once. She understood. She hated that she understood.

"I wanted to," he added, even quieter now. "More than you know."

She never expected anyone to defend her up there. Everyone was supposed to be tough. Unshakable. Bulletproof.

But still.

If Kieran had risen to it—if he'd called Drew out, if he'd defended her like she secretly, shamefully wanted—he would've endangered the flight. He would've done exactly what Drew wanted: made her look unprofessional, made him look unstable, and put one-hundred-and-eighty lives at risk.

And in the end, it wouldn't have hurt Drew at all. It would've buried her.

"You didn't deserve any of that."

Still no answer. He almost left it there. But then something in him shifted—something small, careful, and worn thin.

"I've been...holding things together lately, too. With my kid. With family stuff. It's not the same kind of hurt, but...I guess I know how it feels sitting in the jumpseat and pretending you're fine when you're not."

Morgan's jaw flexed. Her throat moved like she was trying to swallow something sharp. He wasn't comparing. He wasn't deflecting. He was giving her a foothold. A flicker of truth in a day full of power games.

He didn't ask how she was. He just stood there, beside her. Steady. Quiet. With her. And when she finally turned to walk toward the crew elevators, she didn't say a word. But she walked a little slower.

"I need to get out of here," she muttered. "Before I do something regrettable."

Kieran looked over, deadpan.

"What kind of regrettable?"

"Like kicking him in the balls," she said.

"I hope you're not asking me to hold you back, cause I'll be right there with you."

She didn't laugh. Just stared listlessly.

"I know a place."

"To hide the body?"

"A place to kill time for a five hour layover."

She narrowed her eyes.

"We're in Des Moines," she said, tempted to add *again* with an eyeroll.

They'd been grinding through classic out-and-backs from Chicago all week, like Des Moines was the center of the damn universe.

"Correct."

"There's nowhere to go in Des Moines."

Kieran didn't flinch.

"You're just not looking hard enough."

"You're from Michigan. Your standards are compromised."

"And you're from Chicago," he said, pulling out his phone. "Which means you'll complain the entire ride and still order pie at the end."

She opened her mouth. Closed it. "Is there pie?"

"Yes."

She followed.

14

The pie was better than it had any right to be. Crust flaking apart under the back of his fork. Cinnamon-heavy and just barely warm. The kind of pie that reminded you someone still cared about flour ratios and butter temperature.

Across the table, Morgan sat with her shoulders still squared like she was in a boardroom. Top button undone. Jaw clenched tight enough to crack a wine bottle. She hadn't touched her slice.

He didn't speak. Didn't push.

Then, quietly—like the sentence had been trying to form all day—she said: "He used to wait until I was tired."

Kieran looked up.

She wasn't looking at him. Not quite at anything.

"That was his favorite trick. Wait until after a twelve- or sixteen-hour work day, then pick a fight."

Her fork still hadn't moved. She was saying it like she wasn't sure she was allowed to.

"I used to think I was just bad at relationships. But no. I was just too exhausted to argue."

He didn't flinch. Didn't nod. Just listened. And because he was listening, he saw it—how much it cost her to say it. How it scraped against every instinct she had.

This was the woman who could de-escalate a failing reroute in six minutes, who'd kept her whole operation afloat during a Category Four storm without once raising her voice. And here she was, talking about exhaustion like it was something sacred. Like it was where her worst memories lived.

She knew he knew. About Drew. About what it had been.

She hadn't said it, but she didn't have to. He'd seen it the moment Drew smiled at her like he owned her name. And now she was trusting him not to make her say the rest out loud.

She stared at the pie like it might offer absolution.

"He told me I was miserable so often, I started believing it," she said with a small laugh. "I even said it to the board once. During a pitch deck. Like it was something I thought."

Kieran swallowed.

She was ashamed. Not of what happened—of what it meant. That someone like her, sharp as hell, unshakable, could be brought that low by a man. By love. By whatever grotesque version of it Drew sold her.

She was ashamed that she hadn't seen it coming. That it had worked.

And all Kieran could think about—besides the ache in his jaw from not driving back to the airport and slamming Drew's skull into the tarmac—was this:

"What he did wasn't right."

She didn't look at him. Just took a bite. Finally.

After a long moment, she said: "It's not like he hit me."

Kieran set his fork down, slow.

"Doesn't make it okay."

Not a question. Not an opinion.

Morgan went quiet, the kind of quiet that only comes after saying something that's been locked in a chest for years. The kind that still echoes after it leaves your mouth.

Kieran wanted to tell her more. He wanted to offer something back.

But his phone buzzed.

Not a call. Not even a full message. Just one word.

"Hey."

He didn't open it right away.

"I'm sorry," he said instead.

Not for her. For himself.

She looked up, finally.

He didn't say what he was thinking: That this was the worst kind of split-second calculation—when someone you care about finally lets you in, and someone else you love might be falling apart somewhere else, alone.

And then—quiet, but steady: "Is it your kid?"

Kieran paused, thumb hovering over the screen.

"Yeah."

Morgan didn't ask anything else. She just pulled a napkin from the dispenser and slid it toward him.

"Go. I'm not about to be the reason you ignore that."

He huffed—half a laugh, half a breath.

"You sure?"

"I'm not going anywhere," she said.

And for the first time since their falling out in Traverse, he believed it.

～

THE AIR outside the barn was flat, the way Midwest wind got when the sun was low and the clouds couldn't be bothered to form.

Gravel crunched under his black leather shoes.

Around him, the parking lot was ridiculous—like a Pinterest board for "rustic charm." A rusted milk can sat next to a bale of straw wrapped in fairy lights. Two plywood cows danced in overalls near a photo stand where you could stick your face through a hole and become "Farmer of the Month."

The phone was already ringing. One ring. Two. Three. Voicemail.

He stopped walking. Pinched the bridge of his nose.

The screen blinked up at him like it was trying to be gentle.

"Your call has been forwarded to..."

Beep.

Kieran's voice came out low. Too careful.

"Ren, buddy. What's going on?"

Silence. Then a swallow.

"I got your message. Just...call me back, okay? You don't have to explain anything. I just want to hear your voice."

He ended the call. Dialed again. Same result. The second beep hit harder.

"Bud, we've talked about this," he said into the next voicemail. "You worry me when you go quiet like this. I know you're busy, I know you've got a lot on your mind—but just shoot me a thumbs up. Let me know you're okay."

He paused. The wind stung his ears. His hand tightened around the phone. And then—his chest didn't open the way it should have. A breath caught. Just a little. But enough. The gravel under his shoes blurred. The air got thinner, drier, too loud. The sky was too big all of a sudden.

Somewhere, under the present, an old memory roared back to life:

That Sunday. The missed call. The voicemail from his brother he still hadn't deleted. The way the silence afterward felt like being held underwater.

His body remembered. Not with thought—but with muscle. With heat. With that crackling feeling under the skin, like something was about to break loose. He pressed his thumb hard against the edge of his phone. Ground himself there.

"I'll ride standby up to Detroit tonight if I don't hear from you."

It came out steadier than he felt. He exhaled—too fast. Had to pull back. Softened the next part.

"Not to interrogate. Just to check in. Bring groceries. Say hi to that garden of yours."

He cleared his throat. Swallowed the rising static behind his ribs.

"I'll bring pie. I know you say gluten makes you tired, but come on—it's from Pie Barn."

He let out a shaky breath. A needling jolt of pain shot across his chest.

"Call me, bud. Please."

He ended the call.

And stood there, in the parking lot behind a kitschy pie barn, hands trembling, lungs tight. Letting the wind whip through his jacket and take the rest of his composure with it.

AT THE RIDESHARE drop-off point back to the airport, Kieran and Morgan stood side by side. Not speaking. Not quite touching.

The breeze off the fields carried the smell of hay and exhaust.

Morgan shifted her weight from one foot to the other. Her tablet was clutched against her chest like armor.

Kieran hadn't said anything since the parking lot. He looked steadier now, but she could still see the tremble in the corner of his jaw—the kind that only shows up when you're trying to look fine.

The terminal shuttle pulled in. Headlights swept over the pavement.

She turned toward him, but not fully.

"You don't need to fly standby," she murmured, eyes still on her tablet. "Last flight to Detroit's technically full, but I bumped you up. I'm still flagged priority from the audits— you'll have a seat."

His mouth parted slightly. Somewhere, a gate agent was about to shove a seven-hundred-dollar voucher in a passenger's hand and promise it was their lucky day.

Before he could acknowledge what she just did, she added—

"Text me when you get there. And, if you don't mind...let me know your kid's okay."

Her voice was steady. Light, even.

But her eyes flicked up once—just long enough to show that she meant it.

Kieran nodded.

"I will."

Morgan stepped in first. Not much. Just a half-shuffle on the asphalt. But it was enough.

Kieran hesitated—just long enough to make sure this wasn't a mistake. Then he stepped forward too.

It wasn't dramatic. No sudden closeness. No cinematic swell. Just a slow, awkward arrangement of limbs.

His arms went low. Not around her waist—he wouldn't presume—but lower than shoulder height, palms resting carefully between her mid-back and elbows. Secure. Solid. Braced, like he'd done it a hundred times before and still didn't quite trust himself to get it right.

Hers went higher, folding loosely over his shoulders—careful not to add weight.

It was a gesture meant for an acquaintance. Like someone afraid of being misunderstood, but needing the anchor anyway.

Their height difference—maybe eight inches—meant she tilted her chin against the fabric of his jacket, just beneath the collarbone. Not quite resting there. But close. Closer than she meant to be.

He kept his head angled away, jawline to temple, like even breathing too directly might make it too much.

It lasted three seconds. Maybe less.

It was supposed to be a courtesy hug. Brief. Respectable. Noncommittal. But it stayed a second longer than safe. He let go first. She loosened after.

They both stepped back at the same time. Immediately reoccupied themselves—adjusting a sleeve, re-gripping a tablet, checking a phone.

And neither said anything about it.

"Blue skies, Captain."

He half-smiled. The real kind. Tired, but honest.

"You too, Delgado."

15

The streets were slick from earlier rain, but the air still held that stubborn smoggy bite that stung her nostrils.

Morgan walked with her blazer folded over one arm, heels clicking against uneven concrete. The hem of her pants skimmed a puddle. She didn't care.

This was her favorite part of the city—after midnight, after meetings, after having to be useful to anyone.

Humboldt Park didn't ask her for anything at this hour.

The traffic lights cycled for no one. Corner stores shuttered behind metal grates. A wind chime rattled somewhere overhead like it was trying to remember a song.

She took the long way home, past the lot where her uncles used to hold cookouts. A cat darted across the street. A bus rumbled by, empty but lit up like a theater set.

With every few steps, her body unclenched in small increments—shoulders, jaw, the knot at the base of her spine. She hadn't realized how tightly she'd been holding herself, still bracing from the hug. From the pie. From the quiet ache in Kieran's voice when he said, "Call me, bud. Please."

She exhaled, slow.

She'd listened in—not out of curiosity, and not because of something unnamed she wasn't ready to face yet. She was just built that way.

Trained, really. The moment someone looked like they were unraveling, her first instinct was to reach for the thread and start braiding it back together. Quietly. Without being asked.

She couldn't remember when it started—only that it was always expected.

The youngest cousin cried, and she rocked them. A teacher faltered, and she stepped up. Her mother burned herself on a pot of rice, and Morgan was the one who ran cold water, and cleaned the stove, and held the silence.

Her mother used to say, "Don't just watch—help."

And so she did. She helped, and helped, and helped, until help became habit.

Until every room felt like it was hers to manage, every silence hers to break, every emotion hers to absorb and smooth and carry.

They called it maturity. Leadership.

They never called it work.

Even now, in the quiet aftermath of someone else's grief, her body moved like a machine tuned to ache.

She didn't mean to take it on.

But she didn't know how not to.

THE HEELS CAME off before the door clicked shut.

One hand braced the frame as she nudged them off with

her toes—Jimmy Choo pumps, black suede, with a sculpted stiletto heel sharp enough to draw blood.

She was five-six, which still meant she had to physically look up at most men. That's why she wore heels—to even the field without giving them a chance to notice.

One thunked against the baseboard, the other landed sideways, laces tangled like they were too tired to try. She scooped them up and set them neatly beside the shoe rack anyway—a small ritual of order, a quiet offering to the woman she was becoming again, piece by piece.

Her house was dim, but warm. One light above the kitchen sink cast a soft golden arc over the hardwood floor, which creaked familiarly beneath her bare feet.

The scent of lavender and leftover garlic lived here now, along with the hum of a well-used refrigerator and the faintest trace of laundry soap still clinging in the air from earlier in the week.

This was her home: a remodeled worker's cottage on a block she knew like her own pulse. Low ceilings with exposed beams. Painted cabinets in sage green. A couch that hugged you whether you wanted to be hugged or not.

Her people lived next door—grandma, aunt, and two girl cousins in their twenties—and they had keys, which meant she was never quite alone, even when she needed to be.

She opened the fridge and smiled. There it was. A foil-wrapped jibarito, nestled like a secret. A paper towel note folded beneath it: "Love you! – Tía V."

She didn't bother to heat it. Just unwrapped it and leaned against the counter, eating slowly, savoring the crunch of plantain, the vinegar tang of aioli, the roast pork still clinging to its warmth.

She ate with one hand, the other flipping on the

Weather Channel like muscle memory. A low-pressure system was moving in from the west. Storms by morning. She liked knowing these things before the rest of the city did. It made her feel ready. Steady.

THE LIVING ROOM was a soft sprawl of throw blankets, framed art, and scuffed furniture with character.

It held its stories in frames.

Above the mantle, her Penn diploma hung slightly crooked—she'd hammered the nail in herself one night after too much ambition and not enough sleep.

Just below it, a shelf displayed her past like a quiet timeline.

There was a photo of her and her stepdad in matching aviator jackets, sitting in the cockpit of a training plane, his beard still dark, her braces gleaming under a crooked smile —and Amari in the jumpseat, her younger brother, still too young to get his license but tagging along to get ahead, and maybe ease the sting of suddenly not being the only kid anymore.

Her mom, tear-streaked and proud, had her arms wrapped around Morgan after graduation, both of them in dresses that didn't quite match but somehow still belonged together.

A grainy Polaroid of her father from the '90s showed him grease-stained and grinning in front of a disassembled jet engine, like he could rebuild the whole damn world from bolts and memory.

And tucked at the edge, a New Year's Eve photo of Vee: glitter smudged on her cheek, kissing Morgan's temple while Morgan grinned—wide, ridiculous, carefree, like someone who hadn't yet learned to hold herself together all the time.

That girl felt a million miles away. But she was still in there, somewhere. She let her fingers graze the frame, then moved to the bathroom.

STEAM BUILT QUICKLY. She didn't rush. Lavender bath salts. A rose clay face mask she only used when she remembered she deserved it.

Her Sad Girls with Brass Lungs playlist echoed off the tile in low, honeyed loops—Etta James growling like she knew your secrets, Dinah Washington cutting smooth and cruel, Billie Holiday dragging every syllable like a smoke ring, Ruth Brown bending notes like wire. Voices that didn't just sing—they wailed, strutted, survived.

She dipped her toes in first, then sank down into the tub inch by inch, like a ceremony.

No urgency. No audience.

Just water, and the hum of her own breath.

Later, she stood in front of the bathroom mirror. Hands on hips. Studying the curve of her waist like she was tracing someone else's story.

She leaned in, touched the corner of her lip—tilted her head like she might try to see herself through Kieran's eyes.

He'd seen her naked. Really seen her. Traverse City. The hotel room overlooking the tarmac. The way he hovered before touching—heat barely held in check by sheer will. That reverent silence, like he was afraid too much might break her.

He'd waited, breath caught, until she told him exactly what she needed. And then he unleashed it. The hesitation vanished. What replaced it was precision. Control. Hunger.

He'd left bruises like waypoints on her hips and thighs, and even now, she could still feel the ghost of his fingers anchored above her collarbone—a firm claim she couldn't deny.

She shook her head and wrapped the towel around her body. Let out a breath that wasn't quite a laugh.

Barefoot, she padded back into the kitchen.

Poured herself a glass of cold water and stood there for a while, the fridge light throwing long shadows across the floor.

The city murmured around her—an occasional car, a far-off bark, basslines from a party still going somewhere down her block.

Cumbia, maybe, or a warped old salsa track, dragging itself through the humid dark.

Too tired to dance anymore. Too stubborn to quit.

Her towel was starting to slip, but she didn't adjust it.

She was almost ready to go to bed.

Her body was tired, but her brain still clung to the day like static.

Morgan and Kieran had flown enough routes now to build a case—logs compiled, incident-free, ready for review by the PAWG.

Proof, on paper, that the airline could trust her decisions. That she could trust herself.

Though now, apparently, Drew was trying to tear it down—whispering about failures that weren't real.

Drew. The kitchen tile again. Cold. His body in the entryway. The sizzle of burnt onions in the pan.

He was holding a chef's knife. Not raised. Not threatening. Just...holding it. Casual. Familiar. Like it was any other night.

And he was explaining himself. So calmly. So rationally.

"I just think you're misinterpreting me. You always do that."

She remembered nodding.

She remembered the smell of rosemary.

She remembered realizing—viscerally—that she couldn't leave.

In her real kitchen—now warm with safety, now hers—she blinked fast. Her hand gripped the edge of the counter. Hard.

She forced herself to look around. The photos. The diploma. The jibarito wrapper still on the counter.

Her people. Her proof. Her life.

He didn't live here. He had no key.

She exhaled, long and slow. Ran both hands through her hair, still damp from steam.

Tomorrow would be brutal. But tonight—tonight she still had her face mask, her jibarito, and the quiet, undeniable truth: She made it home.

16

Kieran got to Detroit after midnight.

Ren's co-op still didn't have a working lock, just a scuffed door and housemates who knew Kieran. He found them curled under a heap of blankets, eyes puffy, phone dead. Not a crisis. But close enough that he sat on the floor.

A roommate passed by, barefoot and kind, and said something about eighteen-hour sleep cycles and a Berkeley grad student who'd decided Ren had "no drive."

That landed like a slap.

Kieran didn't say much. Just cleared a path to the bed, untangled the charger. Waited.

Eventually, Ren stirred.

"Am I a loser?" they mumbled, eyes half-closed.

"No," he said. "You're doing more for the world than anyone in our family ever did."

They didn't answer. Just rolled over.

He tucked the blanket back over their shoulder.

On the porch, he called Naomi. She picked up on the second ring. Always did.

"Did I call at a bad time?"

"It's one in the afternoon here in Bali," she said. "What's wrong?"

"Ren got dumped," he said. "They're spiraling. No danger, but not great either."

There was a pause. Then: "God. That little Berkeley shit?"

"Yeah."

Naomi's voice dropped. "Did Ren say anything?"

"They asked 'Am I a loser?' Like they were asking about toast."

Naomi exhaled slowly. "And you panicked."

He didn't respond.

She filled the silence. "This isn't your brother."

"I know."

"They're Ren. Messy, brilliant, hurting—but here."

He closed his eyes.

"Tomorrow," she said, "make them breakfast. Do the bacon thing. Burn it a little."

He almost smiled.

"That's the only way I know how."

"Exactly. Let that be enough."

She hung up.

Kieran sat a little longer. Then he went back inside and made sure the blanket hadn't slipped off Ren's shoulder.

Before that, he texted Morgan: *Thanks for getting me here tonight. Everyone's alright. I owe you one.*

17

The storm hadn't let up in twenty hours. Lightning veined the radar like a threat. Flights grounded. Crews timing out. Four cities frozen.

Even the lights in the Heritage Command Center felt hostile—buzzing fluorescents casting everything in surgical white. The air was stale. Everyone was running on caffeine and nerve. Printer jammed on the hour. Someone ripped into trail mix like it was doomsday prep.

Morgan Delgado hadn't sat down in six hours.

Her heart hammered steady and brutal, punching against her ribs like it was trying to warn her. Her right wrist buzzed with faint pins and needles. She ignored it. Ignored the tremor in her knees, the shallow pull of every breath.

Her blazer was MIA under a flood of reroute packets. Sleeves rolled, headset clipped to her jaw, she stood dead center—war room spine, coffee cooling in one hand, tablet buzzing every six seconds in the other.

The FAA liaison was mid-tantrum. Not at her, but loud enough that it may as well have been.

"No, what you're not hearing," he snapped, "is that this is a compliance issue. If Heritage keeps—"

She cut in. Calm. Precise.

"Tower issued a ground hold. Crew complied. We rerouted per protocol and confirmed with dispatch. If you want to push compliance, I'll pull the ATC transcript and loop Newark. Next."

A quiet "damn" floated from east desk.

Her heart kept slamming against her ribs like she was fighting for oxygen at thirty-five-thousand feet.

She forced the world to hear control, even as her body tried to mutiny.

Revenue ghosts lurked near the corner, one brave enough to approach—printout in hand, brow furrowed.

"Morgan, with all due respect—if we keep delaying D.C., we're looking at a loss of—"

She didn't look up.

"If I hear 'net loss' again while passengers are stranded and crews are timing out, I'll reroute you to the sidewalk. Clear?"

Silence. Heads down.

She moved on. Later—when it was safe—she could fall apart.

"Denver?"

"Trying to refile. Four aircraft up, nowhere to send them. COS is full."

"Try Kansas City. Tight, but we've landed worse. Watch the burn rate. Get them down—I'll eat the PR."

Somewhere across the ops floor, someone shouted about *paczki* in the break room. Ava Thompkins had dropped them off earlier that morning, someone added. She'd asked Morgan for a visitor badge last week. Just wanted to say hi to the dispatchers.

Morgan hadn't even seen her. A flicker of guilt surfaced —quick, sharp—and she shoved it down. She didn't have time for guilt. Not today.

She could almost hear it ticking now—the countdown to that stupid PAWG report.

All she could do was keep the rest of the machine standing before they came for her throat.

"Heritage 188—Buffalo captain's refusing. Union wants a rep looped."

"Loop them. And tell them I don't want one tired crew flying. Not on my rotation."

She didn't yell. Didn't pause. Just moved—decisive, relentless, like a conductor keeping time in a room that had forgotten the rhythm.

18

He showed up at the far end of the room around half past seven in the evening, quiet and unnoticed at first—just another tired man in a worn jacket, flight bag slung over one shoulder. His eyes swept the chaos, the faces, the stress. And then he saw her.

Morgan, in her element. Not polished, not posed—just powerful. Sweat at her temples. Sharp around the eyes. Tired in a way that made her beautiful.

She hadn't seen him yet.

He stood still, just for a moment. Just long enough to watch her take control of a system that should've collapsed three hours ago—and bend it back into order.

When she saw him, her eyebrows went up—tired, unsmiling. He told himself it was about the meeting they'd been postponing, not about him. Still, he wasn't thrilled with the flicker of disappointment on her face. It hit lower than he expected.

They both knew it couldn't be put off any longer. The joint PAWG report was due in seven hours. No more excuses. No more delays.

He gave a tired smile.

"I'll wait."

She didn't say anything—just gave him a look. Not warm, but grateful. And that was enough.

SHE GENTLY SHOOK him awake around midnight.

He'd nodded off in the reception area of the ops center —head tilted back, arms crossed, the picture of controlled exhaustion. Like many men in his field, he'd mastered the art of sleeping anywhere, anytime, stealing rest in the cracks between chaos.

He yawned, slow and groggy, blinking up at her. He couldn't help it—a grin pulled at his mouth, easy, helpless. Seeing her standing there felt like the first good thing to happen all day.

"I'm sorry," she whispered. "Just got off my last call with ATC. They wouldn't shut the fuck up."

"You always this charming after a sixteen-hour shift?"

She rolled her eyes and gestured for him to follow her.

The chaos had finally quieted. Down the hall, the fleet control room was now a low buzz. Most had gone home, replaced by a skeleton crew. Phones silenced. Printers sleeping. The storm hadn't let up, but the worst of the reroute scramble was over.

Crew changeovers had begun. Union calls were postponed. The world had stopped asking Morgan for things—for now.

Her office door clicked shut behind them.

It was a different world in here. Soft. No fluorescent lights. Just the warm glow of a curved Ikea lamp in the corner, casting honey-gold light across the small, cluttered space.

It smelled like bergamot, printer ink, and paper—warm, lived-in, familiar.

Pictures lined the shelves and walls in quiet tribute: teenage Morgan and her stepdad—a bearded Black man with a crooked smile and infinite patience—in matching flight jackets, standing in front of a tiny single-engine plane; a framed Polaroid of her father, Puerto Rican through and through, in mechanic overalls with a grin that matched hers exactly, both of them oil-smudged and radiant; a Tuskegee Airmen dedication poster, its corners laminated from years of being pinned and unpinned.

Above her desk, framed in walnut: a copy of her *Air & Space* profile. The headline read: *Skybound: How Morgan Delgado is Redefining Control.*

Kieran stood just inside the doorway, jacket still on, hair windblown and damp at the edges.

Her office wasn't large, but it was full—photos, papers, pieces of her he hadn't seen until now.

He didn't feel like an intruder. He felt like someone being let in. And for the first time in a long time, he wasn't just seeing her—he was understanding her.

She'd kicked off her heels. Her legs were folded under her in the rolling chair, her blouse slightly wrinkled, eyes dark with exhaustion. Still, she looked radiant—illuminated from within by the fire she'd just carried an entire system through.

She glanced at him, half a smirk tugging at her mouth.

"Well?" she asked. "You here to do the vector or just brood dramatically?"

He stepped closer. Set his bag down.

They sat shoulder to shoulder at her desk, the only light a warm arc from the lamp behind them. Her office was still —quiet in the way most places never were anymore.

His jacket hung over the back of her chair. Her tablet lay between them like a shared weapon, both their thumbs moving in tandem as they revised line items.

"Do you want to reword the mitigation clause?" she asked, voice hoarse but focused.

He squinted at the phrasing.

"It's fine. Reads neutral."

"It reads like you didn't want to sign off on it."

"I didn't," he said. "But I trust you."

She paused, blinked at the screen, then kept typing.

They finished the route notes in silence. The kind of silence that felt too full. Too intentional. Like the sound-proofing in the walls was doing too good a job keeping the rest of the world out.

Morgan hit save. Double-checked the formatting. Her cursor hovered over *Send for Review*.

"You ready?" she asked.

"Yeah."

She clicked it. Done. Final. Gone.

They sat there for a moment. Not moving. Not speaking. Just breathing in the scent of vanilla, ink, and old paper— the quiet sanctuary of her office holding them like a warm hand.

They both exhaled at the same time. Looked at each other. Laughed—soft and startled, the kind of laugh that only happens late at night, when everything is finished but nothing feels over.

"This was airtight," he said. "Maybe now they'll let you do your job in peace."

A shadow passed over her face. Doubt. Dread.

"Sometimes..." she started.

"What?"

She shook her head, eyes flicking back to the rain streaking the window.

"Never mind."

But he knew. Or thought he did. *Sometimes I don't think they'll ever leave me alone.*

He didn't say it. He didn't have to.

They sat in silence again, watching the blue runway lights shimmer behind the glass, blurred by rain.

Then—quietly, unexpectedly: "I haven't stopped thinking about it."

Morgan blinked, the words taking a second too long to land.

"What?"

"Traverse."

The word hung there. Soft. Dangerous.

She looked away. Pretended to pull up the report. But the air had shifted. Her shoulders didn't drop. Her breath went shallow.

"I know," she said, too casually.

He leaned closer. She didn't stop him.

"I remember every second," he said. "You?"

She looked up. There was something raw in her face. Not fear. Not surprise. Just the quiet ache of someone who'd buried the memory deep and still felt it humming under her ribs.

"Yeah," she said. "I remember."

For a long moment, neither of them moved. The only sound was the soft whirr of the air vent, the occasional crack of thunder outside.

He let the words hang between them. Didn't push. Didn't move. Just said, low and rough: "I haven't been with anyone since."

She blinked, like maybe she hadn't heard him right.

Then she swallowed, hard enough he saw it in her throat.

"Me either," she said, voice barely above a whisper.

He was close enough now to see the edge of a bandage on her wrist—tension from hours of tablet work. Ink smudged on her thumb. A faint crack on her bottom lip from too much dry air, too much biting back. She looked real. Worn. Undeniably beautiful.

And then she reached out, grabbed the collar of his shirt, and pulled him in.

Her gaze locked onto his—unflinching, deliberate. Her lashes brushed his cheek as her lips ghosted over his. A question asked without words.

He answered by kissing her, slow and deep, cradling the back of her neck as if she might vanish if he let go. She melted into it, all control slipping, her hands tangling in the fabric at his shoulders.

When he lifted her—effortless, like he'd been waiting months to do it—she wrapped around him instinctively. One hand stayed steady on her waist, the other cupped the curve of her ass, guiding her onto his lap as the chair rolled violently back, crashing into the wall.

A plaque rattled loose and hit the floor. Neither of them looked.

Her fingers were already working at the buttons of her blouse, impatient. He yanked his tie off with one hand, not breaking contact.

And then she was bare from the waist up, save for the sheer, dark thing clinging to her skin. Iridescent, barely there, embroidered with flames—or maybe feathers, or wings. It caught the light like oil on water. Not just lingerie. Not for anyone but her.

He hesitated.

It was beautiful. So was she. And the fact that she let him see it? That nearly brought him to his knees.

He fumbled at the clasp, careful like he was undressing something sacred—not from fear, but wonder.

When her breasts fell free, he froze, breath caught.

They were as perfect as he remembered—not just the shape or softness, but the way they made him forget everything else. He leaned in, brushed his lips around one dusky peak, his tongue circling, savoring.

Her breath hitched, that not-quite-moan catching in her throat like a truth she hadn't said out loud.

Then: a knock.

Soft. Polite. Wrong.

He was still fully dressed, save for the missing tie. Her hands hovered over his belt, now unclasped. The outline of him was obvious—thick, urgent, straining. Her slacks had already slipped down her hips.

"One moment!" she called, leaping off him in a single, furious motion.

She darted across the room and locked the door.

"Ma'am, can I take your trash?"

"No trash," she snapped, then grimaced. "Thank you, Olga!"

"No problem, ma'am."

They waited in silence until the hum of the custodial cart disappeared down the hall and the distant door clicked shut.

She exhaled and pressed a hand to her face, chest still heaving. Topless. Still flushed.

He didn't move. Didn't say anything.

Was this the walk-back?

Instead, she let the rest of her slacks fall.

Then she turned and looked at him—eyes fierce, body bare but unflinching. That look said everything.

He rose and closed the distance.

One hand cupped her jaw, thumb brushing her lip before he kissed her again, deeper this time—like possession, not a question.

His other hand slid over her hip, down her stomach, between her thighs. Her panties were soaked. He pressed his thumb against her, slow and deliberate.

Her knees buckled. He caught her.

"You rerouted an entire fleet and probably made a grown man cry on the floor...and all the while, you were this wet for me?"

"Fuck off," she hissed, equal parts mortified and aroused.

"Filthy mouth, Delgado," he murmured, voice rough. "Makes me want to bend you over that desk and fuck you until you forget how to speak."

She bit her lip. Didn't argue.

He stepped behind her, one arm sliding around her waist, the other pinning her elbows behind her. She let her head fall back against his chest with a breathless sound he remembered too well.

His hand slid lower again, fingers circling in a rhythm that made her hips stutter.

She whimpered—high and wrecked.

"Fucking do it, Kieran," she whispered.

No more formality. No more armor. Just need. And that was it.

He turned her, guided her forward to the desk. She braced herself against the surface, papers crumpling under her palms, her hair spilling down like silk. Her nameplate clattered to the floor.

He leaned over her back, one hand guiding her forward, the other skimming her spine. Her body shivered, gave in.

She whimpered again, a low and guttural sound of surrender. She shifted under him—hot, slick, open—and he felt her body jerk tight.

His brain, fogged from how fucking good she felt, still caught it. Still stopped. He braced his forearms on either side of her head, panting against her hair.

"No condom," he rasped. His voice sounded wrecked, half-choked.

She stiffened under him, air slicing between her teeth.

He pressed his nose to the back of her neck and she shivered.

"I had a vasectomy," he ground out, like it physically hurt him to slow down. "Years ago. Safe."

He stayed frozen, muscles straining, not moving an inch until she gave him something.

She tipped her head back just enough to look at him.

Eyes glassy. Wide. Scared—but not of him.

"You're sure?" she breathed.

He nodded, rough and desperate.

She moved her hips back, a slow wet grind that made him black out for a split second.

"Okay," she whispered. "Okay."

The noise he made wasn't human.

He caught her mouth with his, swallowed the sound she made, and finally—finally—let himself move.

She was hot, soaked, tight—too tight for how easily she took him. There was no resistance. Just that maddening slide of him sinking in, all at once, deep enough to make his legs shake. One slow stroke and she was already fluttering around him, wrecked before he even started.

"Fuck," Morgan gasped, writhing under him. "You're doing that on purpose—"

"I am," Kieran said, voice low.

She cursed again and tried to push back into him. He didn't move.

"Now you're just wet and whining for it," he murmured, grinding slow and deep, his grip iron on her wrists.

She hissed, a sound somewhere between humiliation and hunger, and he smiled—cruel and satisfied. He kept it slow. Not to tease, but to punish. Every thrust a deliberate torment.

She thrashed under him, hips rolling, breath hitching. Her voice broke when she moaned—high and slurred and real. She wasn't talking anymore. Just gasping, clawing at the desk, lost.

And when she finally stopped fighting it—when her body gave up the last thread of control—he felt it. That shift. That surrender.

He snapped his hips forward, brutal and sharp, each stroke a jolt through her spine. She sobbed out a broken sound that hit him like a lightning strike—honest, unfiltered, raw.

He didn't speak. Didn't need to. Just the slap of skin, her breath catching, the desk rattling under their weight.

And her. Bent over her work. Shaking from the inside out.

By the end, there were no words left.

Just the wreckage of both of them.

THEY MUST'VE FALLEN ASLEEP.

The last thing he remembered was her body curled into his, skin still damp with sweat, the storm outside burning itself out. Now, the office was dark but not dead—just quiet in that early-morning way, before anyone had reason to demand anything.

Her office couch was far too narrow for this, but somehow they'd made it work. His arm was pinned under her neck, her leg slung over his hip. Their skin tangled, familiar now.

At some point, the last of their clothes had come off. Not in a rush. Not for sex. Just that slow, post-coital drift when fabric starts to feel like a threat and skin feels like home.

He'd been awake for a while, eyes fixed on the thin slice of hallway light under her door. Not thinking. Not spiraling. Just...there.

When she stirred, she didn't say anything. Just inhaled, long and slow—like she knew he was already awake.

Then, voice low and amused: "You know the CEO's sat on this couch, right?"

He blinked. "What."

"Yeah. And I'm pretty sure at least two board members. We used to do debriefs in here before I made them use the conference room."

He went still behind her. Like her words physically landed.

"That's disgusting," he muttered.

She laughed. He didn't.

"You're getting possessive over a sofa?" she teased, twisting just enough to glance back at him.

"No," he said—too fast. Then, quieter: "I don't know. I just—marked the territory and everything. Figured—"

"Ew!" she shrieked, grabbing the throw pillow and smacking him in the ribs.

"I didn't mean like—"

Thwack.

"Okay, okay. I deserved that."

"You absolutely did."

They were both laughing now, too high on endorphins and little sleep. It shook through them—her shoulders, his chest, the space between them.

The tension finally broke. He tightened his arm around her without thinking. She didn't pull away.

They didn't talk about what happened. Not yet. But something about this—her laugh, his warmth, the sheer chemical relief of it all—made it less terrifying.

Her skin was soft against his. Still slightly damp. And somehow, they both looked better than they had in days. Like something had been knocked loose.

She yawned. Murmured, "The graveyard mechanics might come through soon. To drop off a manifest."

His body tensed, just a little. He started to move—ready to untangle, to go. But her hand reached back, rested lightly on his thigh.

"I didn't mean you had to leave," she said. "I just meant —do you want to get breakfast?"

He froze. And then—God help him—he flushed. The kind of flustered that should've felt ridiculous on a man his age. But it hit him square anyway.

"Uh. Yeah. Yeah, I'd like that."

She pulled away slowly, sat up to gather the scattered remnants of her outfit, her hair a haloed mess of waves and static.

Watching her dress was a special kind of torture. Every inch she covered felt like something he was losing. His hand twitched uselessly at his side, aching to pull her back in and keep her warm. Keep her his. He watched her, completely gone. Then grinned without meaning to.

19

By the time they reached Morgan's front porch, the sky had cracked open into morning—soft light glinting off wet pavement, tree branches still heavy from the storm. Everything smelled rinsed. Like the city had finally exhaled.

She unlocked the door with a quiet ease, shouldering it open the way someone does when they know every creak and catch. Kieran followed, stepping into warmth.

It hit him all at once: vanilla, black tea and garlic, something faintly floral under that—maybe her shampoo—and the unmistakable comfort of a house that had always been lived in. A house that held people. Not staged or sterile. Just worn in.

He stood just inside the doorway for a breath, taking it in. Morgan was already peeling off her blazer, hair still damp from the storm.

"Shower first," she said, casual. "Then breakfast."

He raised an eyebrow. "Together?"

She gave him a shrug over her shoulder, like it wasn't a question worth fussing over. "Hot water's not free."

The bathroom was small, clean, already a little humid even before the water ran. They didn't say much. That felt right.

He watched her step beneath the stream, eyes closed, shoulders finally starting to loosen. He gave her a moment before joining, careful not to crowd. Somehow, they fit into the narrow space like they'd done it a hundred times—even if this was the first.

Her fingers found the back of his neck; his hands drifted over her waist. Not greedy. Just sure.

He shampooed her hair slowly, like it was something he'd trained for. She stood still beneath his touch, trusting him completely. That alone sent something hot and quiet surging through him.

Eventually, he couldn't help himself. He dropped to his knees—silently grateful he always looked after them, or he'd never pull this off at his age—and pressed his face between her thighs. His tongue teased her open, slow and methodical, a torment he knew she craved.

She groaned, low and helpless. Thank god for the shower ledge—she sank onto it, legs gone boneless. Her cries echoed off the tile, sharp and desperate. He could've sworn they made the neighbor's dog bark.

They dried off without ceremony, but that didn't mean the show was over.

She tossed him his pilot bag, already grinning like she knew what came next.

He moved through his routine with quiet precision, the kind that said 'I've done this a thousand times, and I'm always this good at it.' Uniform pants first—smooth, dark, sharp lines hugging his hips as he fastened the belt. Then the shirt: starched and spotless, the white so crisp it made the ink on his forearms look darker by contrast.

She watched the way the tattoo sleeve disappeared inch
by inch as he rolled the fabric down, buttoning slowly,
deliberately, like he knew exactly what it did to her. He did
know. He was starting to figure it out—that the way he
moved, the way his hands worked, was a kind of foreplay
she couldn't resist. The more precise he was, the more
unraveled she became.

He tugged his collar straight, slipped the tie into place,
slid the pin through with practiced grace. Every movement a
small performance—not cocky, just calculated enough to
rile her up again.

She sat at the edge of the bed in lingerie that looked less
like fabric and more like art—delicate blooms, the exact
color of her skin, pressed like living tattoos over the most
dangerous parts of her body. She blow-dried her hair
without a shred of subtlety, eyes locked on him like he was
the only thing in the room worth watching.

He gave her the faintest smirk before smoothing his
shirt across his chest—just to twist the knife.

She exhaled a single word, low and filthy.

He groaned.

Two hours until her first war room briefing of the day.
And he needed to be wheels up in three.

She didn't make him take it all off again. But she did step
close, eyes on him like a promise. Her fingers moved to his
belt, slow and careful, unbuckling it with deliberate precision—matching his own. She unzipped his pants gently,
mindful not to wrinkle the fabric. Then she sank to her
knees.

Her hands wrapped around him, both palms cradling
his length with a kind of quiet worship. She took him into
her mouth without a word, steady and unhurried, like she

had all the time in the world—and knew exactly how he liked it.

THE HEAT between them had lowered to a simmer—for now. They had an hour before clock-in.

The kitchen was narrow, sunlit. He opened the fridge and blinked. Nothing except eggs, soy milk and condiments. He tried the freezer. Containers, stacked with militant precision. Bright labels in a mix of handwritings. Some marked with dates. Others with warnings.

"Your food system is..." he began, trailing off, unsure how to finish without sounding out of place.

"Terrifying?" Morgan offered, deadpan, stepping into the kitchen.

He just stared.

She wore one of those suits—the kind he never had the right words for, just the visceral reaction. This one was pale tan, like sand after a storm, and it fit her like it had been built for her from the bones up. Sharp lines. Soft curves. Somehow both.

The jacket cinched at the waist, then tapered just enough over her hips. The pants clung in all the right places before falling long and clean over her legs. Her blouse underneath was half-unbuttoned, revealing just enough collarbone to make his mouth go dry. He didn't think she usually wore heels that high—nothing dramatic. Just enough to tilt her forward like a promise.

"I was going to say 'impressive,'" he managed, smiling.

She leaned against the counter, slipping in a pair of diamond studs. "It works."

He pulled out a plate labeled in Sharpie: *Garlic rice + tocino – from Mom. I cooked, you better eat.*

She nudged him toward the stove. "Can you fry a couple of eggs? I'll microwave."

"You trust me with it?"

"Can't be worse than me. I always overcook it or it sticks to the bottom."

"You're saying this country can trust you with keeping planes in the sky—but not a frying pan?"

She shot him a look. "Delegation is a leadership skill."

He chuckled, cracking the egg one-handed. "Says the woman who never lets anyone do things for her at work?"

"I'm literally letting you cook for me."

He didn't argue. The kitchen filled with the smell of sweet pork and garlic—rich, grounding.

They moved around each other with quiet efficiency. He didn't need to ask where the plates were. She didn't need to ask if he wanted coffee—she just poured two mugs from a fresh pot without looking.

Just then, a front door slammed. Quick footsteps. Laughter. A blur of color streaked past the kitchen window.

"My cousins," Morgan said, rolling her eyes. "Yarelis is eighteen, Kiara's twenty-five."

The younger one—Yarelis, he guessed—darted across the yard with a backpack nearly bigger than her body, hair still damp and slicked back, yelling something about being late for biology.

The other followed a moment later in a CTA station worker uniform, cap tipped back to reveal a crown of intricate braids, neat and gleaming. She balanced a travel mug in one hand and her phone in the other without missing a step. Both headed toward the station.

They paused at the edge of the sidewalk, glanced up at the kitchen window, and spotted her. They waved coyly.

Morgan, already halfway to the sink, gave a tiny wave back through the screen. They immediately turned to each other and started whispering—then broke into a synchronized cackle.

"Gremlins," Morgan muttered.

Kieran bit back a grin.

They were just plating when a voice rang out through the window screen—he'd cracked it open to let some of the smoke from the fried egg drift out.

"Morgan!"

She stiffened. Then gently nudged him away from the window with her hip.

"Morgan! Is there someone else in there with you?"

Kieran glanced at her with a neutral expression. She didn't flinch. Just turned toward the sink and shouted, "Sorry Tía V! Can't talk! Gotta go to work!"

There was a moment of silence from outside. Then a drawn-out, knowing: "Mmhmm."

Morgan turned back to the stove with surgical focus, lips pressed into a line. Kieran tried not to smile.

"They always just show up like that?"

"It's their neighborhood," she said. "I just pay the mortgage."

When they sat down on the couch—plates balanced on knees, the Weather Channel humming low in the background—Kieran felt something shift in him.

He looked at her, eating garlicky rice like it was nothing, like this was any morning, like he belonged in it.

"You okay?" she asked quietly.

He nodded. Took a moment. Looked around the room again—not at the furniture or the framed degree on the wall, but at the whole of it. The feeling.

"Yeah," he said.

She didn't answer. Just reached out and brushed her hand over his wrist, thumb warm against his pulse. He leaned into it, like he was allowed. And for the first time in a long time, he didn't feel like he was borrowing someone else's peace.

20

Morgan reviewed a reroute matrix on the wallboard, eyes flicking across flight numbers, delays, weather maps. She was three hours deep into storm response rotation, brain half-distracted by the still-silent inbox where her PAWG board decision was supposed to land. Any minute now. Any day now.

And yet—

Her mind kept tugging at the morning. Specifically: garlic rice. Tocino. The egg, perfectly done. And the way he hadn't even asked—just pulled the Tupperware from the freezer like he knew what it meant.

Which, of course, he did.

Kieran O'Hara. All that hot Midwest dad energy plus a flight history that touched every major Asian and European hub. Manila, especially—six months flying Detroit to NAIA. She'd clocked it early, filed it under probable ex-girlfriends and worldly white boys who think they know everything.

So no, she wasn't naive. She knew exactly how men like him wove bodies and border crossings into the same fraying story, and called it a life well-lived.

Still. She hated how impressed she'd been that morning. The subtle ease with which he'd moved through her kitchen. No grand declarations. No "What's this?" or "I've always wanted to try Filipino food"—God forbid. Just: garlic rice and tocino. Opened the window when it got smoky. Knew how to fry the egg without a word.

She should not be impressed. Girls like her were always being told—subtly, relentlessly—to be impressed when white people knew the bare minimum about their culture. And most of the time, it was unbearable. A well-pronounced *adobo* did not make someone soulmate material.

But this had been different. Infuriatingly so. He hadn't said anything about it. No weird commentary. No delighted discovery of her as an anthropological experience. He just...did it. Like it wasn't remarkable. Like it was normal.

And of course it was easy for him. Of course he could pull out the tocino and garlic rice from the freezer like it was no big deal. Like he already knew it was breakfast food. That was privilege—quiet, casual fluency in things he never had to fight for.

Still. He hadn't made it weird. He hadn't made her weird. And that, somehow, was harder to shake.

BY THE TIME the board feedback for the PAWG landed in her inbox, Morgan had already replayed that morning too many times. She clicked out of the report, lips pressed so tight they ached. Clean. Immaculate. A textbook case of how to manage crisis at thirty thousand feet. She knew it like muscle memory. She'd written the book they all plagiarized now, quoting her without knowing her name.

Still, she waited. A foolish, stubborn part of her waited. For a call. For a thank you. For the kind of rare, accidental decency that might mean the last decade hadn't hollowed her out for nothing.

She had scoured the feedback, looking for it—some sign of dissent, a leak, the hand Drew had threatened to play. Nothing. He hadn't filed a single objection. Hadn't even gotten himself CC'd. The threats had been just that: noise. Enough to make her flinch even when she'd done everything right.

Then: a FaceTime ping.

Dickhead (Work), flashing across the screen like a bad joke.

Officially: Chief Operating Officer David Enright.

The camera opened on a golf cart jolting across some sun-bleached green. Wraparound sunglasses. Too-white teeth. A man who hadn't touched real work in years, waving like she was the beverage cart girl.

"Heyyy, good work. Everything came back solid. Appreciate it."

Morgan blinked. "Thanks—"

But he was already swiveling the phone away, disinterested, wind carrying half his words.

"Anyways, we're running behind—double bogey on nine, can you believe that?"

And then it ended. No follow-up. No official commendation. Not even the courtesy of a CC to the board—a paper trail that might've said she saved their asses.

Morgan stared at the blank screen. Her reflection stared back: drawn, sharpened at the edges, a woman slowly dehydrating in a system that drank girls like her down to the pulp.

She had rerouted a jet bleeding altitude through clear

air, pulled them away from the heart of the storm before it could shatter them against the ground.

People had been hurt anyway—tossed into ceilings, wrenched from their seats. One man had only just clawed his way out of a coma. His brain would never heal the same way.

It could have been a mass casualty event. It could have been worse.

It wasn't. Because of her. And still, they doubted her.

A pilot who couldn't fly manual blamed the detour she'd ordered. A pilot with a board member uncle pulled strings to make sure she bled for it.

The turbulence that had cracked ribs and skulls was forgotten almost overnight—buried under newer scandals, fresher outrage, a million other things clawing at the news cycle. Not forgiven. Just replaced.

The board stopped worrying once the headlines moved on, once she made herself small and blameless enough to survive it.

Of course it would end like this. Good girls didn't get trophies here. They got a brief nod on the back nine and a pink slip when the stock price dipped.

She stared at the blank screen for a moment longer, then clicked back into the PAWG summary she and Kieran had scrubbed line by line.

"Meridian 7X, tail #489."

Her eyes scanned the ops recap. Same aircraft she'd rerouted. Same aircraft flagged last quarter for sudden altitude-drop anomalies. Flagged—and cleared.

Her jaw tightened.

She filed it away without knowing why. Only that it didn't sit right. Not at all.

21

Morgan's office door swung open so hard it bounced off the wall.

Vee stormed in, a half-crushed granola bar in one hand and a Thai tea sweating all over her other. She dropped both onto Morgan's desk like a sacrifice.

"Here. Food. Drink."

Morgan didn't look up. Just kept stabbing the same three lines into her notepad, over and over, until the paper tore.

Vee flopped onto the couch, boots hitting the armrest. She kicked a pen onto the floor. Didn't even apologize.

Before Morgan could say anything, Vee sat up, nose wrinkling.

"...Ew."

Morgan squinted. "What?"

Vee pointed at the couch, eyes wide. "Did you—you did! I can feel it."

"Feel what?"

"My mechanic saw you and Captain Age Gap leaving the building at five in the morning."

Morgan still didn't move.

Vee's eyes went sly. "Oh my god. You did it. You finally let Michigan zaddy fly into your command center."

Morgan jerked her head up, murder in her eyes.

"Shut. Up."

The door slammed closed with a hollow thud that echoed too long.

Vee just grinned, all sharp teeth and bad ideas.

"Seventeen-year-old you would slap the shit outta you," Vee cackled.

"Midway Magnet's finest. All that hustle, all that ambition—and you're risking it all for somebody who probably qualifies for the senior discount at IHOP."

Morgan pointed a pen at her like a weapon.

"I swear to god, if you don't shut up, I'll have you fixing toilets in Newark all summer. Ninety degrees. No gloves."

Vee snorted.

"Please. Newark's still less toxic than this hellhole."

Morgan dropped back into her chair with a hiss, pen clattering onto the desk.

The grin slid off Vee's face.

She leaned in, elbows on her knees, voice dropping into something almost gentle.

"Hey," she said. "Congrats. For putting nepo baby pilot Hayes in his place."

Morgan barked a laugh—ugly, hollow—and scrubbed both hands down her face.

She wanted to scream. She wanted to flip the whole fucking desk and tear the drywall down with her bare hands. She was hanging on by a thread—seconds away from crashing so hard they'd need a mop, not a recovery team.

"You ever get tired?" she asked, voice wrecked and raw.

Vee watched her for a second.

"Like, sleepy tired or 'the system is built to extract and discard me' tired?"

Morgan didn't answer. Didn't have to.

"You remember when we thought ambition was gonna save us?" Vee asked with a laugh. Mean and small.

Morgan flinched like she'd been slapped.

"Turns out it just made us easier to chew up."

Morgan tapped her pen against the desk, wild and uneven.

"Enright called me on FaceTime," she started.

Swallowed.

Started again.

"He couldn't even look at me. Not even long enough to admit I saved his fucking ass."

Her voice cracked on the word saved. She slammed the pen down, hard enough to splinter it.

Vee stood up too fast, rattling the desk. She opened her mouth to say something—some shitty half-joke, some battle cry—and caught herself. Caught the way Morgan's hands were trembling. So she just picked up the Thai tea and held it out again, this time gentler. No jokes. No smugness. Just offering something, anything.

Morgan took it. She didn't say thank you. Didn't say anything at all. Vee slung an arm over her shoulder, rough and too hard, and said, "Come on. Let's get drunk enough you forget what FAA stands for."

Morgan exhaled something halfway between a laugh and a sob.

"You're buying," she said.

Vee grinned.

"Don't be absurd. You make three times as much as me."

Morgan elbowed her—hard.

"Fine, I'll buy. But no more mentions of the Unmention-able. Or I will murder you."

"Bitch, you've been trying since junior year. Get in line."

Morgan finally smiled—a real one this time. Bent and broken and real.

They left together, slammed the door, and didn't look back.

THEY PULLED INTO THE GENE & Jude's lot like they'd done a hundred times before, Vee taking the corner too tight just for fun.

Morgan didn't bother looking up from her phone—she was already unbuckling.

"Same thing?" Vee asked.

"You already know," Morgan said, slipping off her heels, and handing Vee two fresh twenty dollar bills.

Five minutes later they were posted up on the tailgate, paper-wrapped hot dogs balanced on napkins, the smell of fresh fries rising like incense.

"You think this job's killing us?" Vee asked, mid-bite.

Morgan chewed. Swallowed.

"If it is, at least we're eating good on the way out."

They clinked cans of root beer and let the moment stretch.

Planes flew overhead—low, distant, impersonal.

Then the music went up. The windows came down. And the road unfolded beneath them like a promise.

The city swallowed them in light and noise. Dorothy's blinked from its spot on the corner like a secret—fuchsia glow, mirrored windows, and the promise of anonymity wrapped in bass.

Inside: sweat-slick bodies, perfume, whiskey, and the kind of queer joy that felt half-holy.

Vee spun Morgan into the crowd without warning.

"Let it all out!"

And she did. They both did—like they hadn't worked fourteen days straight, like their careers weren't held together with speed tape and spite.

The music kept pulsing. Time went sideways. Eventually, they surfaced—breathless, glowing—and made their way to the bar. Somewhere in the back, a bartender was torching an orange peel.

Morgan didn't notice at first—she never did.

She laughed at something Vee said, her head tipping back, her collarbone catching the light. Her heels clicked softly on the worn floor when she shifted, legs crossed just so. Casual. Unbothered. A little too polished for the bar stools they were sitting on.

Three people were watching her from the other end of the bar. Two more from the patio. One had just changed her seat to get a better view.

Vee sipped her whiskey soda with a sigh. "You're doing it again."

Morgan blinked.

"What?"

"That thing where you exist."

"I'm literally just sitting here."

"Uh-huh. In custom tailoring and a satin camisole. With your hair like that."

Morgan reached up instinctively, smoothing the perfectly wavy line behind one ear.

"It's just blow-dried."

"Sure, and I'm just queer."

A brave, hopeful voice interrupted them.

"Hey, sorry—this is awkward, but are you two together?"

Morgan looked up, startled.

Vee didn't even flinch. She leaned back against the bar, smiling with the long-suffering air of a woman who had witnessed this exact moment too many times to count.

"We tried," Vee said, raising her glass. "Didn't take. Tragic, I know."

Morgan gave an apologetic smile.

"It was a long time ago. We were both confused."

"I wasn't confused," Vee muttered into her drink.

"But I am straight," Morgan added quickly, wincing. "I mean—I think I am."

"Fully. Utterly. Painfully," Vee sighed, then to the crestfallen stranger: "Sorry, babe. I've already lost that war."

The stranger gave a soft, broken laugh and nodded like she was trying to be chill while quietly absorbing heartbreak. She returned to her table, whispering to her friends like she was relaying a ghost story. Across the bar, another onlooker sighed.

Morgan toyed with her napkin.

"Do I need to start wearing a sign?"

"No," Vee said, grinning. "They wouldn't believe you anyway."

Morgan laughed, but it didn't quite reach her eyes. Her drink was nearly gone. The bar was getting loud again—too many bodies, too much heat.

"I'm gonna get some air," she murmured.

Vee nodded, already distracted by a familiar face near the DJ booth.

"Don't fall in love with anyone out there."

Morgan didn't answer—just slipped through the crowd, heels soft against the floor, breath tight in her chest.

· · ·

OUT ON THE PATIO, the air was cool and damp, the thrum of synth bass muted through the glass. Morgan stood near a fan, sipping her drink slower now. Behind her, a stranger was mid-rant at the smoking table—sharp eyeliner, sharper tongue. She'd been talking about an ex for at least five minutes.

"They always say it came out of nowhere," the woman snapped, flicking ash into a tray. "But that's never true. The signs were always there. Someone just didn't want to call it. Didn't want to be the bitch who said, 'This isn't safe anymore.'"

Morgan froze, her glass halfway to her mouth. It's just a breakup, Morgan. Not everything's a conspiracy. Her brain said it. Her body didn't listen. Because cover-ups and bad relationships ran on the same fuel: denial, misdirection, blame. Make it someone else's fault. Pretend everything's fine. Smile wider. Lie harder. Tail #489. Flagged. Cleared. Not safe. Cleared anyway.

Her hand tightened around her glass. Someone knew. Someone always fucking knew.

Vee found her a minute later, flushed from dancing, drink in hand.

"Why do you look like you just saw a ghost?"

Morgan blinked.

"I didn't. I just—"

She glanced back at the stranger, who had already moved on to another story, laughing now like she hadn't just ripped Morgan's whole world sideways.

"Never mind."

Vee studied her for a breath, unimpressed.

"Absolutely not. Whatever disaster you just put together in your head? It can wait."

"I didn't say anythi—"

"Yes, you were. Your face is doing the thing. The 'if I don't solve this mystery tonight I'll explode and take everyone with me' thing."

Morgan didn't argue. She just sipped her drink, too fast.

Vee leaned in, voice low and pointed.

"Not here, babe. Not tonight. My ex is at the bar, her ex just walked in, and I am officially off-duty from managing your anxiety spiral."

Morgan's voice was a whisper.

"I think the turbulence wasn't weather. I think something was wrong with the Meridian."

Vee's smile faded. Serious now. All business.

"Okay. We'll chase it tomorrow. When our brains aren't full of sweat, vodka sodas, and sapphic melodrama."

Morgan opened her mouth.

"I mean it," Vee said, cutting her off. "You want to pull the thread? Fine. I'll help you unravel the whole damn sweater. But not in a bar where I can literally see three people I've hooked up with in the last decade."

She drained her drink, slung an arm around Morgan's waist, and steered her toward the exit. Morgan didn't argue. Didn't explain.

As the door swung shut behind them, the bass gave out, and the silence swallowed her whole. She was already building the case in her head.

Tail #489. Flagged. Cleared. Buried?

22

Kieran was up before the dogs.

The house was still, early light filtering in through the kitchen blinds, quiet enough to hear the hum of the fridge and the faint click of the thermostat kicking on.

He moved slow—socked feet, flannel pajama pants, hoodie pulled over his head—just a man and the coffee machine he understood better than most of his relationships.

The dogs stirred when the beans ground.

He let them out into the yard—Daisy first, stiff but determined; and Scout, who needed three verbal affirmations and a pocket treat before stepping paw onto the porch.

Same routine, every morning. Predictable. Comforting.

The not-book-club guys would roll in at five, dragging coolers, cornbread, and paperback sci-fi with underlined passages. They rotated between space operas and books about unlearning toxic masculinity—*Octavia Butler*, and *I Don't Want to Talk About It*, the one where Terry Real explains how boys learn to shut down before they ever grow up.

By the third serving of brisket, they'd be unpacking father wounds like old toolboxes: dented, but still functional.

No one flinched when a grown man cried for the first time since junior high. They just passed the tongs, nodded slow, and let him have his dignity.

His phone buzzed. Ren. FaceTime.

He picked up, leaned against the counter.

"Hey, bud."

They looked tired. Hood up. Dark circles. But smiling.

"Hey, Dad. Quick—do you remember how to restart the pilot on the stupid water heater in the basement? It's being homophobic again."

He walked them through it. Talked them through lighting it. Talked them down when they got frustrated and called it a capitalist relic designed to fail.

They were in a mood—post-breakup, low sunlight, too much on their shoulders for someone so young. But still showing up. Still managing a community garden and a block full of elders who called them "baby" and left vegetables on their porch.

"You good otherwise?" he asked when the flame finally held.

Ren shrugged.

"I mean, depression's depression, but yeah. The collards are finally taking off. The kids from the middle school are coming to help next week."

He smiled.

"That's amazing."

"I'm trying."

"I know. Proud of you anyway."

They nodded. Didn't cry. He wouldn't have minded if they did.

"Love you," they said.

"Love you more."

They hung up.

He stood still for a long moment, hand wrapped around his mug, heat fading.

THE SPIRAL DIDN'T COME ALL AT once. It never did. It was small things. The way the sun hit the hardwood floor. The way Scout rested his chin on Kieran's foot like he could feel a shift in the air. The faint buzz of his phone when he wasn't looking at it—muscle memory said Morgan before he even picked it up.

She hadn't texted. Of course she hadn't. She was working. Always working. Probably deep in something that mattered.

He sat at the kitchen table, dogs tucked around him, watching the smoke curl lazily out from the grill vent. He tried to stay there—present, grounded, grateful—but his brain wandered. To her. Again.

He needed to move.

Kieran stood, sliding into the familiar rhythm of small tasks. Grabbed five folding chairs from the garage. Hauled them down the worn flagstone path that curved around the side of the house, past the garden where the tomatoes always died too early. Scout trotted after him, tail up, nose twitching.

The house wasn't fancy—old wood siding, a metal roof that sang in the rain, a wide porch that wrapped around back. It sat tucked between tall pines, the dock just a few steps off the grass, leading out to a narrow lake so still it looked painted most mornings. He set the chairs up at the end of the dock—spaced out sloppy, no real plan. Just enough for whoever wanted to sit close to the water while they picked apart sci-fi novels and their own childhood trauma.

The boards creaked under his feet, old but holding. The dogs flopped down in the shade without being asked. He stood there a minute, mug in hand, letting the breeze lift the hair at the back of his neck. It was beautiful. It should have been enough. But his brain was already back with her.

He remembered how she looked, back arched over the desk that had command over three hundred plus staff on a daily basis. Her lips parted and eyes daring him to do more than he should've. She'd kissed him first. Sharp and sure. Like she needed to quiet her brain by occupying his mouth. He'd let her take control—for a minute. Then put her onto his lap, fingers in her hair. When she stilled—he'd taken over. Hand on her throat, not to choke, just to keep her tethered. Thumb under her chin. The way her breath caught when he said, "Keep looking at me."

She had. Until she couldn't. Until she threw her head back shaking, silent, shattered, undone.

She hadn't said a word after. Just rested there. Let him hold her.

But now? He wasn't just thinking about what happened. He was thinking about what he wanted next. He wanted her on her knees, heels still on and nothing else. Watching him like the question was whether he'd make her ask again. He wanted to hear her say, "Please," and know it wasn't weakness—it was trust. Control she chose to give. He wanted to pull her wrists above her head, wrapping them in silk, and kiss her until her whole body softened. Until she couldn't keep up the act, couldn't hold the line, couldn't do anything but come apart and let him see her.

And maybe that scared the hell out of him. Not the wanting. But the fact that he'd wait for her to ask. And burn in the meantime.

His phone buzzed.

Not Book Club Book Club Group Chat

Chuck: I'm bringing pie. Store-bought. Sue me.

Rick: Don't forget the good tongs this time.

Doug: I'm not using the "good tongs" on your dry-ass brisket, Rick.

Kieran: God forbid a grown man brings his own damn tongs.

Gary: Reminder: No union talk tonight. Doug's blood pressure can't handle it.

Chuck: Deal. As long as Kieran promises to bring his lady friend next time. I'm tired of you all.

Kieran shook his head, smiling despite himself. These idiots. God help him, he loved them. It helped. For a minute. But the second he set his phone down, the quiet crept back in.

Lady friend.

It was too easy to think about her. Too easy to fall back into it. They hadn't talked about what they were. And maybe that was the smart move—two grown adults with jobs that didn't allow for softness. If they got caught, HR would have a field day. She'd be under scrutiny. He'd get off easier. And that imbalance made his skin itch.

Still, it didn't feel like nothing. And pretending was worse than saying it out loud. He'd been a man who liked the in-between once. Drink enough, flirt just right, ghost before sunrise. He told himself it was cleaner that way. Less harm. Less risk. But that was a lie, too. He wasn't that man now. He didn't want almost. He wanted her. With all the mess, all the truth. But he didn't want to pressure her. Didn't want to be one more man expecting her to carry both her own heart and his.

He stared at his phone.

Typed: *You good? Sent you that follow-up data. Let me know if you need anything else.* Read it twice. Looked at the unsent message underneath: *I love the way you look at me right before you let go.* He deleted it. Sent the first. Set it down like it bit him.

It buzzed a second later.

Morgan. Calling.

He hesitated—just a breath—but his heart already knew what it wanted. He grabbed the phone like it owed him closure.

"Morgan."

Silence. A pause filled with breath and static and everything she wasn't saying.

"Hey."

That voice. It pulled something tight in his chest. He pictured her instantly—big honey eyes shadowed with too many hours and too little sleep, lips soft but pressed into that line she wore when she was holding everything in place. He wanted to kiss the tension off her face. Just once. Just to see her smile again. But her silence kept hanging there.

"You alright?"

Another pause.

"I don't know," she said finally. "But it's something. Might be big. Definitely scary."

That wasn't how Morgan talked. She was always surgical with her words—this was fog. He straightened, pulse ticking up.

"You want to tell me what it is?"

"I shouldn't," she said. Then, a weaker add-on: "Not yet."

He felt the heat rise in his chest, somewhere between frustrated and hurt.

"Then why'd you call?"

She didn't answer. Not really.

"I just—" Her voice broke, then she caught it. "I saw your text."

So that was it. Not about work. Not about them. Just her, reaching out without saying why. His jaw clenched, but his voice stayed calm.

"You don't have to shield me."

"I'm not shielding you," she said quickly—too quickly. Then softer: "I'm trying to."

"Morgan."

Silence, again.

"I'm not saying this goes anywhere," she said, voice clipped. "But if it did—hypothetically—I need someone who could verify some things. Off the record."

He didn't hesitate. "I can do that," he said.

She exhaled, quiet but shaky.

"I wouldn't ask if I didn't think you could handle it."

That should've felt like a win, but it didn't. It landed like a half-door open in a windstorm—inviting, but full of warning. She wasn't asking for help. Not really. She was trying to not be alone, without admitting she needed someone. And he hated that part of himself that wanted it to mean more. Wanted this to be something other than two professionals trying not to fall into each other while everything burned down around them.

So he treaded carefully. No pressure. No assumptions. Just the truth.

"I know this probably doesn't mean much," he said,

voice low, "but I've always known you were the one holding this airline together. From day one. And even if this...whatever this is...stays casual—I still trust you. I still want to help. If that's okay."

A long silence.

Finally, she said, "Fine. Look into the Meridian 7X. Stabilization issues, especially in crosswind climbs and descents. You ever flown it?"

"Yeah. I'm certified on it. Flew it when it first rolled out a couple years ago. It's twitchy as hell. I filed reports."

She went quiet. Too quiet.

"There's no record of any reports from you."

His stomach dropped.

"That's not possible. I wrote them. Logged them. Hell, I argued with maintenance about it more than once."

"Try again," she said. "File another one. Just...see what happens."

"Copy that," he said.

"You think they're deleting them?"

She didn't answer. She didn't have to.

"Kieran..."

Her voice softened.

"Are you sure? You know what happened to the Boeing guys. The ones who talked."

He could hear her shifting, probably pacing. That thing she did when she was trying to stay professional while the world cracked underneath her.

"I'm sure. The whole point of this job is to get people home."

The rest he didn't say out loud.

And because it's you. And I might just burn my career to the ground if it meant keeping you safe.

23

Morgan hadn't slept in...what, a day? Two? Time had melted into a blur of reroute logs, radar playback, and maintenance reports she wasn't even supposed to access. But she did. Because no one else was going to.

Her skin felt tacky with dried-up stress sweat. That sour, lived-in stink of old deodorant and adrenaline that clung to her clothes like static. Her mouth tasted like bad coffee and regret. She wanted to brush her teeth so hard her gums bled. She wanted to scrape off this entire day—week?—with a scalding shower and clean sheets that didn't smell like jet fuel. She wanted to eat something that wasn't vending machine peanuts or cold leftovers scavenged between panic attacks.

And—God—she wanted a hug. From Kieran, specifically. Big arms, stupid reassuring warmth, someone to say, "You've done enough, you can stop now." But even that thought stung. Because it wasn't just a hug she wanted.

It was him, the way his voice dropped—low, firm—when he said, "Keep your hands there." The way his mouth grazed her collarbone before he told her to look at him. And she had. She always did. Not out of fear. But because it was him. Because he asked like he meant it—and he always did.

He didn't rush. He let the silence stretch, taut and loaded. Kept her on edge, slow and deliberate. One hand gripped under her thigh, bruising; the other pinned her still between her neck and shoulder. She was unraveling—hips chasing his rhythm, breath caught on every drag of contact —and he just watched. Waited. Until she begged. And when she came—shaking, undone—he said nothing. Just fisted the back of her hair and kept driving into her, steady, relentless, while her whole body trembled beneath him.

And now? That memory wasn't comfort. It was a threat. A dangerous, damning little film reel that lived under her skin and hit play every time she let herself feel too much.

So she shut it off. She was not allowed to miss him and expose a federal conspiracy at the same time.

THE HANGAR SMELLED LIKE OIL, burnt coffee, and too many vending machine dinners. The soundtrack was power tools and profanity. Fluorescents flickered overhead like they were as exhausted as everyone beneath them.

Vee was in the center of it all, radiant in a way only someone covered in grease and purpose could be. She had a smudge on her cheek, a wrench in one hand, and three men twice her size standing at attention while she laid down protocol like scripture.

"I don't care if it's your brother-in-law's shop," she barked. "You don't sign off on work that didn't happen. Period. That's your name on the paper. They'll fire you, not him."

A junior mechanic hovered behind her, trying not to look like he was taking notes on her every word. Vee clapped a hand on his shoulder. "And you—keep asking questions. That's how you stay alive in this place."

Morgan didn't say anything. Just watched, quietly in awe. Vee clocked her immediately, gave a chin tilt, and jerked her head toward the office.

"Let's go, boss lady."

Inside, the office was chaos with meaning. A dusty corkboard covered in grievance notices and ratty union flyers. A Heritage rainbow mug full of pens next to a "Proud to Be Union" thermos. A picture of Vee and her ex taped to the filing cabinet, both of them young, messy, and still in love. A red toolbox repurposed as a seat. A Snap-on calendar from 2009 that had never been replaced.

Morgan leaned against the desk. "You redecorate?"

"I'm sentimental," Vee deadpanned. "Shut the door."

She picked up a walkie, thumbed it on. "Cabrera. Come in here a sec."

A few minutes later, a broad-shouldered mechanic walked in, wiping his hands on a rag that had already given up. His expression was somewhere between wary and over-it.

Vee nodded toward Morgan. "Tell her what you told me."

He looked at her. Then back at Vee. "You serious?"

"She's not gonna burn you."

He sighed, scratched his neck. "I don't know, boss—I got two car notes, and my boat payment's already late."

Vee didn't miss a beat. "Well, did you really need this year's Dodge Ram with the Tungsten trim for eighty-nine grand?"

Morgan looked away so she didn't laugh.

He blinked. "It was on sale."

"Of course it was."

He huffed. "What I'm saying is—I need this job. So if you come back asking about this later, I'll deny it. Every word."

Morgan raised a brow. "Noted."

He shifted, uncomfortable. "There's something weird with the Meridian 7X. Not just the usual AeroVox cheap-ass build quality—it's the stabilizers. Trim system doesn't hold steady, like it's thinking about what to do instead of just doing it. Pilots have been flagging weird feedback, and I've had to recalibrate the same components at least every couple of weeks." He lowered his voice. "But the reports? They go nowhere. Like someone's clearing 'em before they hit the system. No follow-ups. No flags. Just gone."

Morgan's stomach twisted.

The mechanic shifted his weight from one steel-toed boot to the other, clearly uncomfortable. "Anyway. That's all. But like I said—off the record. I work my ass off, and my stupid ex and the kids take every damn dime."

Vee gave him a look. "We heard you the first time, Captain FICO."

He grinned, sheepish. "So...does this mean I get the hours I asked for?"

She rolled her eyes, grabbed a pen, and scribbled something on a post-it. "Yeah, yeah. Just for this quarter. Don't make me regret it."

"Nice," he said, nodding like he just closed a million-dollar deal.

He ambled out like he'd just saved the day, not casually confirmed a federal crime.

The second the door shut, Vee and Morgan locked eyes. The dread sat between them. Heavy. Inevitable.

Vee folded her arms. "Told you."

MORGAN LAID down on the filthy floor of Vee's office, legs sprawled. One hand on her chest, the other clutching her phone. Not for work. For grounding.

She stared at the ceiling like it might offer her answers or, ideally, an exit. Vee was pacing in the corner, hitting her vape like it owed her rent. Clouds of mango ice swirled around her head. She looked like she was about to combust.

"Tell me I'm wrong," Morgan said finally, voice low, like saying it any louder would make it real. "Tell me I'm reading too far into it."

Vee exhaled a plume of vapor, eyes sharp and glassy. "You're not. I wish you were. But you're not."

Morgan laughed, one short bitter sound. "Great."

Silence. Just the soft hum of the ancient HVAC and the static from the radio.

Vee sat down across from her, legs crossed like she was in a fucking yoga class instead of a moral crisis. She tapped the vape against her thigh. "You know what I keep thinking?"

"What?"

"We worked our asses off to be the kind of people they could trust with this shit. And now we know the truth and there is nothing we can do that doesn't cost us everything."

Morgan nodded, slow. "You ever think about how if we'd just kept our heads down—if we hadn't asked questions— we could still be pretending?"

"I try not to," Vee said. "It makes me want to crawl out of my own skin."

Morgan dragged in another breath—too shallow, too fast. "I have people relying on me. I'm no different than

Cabrera, if you think about it. I've got a mortgage. I've got a shoe collection worth more than a base model Kia. And no, I don't want to sell them. I can't just switch careers. This is the only thing I know how to do."

Vee didn't even pause. "First of all, don't ever compare yourself to Cabrera again. That man does not wash his ass."

Morgan let out a hollow laugh.

Vee wasn't done. "Second—you think I don't get it? I've got my two little sisters living in my spare room. My ex is still on my damn health insurance. I put my union card on the line every time I even blink at the wrong supervisor. And now I have to pick between keeping my job and letting people die?"

Morgan pressed the heels of her hands to her eyes. "We report it, we're done. Blacklisted. Labeled difficult. Liability. Can't even get a job sweeping hangars after that."

"And if we don't?" Vee's voice cracked. "And a plane goes down? And it's our names on the logs? Our decisions in the debrief?"

Morgan didn't answer. She couldn't.

Vee let the vape fall into her lap. "You remember when we were coming up? All that bullshit about how if we just worked harder, were better, more competent, more prepared —we'd be safe?"

"I remember," Morgan said.

They sat there in silence again, both of them vibrating just under the skin.

Finally, Morgan spoke. "I can't save the company. But I can try to save the people."

Vee raised an eyebrow. "That sounds dangerously like a plan."

"Not a good one," Morgan said. "But maybe the only

one. We do what we can. Quietly. We bury the 7X in paper-work until it chokes. Document everything."

"And then what?" Vee snapped. "Wait around until someone else grows a spine?"

"Maybe," Morgan said. "Or maybe we wait until we've got enough ammo to make sure they can't bury it. But we do not go out like martyrs. We do not let them turn us into villains in our own story."

Vee stared at her a long time. Then nodded, once. "Alright. Fine. We play the long game. But if I die from the stress first, you better give a bomb-ass eulogy."

Morgan let out a breath that might've been half a laugh. "You get one Beyoncé song and a slideshow. That's it."

"Deal," Vee said, and picked the vape back up. "But you're making the PowerPoint."

24

S etting up the dead man's switch wasn't heroism, and it wasn't strategy; it was survival, plain and sharp-edged, and Morgan knew exactly how ugly survival looked once you stopped lying to yourself.

A backup file, rigged to send itself to the FAA if she vanished, if she got fired, if she so much as flinched wrong inside the machine she had spent her whole life serving.

The walk to Systems Admin was longer than it needed to be, an architectural afterthought tucked into a corner of the building even the security cameras barely bothered with. Morgan kept her pace steady, kept her breathing even, like there weren't knives tucked into every second of what she was about to do.

Marisa's office was at the end of the hall, a tiny glass-fronted pocket of civilization carved out from the chaos of the server room beyond.

While the other admins languished in an open-plan hell of extension cords and Mountain Dew fumes, Marisa had quietly—brilliantly—made herself indispensable. Half the planes in Heritage's fleet would not have made it off the ground without her silent maintenance, without the constant push of patches and overrides she controlled with a few keystrokes and a stubborn smile.

No one said it out loud, of course. You didn't put things like that in writing.

Morgan pushed open the door without knocking.

Marisa looked up from her desk, the air sweet with something citrusy and defiant.

"Is it done?" Morgan asked, her voice sharper than she meant it to be.

Marisa nodded, lazy and unbothered, as if they were talking about lunch plans.

"Everything you flagged is uploaded," she said, her fingers drumming a slow rhythm against her ceramic mug. "Secured. And let's just say...it's outside of anyone's reach."

Morgan let herself breathe once. Only once.

Marisa hesitated, just a second too long to pass unnoticed.

"By the way," she added, almost casually, "when I pulled the maintenance logs for the Meridian files—you weren't the first one to sniff around."

Morgan stiffened. "Who?"

Marisa shrugged, the motion loose but her eyes too sharp. "Couldn't pin it exactly. Admin access covered the trail. But some of those folders had old access stamps—years older than your clearance."

Morgan filed it away the same way she'd file a system failure mid-flight: triage now, investigate later.

She turned to go, but Marisa caught her with a tilt of the head, a soft little betrayal of the poker face she usually wore.

"It'll be sad when you're gone," she said. "Nobody else brings mochi donuts."

Morgan almost smiled. Almost.

Instead, she tightened her grip on the doorknob, nodded once like they'd just completed a transaction instead of something that might cost her everything.

The door clicked shut behind her, and the weight of it—the finality—hit harder than anything she'd ever faced.

The nausea came fast and merciless, a cold punch right below her ribs. It didn't build, didn't give her time to reason with it; it rose in a tidal surge that hollowed her out from the inside, a betrayal of muscle memory and iron discipline.

Her breath caught, fractured into something shallow and useless. She pressed a hand against the wall, willing herself to stay upright, willing her lungs to pull something —anything—out of the heavy, recirculated air.

But it wasn't just her body revolting. It was her brain too.

The math hammered itself out behind her eyes, brutal and simple: Her, a single woman, a single title, a single HR file—versus a billion-dollar corporation.

There would be lawyers. There would be private investigators. There would be backroom conversations where her competence, her loyalty, her character, would be gutted and served up on a tray.

The whisper network would flick its tail, and suddenly every mistake she'd never made would be hers anyway. Her name would become shorthand for "trouble." Her career would become a cautionary tale.

Morgan lurched forward, heels scuffing clumsily against the cheap industrial carpet. She found the nearest emergency exit with the desperate instinct of a trapped animal.

The bar pushed open under her weight with a clang that echoed down the stairwell, sharp and too loud. The air was suffocating. She staggered two steps into the service alley before her body gave up pretending.

She doubled over near the dumpster, one hand braced

against the concrete, and vomited—violent, relentless, the kind of retching that scraped out her throat and left her gasping for air that refused to come.

It didn't feel cathartic. It didn't feel earned. It felt like losing.

When it was over, Morgan wiped her mouth with the back of her hand, tasting acid and inevitability, and thought: This is the cost.

THE ALL-PILOT STAND DOWN HAD GATHERED them all here like ghosts answering an old, unwelcome summons.

The wide, sterile corridors of headquarters buzzed with pilots in fleece jackets and battered jeans, the smell of burnt coffee and exhaustion hanging thick in the air.

Morgan hadn't expected to see him so soon—had thought maybe she could outrun it a little longer—but there he was, cutting through the crowd like something she couldn't pretend not to see.

Kieran caught her inside one of the empty briefing rooms, all tired eyes and that stubborn crease between his brows. He had a folder in his hand—of course he did—and that familiar wrecked hope written all over him.

"I've been digging," he said without ceremony, voice low and rough. "One of my union buddies found something— some flagged maintenance records—"

"Drop it," she said, sharper than she'd meant, slicing the thread between them with a single breath.

He blinked. His whole body stiffened, like she'd slapped him in front of God.

"Morgan—"

"I don't want you involved anymore."

She didn't let herself look at him. The words were easier when she watched the floor.

"Ride it out, Kieran. You can retire in like what? Five to six years? No point in burning yourself down over something that won't touch you if you just let it lie."

He exhaled through his nose, a short, incredulous sound. "You think I'm just gonna sit on my ass and fly sightseeing tours to my grave?"

"It's smarter," she said. "Safer."

"And when have I ever been smarter?"

His voice broke open then, a little too loud, a little too honest.

"I'm not quitting flying until they drag me out or the day comes when I know it's not safe anymore."

She crossed her arms because if she didn't she'd reach for him, and that would be the end of pretending.

"Then that should be your focus. Not my bullshit."

He stepped closer, crowding into her space until the drywall behind her would fuse into her spine. His hand came up—not touching her, not even close—but braced against the wall beside her head, like he could hold the whole world still if he just pinned it hard enough.

"Stop it," he said quietly. "Stop pretending you're doing this to protect me."

His hand curled into a fist.

"You're pushing me away because you want me. Because there's something here and it scares the hell out of you. And Jesus, Morgan, I get it. I get why you're scared. But you don't have to make me the bad guy just because you don't know how to stay."

Something inside her broke so fast it was all she could do to hold the pieces together with nothing but spite and breath.

"I can't," she said, and it came out so soft she hated herself for it. "Especially not right now."

For a second, he just stared at her, looking like he could cut a hole in the world if he stared hard enough. Then he turned on his heel and walked away, the folder still in his hand.

Morgan didn't move until the door clicked shut somewhere behind him. Didn't breathe until the quiet came crashing down. Then she folded, graceless and brutal, a sob tearing free like it had been trying to claw out of her for years.

THE NIGHT CLUNG to her skin, heavy with heat and the stink of jet fuel. Morgan peeled her blazer off and folded it over her arm as she stepped out of the building, the concrete radiating back every miserable degree. She moved fast, ready to leave the whole day behind, until movement near the hangar stopped her cold.

Vee. Cornered by the side of the building, under a buzzing light that barely cut through the dark. The supervisor standing in front of her was a familiar kind of parasite —the kind that thrived when no one was looking. His posture said casual, but everything else about him screamed trouble.

Morgan stayed back, breathing shallowly against the burnt rubber and sweat in the air.

He was running his mouth, thinking he sounded smart.

"Lot of closed-door meetings lately with that nerve center chick," he said, voice fake-easy, pulling at the sticky air between them. "You think people aren't noticing?"

A pause, just long enough to try and let it land.

"Just do your job. Get home. No need to stir shit up."

And then, quieter, almost kind: "You're popular, but you're not invincible."

Morgan felt her jaw set. She didn't move yet.

Vee stood still, locked tight under the streetlamp's sick glow. Her voice when it came was so flat, so final, it cut through the heat like a straight shot of cold air.

"Talk to me like that again and you'll be eating through a straw." No rise. No shout. Just enough to make him blink.

Morgan was walking before he could say anything else. She closed the gap with deliberate slowness, each step echoing off the concrete.

"Problem?" she asked lightly, deadly. The man tried to square up like he had some kind of right. Morgan smiled at him without warmth.

"I can fire you before your next shift," she said, voice soft enough to cut. "You want to find out how fast your badge stops working?"

He opened his mouth, closed it, shifted like he might try to make a joke. Morgan didn't care enough to stay and hear it. She turned on her heel and caught up with Vee, who was already cutting across the lot without a word.

They reached Vee's truck—and stopped.

All four tires. Slashed straight through, the work of someone who wanted them to know. No half-measures, no chance it could be written off as some coincidence. Just destruction laid out plain under the summer night.

Vee stared at it for half a breath before reaching up and peeling a slip of paper from under the windshield wiper.

She unfolded it, read it once, and handed it to Morgan.

STAY IN YOUR LANE.

They stood there, breathing the same foul air, the heat dragging down their spines.

This wasn't petty. This wasn't politics.

Somebody was scared.

And somebody was stupid enough to show it.

MORGAN STAYED with Vee while they waited for the tow truck, the heat from the pavement crawling up through the soles of her shoes. Vee leaned against the curb, arms crossed, saying nothing. Morgan stood a few feet away, breathing through the weight pressing against her ribs. Neither of them spoke. There was nothing left to say that wouldn't make it worse.

When the truck finally came, Vee gave the driver quick, clipped instructions. Morgan watched the whole thing like it was happening behind glass. She didn't move until the last signature was scribbled and the ruined pickup disappeared into the dark, rattling behind the truck like a body bag.

Without asking, Vee slid into the passenger seat of Morgan's car. Morgan started the engine and pulled out of the lot, headlights carving into the thick, miserable night. The ride was silent. Vee stared out the window. Morgan kept her eyes on the road, the lane lines blurring into one long, endless warning. The air between them stayed heavy, the kind of thick that didn't lift even when the windows were cracked.

When they reached Vee's apartment, Vee got out without a word. She didn't slam the door. She didn't look back. She just vanished into the stairwell, her shoulders set hard enough to shatter.

Morgan didn't move for a long time. She sat there, engine humming low, hands locked tight around the steering wheel. Her phone buzzed against the console. She didn't want to look. She looked anyway.

It was a text message from an unknown number: **Tick tock, sweetheart. Hope you're ready to bleed for it.**

The phone slipped from her fingers into the cupholder.

Her stomach twisted, hot and slow.

They knew.

Morgan sat frozen, staring at the ghost-lit screen until it dimmed itself out of mercy. Her hands wouldn't stop shaking.

It didn't matter. In less than twenty-four hours, she was expected to smile. To sip champagne. To shake hands with the same executives already picking her bones clean.

Heritage had sent a car. They'd sent an itinerary. They'd even picked her dress code: "formal business attire, black tie optional."

She was going to waltz into the Smithsonian like nothing was wrong. Pretend the ground wasn't already cracking open under her heels. Toast the machine that had already written her off.

And if they thought she was going down quiet, they had another thing coming.

organ stood barefoot on the cool hardwood of her walk-in closet, the silence broken only by the distant rumble of the Green Line overhead.

The closet was...a shrine. A reliquary of fashion, precision-organized like her command center. Italian-built cabinetry in walnut, brass hardware that gleamed like ambition, and shelves that carried the weight of war: her suits.

Rag & Bone. Alexander McQueen. A cluster of Theory blazers hanging like steel traps. Loro Piana next to vintage Donna Karan. Shoe shelves that went floor to ceiling— Ferragamo, Balenciaga, Stuart Weitzman, Manolo pumps she'd snatched from the Nordstrom Rack like a lioness with a coupon code.

And tucked in between? Longchamp outlet scores from Gilroy. A MaxMara coat from the clearance rack at Woodbury Commons that made a Saks associate visibly gag from jealousy.

She had been trained for this. Molded in the fires of

outlet warfare by her Filipino mom and Puerto Rican tías who treated holiday weekend sales like combat ops.

Morgan didn't grow up shopping—she grew up executing precision retail strikes across suburban Chicagoland.

Woodfield. Gurnee Mills. Aurora. No store was safe.

She learned early: never trust the mannequins, always start in the back, and if you're not sweating, you're not doing it right. They coordinated carpool strategies. Packed emergency snacks in giant Dooney & Bourke bags. Weaponized coupons with military efficiency.

"Try it on even if it looks ugly on the hanger. Mia, that's Italian wool, who cares if it's itchy? You'll grow into it."

It was a generational ritual. Tiring. Relentless. Kind of traumatic. But sacred.

Tonight was the Heritage gala in D.C. Political donors. Execs. The C-suite vultures.

And the women? The women would be in gowns. Expensive ones. Probably Vera, Oscar, some "quiet luxury" label that screamed nepotism and husband-sponsored wealth.

Morgan reached for the same thing she always did: her navy Altuzarra suit. Double-breasted. Sharp enough to draw blood. She held it against her body and stared at herself in the full-length mirror. Her jaw was clenched. She didn't even know she was doing it.

The suit was her armor. Had been since her twenties. She remembered the first time a regional VP called her "exotic" in a boardroom like she was a cocktail. The time a chief pilot asked if she wore red lipstick to "make things harder for us."

Being twenty-seven, the youngest in the room, and

watching every man glance at her chest before pretending to hear a word she said.

Suits meant control. It meant they had to see her mind before they tried to reduce her to a body.

She didn't wear gowns to work events. Not even when she was off the clock. Because the clock didn't exist when you were the only one that looks like you in the damn command center.

You can't give them a reason to not take you seriously.

Those were the words she'd lived by. Rules handed down by mentors like Ava Thompkins who'd survived worse, learned harder, bled longer.

But as she hung the suit back on the hanger, her chest tightened. Maybe that was the lie. The idea that it would ever be enough.

She could dress like a senator, quote union bylaws in her sleep, run a goddamn airline—and they would still find a way to cut her down.

Too assertive. Too cold. Too pretty. Too intimidating. Too...brown.

The weight wasn't in the fabric. It was in the myth that respect could be earned if you armored up enough.

Her hand reached—hesitant but certain—toward the back of the closet.

Behind the backup suits, behind the rarely-worn heels save for weddings and funerals, she pulled out the dress.

Silk. Midnight blue, almost black. Cut to make jaws lock. Floor length. Plunging back. No sleeves, no mercy. The neckline was pure restraint—but the slit up the side said, "I know exactly what I'm doing."

The tag read LaQuan Smith. Snagged from a Net-a-Porter final sale like it had been meant for her all along.

She held it up. This wasn't just a dress. It was a threat. A reminder that she could still choose how she wanted to be seen—how she wanted to hurt. And maybe he would be there. After the stand-down, after the shitstorm, after everything.

Let Kieran O'Hara see her like this. Let him feel it in his teeth.

Somewhere in the back of her mind, she could already picture it: his hands skimming that open back, his mouth muttering something low and reverent like *Jesus, Delgado,* his eyes hungry and his restraint hanging on by a thread.

The thought made her laugh under her breath.

God, she was being so unserious.

And yet.

She could be serious tomorrow.

Tonight? She was going to let the dress do some of the talking.

26

Kieran hadn't planned to come. The invitation had arrived in a glossy folder, stamped with an old photo—him in full captain's uniform from fifteen years ago. Back when he was riding high on booze, ego, and a new woman every week. Back when he could pretend his kid wasn't dodging his calls and his wife hadn't already left him in everything but paperwork.

He knew why the PR team sent it. Cami Lattimore—Chief Marketing Officer, Martha's Vineyard socialite, and the woman who once rebranded furloughs as "sabbaticals"—didn't do nostalgia. She did narrative control. And tonight, he was the story she needed.

GQ once called him "the pilot you'd want in the air and at your dinner table." There was a photo shoot—tarmac at golden hour, real wind machine. He said yes because the airline asked. Thought it didn't matter. It did. It still does. Google him—that's the first thing you see. Captain Kieran O'Hara, Heritage's golden boy. Their mascot. Their mannequin. Still in the training decks. Still the palatable poster child they trot out when the headlines get rough.

They hadn't even changed the caption. They didn't have to. He still flew. Still smiled. Still white and well-tailored enough to stand next to a scandal and soothe investors' nerves.

And no, he didn't say no. You don't say no to the C-suite unless you're ready to spend your contract flying overnight milk runs out of Peoria. Unless you want to be labeled difficult. Ungrateful. Disloyal. So he put on the suit.

And now here he was—cornered, polished, and scanning his phone like a teenager at a school dance.

Rusty [5:44 p.m.] *Found old logs from your last 7X. Shit's scrubbed, but not well. One note's still in the archive under the wrong tail number. Yours.*

He didn't respond. Just stared, thumb hovering. That tail number—he knew it like a scar. He should've fought harder back then.

He flipped threads.

Kieran [yesterday, 6:03 p.m.] *Ready for the circus?*

The reply had come fast.

Morgan: 🙈

That was it. No follow-up. No "see you there." Just that one damn emoji. He stared at it like it owed him an explanation. A monkey. Covering its eyes. What did that even mean? Embarrassed? Anxious? "I hate this, but I'm going"? Flirty? Avoidant? He refused to Google it.

"Kieran!"

He didn't duck fast enough. Cami Lattimore materialized beside him like expensive smoke—champagne flute in one hand, the other sliding onto his arm like she owned the rights to it. Not the bicep. The arm. Full forearm real estate. She wore the kind of scent that came with a waitlist and a warning label. Radiant in that terrifying way only older women with money and no shame could be—cheekbones like armor, lips lacquered in a wine-red that said third divorce and not one regret. Her silk gown clung like lighting direction. Jewelry like minor planets.

"Darling," she drawled, breath tinged with Grand Cru and ego, "you look divine. Is that Tom Ford?"

He barely had time to answer before she steamrolled on. "Of course it is. You'd never wear off-the-rack. Not with those shoulders."

"I—yeah," he muttered, trying to ease his arm away without making it look like an escape attempt. She wasn't wrong. It was Tom Ford. Slim-cut, single-breasted, tailored in London. He liked things that fit—on the body. And if it cost more than a regional FO made in a month—well. That wasn't his problem. He dipped into the trust fund for suits, not yachts. Nana wouldn't mind. She always said a man should know the difference between cashmere and crap.

Cami's grip tightened. She locked in that Botoxed crescent of don't embarrass me in front of the donors.

"Come. You have to say hello to Senator Markham. He adores pilots. And the Undersecretary of Transportation—she's dying to meet you. Just a quick hello, then we'll swing by the photo booth. We've got props. You'd look so cheeky in the little wings."

And just like that, he was moving. Or rather, being moved. Cami paraded him around like a debutante escorting her prize horse into the paddock. Every few steps, she pivoted, dropping names like confetti.

"This is Captain O'Hara. He's been with us since the pre-merger days."

"Yes, that photo *is* him."

"Wasn't he just so dashing in that uniform?"

Kieran smiled the way trained dogs heel. Polite. Predictable. Waiting for the next command. He shook hands. Nodded. Repeated the same three talking points like a pull-string doll in a double-breasted suit.

By the time he saw the bar, it looked like a life raft. He peeled away with the grace of a man who's done this before —three paces back, pivot, pretend he spotted someone across the room. Sanctuary secured. Bartender silent. Bless him.

"Coke. In a rocks glass," he said, voice low.

It came back with a lime wedge and enough ice to keep his hands busy. He sipped it slow. Let the fizz bite. The ritual helped—hands busy, mind quieter, no questions. *Play the tape forward. It never ends with just one.* He wasn't tempted. Not really. But he still kept score. HALT. Lonely. Tired. Classic combo.

He didn't look up until he heard his name again.

"Well I'll be damned. O'Hara."

He didn't need to turn. That voice had the warmth of cheap bourbon and the timing of a trap.

Jim Callahan. Former VP of Fleet Safety at Heritage. Now playing dress-up as the Associate Administrator for Aviation Safety at the FAA. Permanent fixture on the conference circuit. Walking conflict of interest. The kind of guy who knew where the bodies were buried—because he personally signed off on the shovel.

Kieran turned, polite mask in place. "Jim," he said. "Didn't realize you were still making the rounds."

Jim laughed too loud, too fast, clapping Kieran on the back like they were old drinking buddies instead of mutually tolerated family acquaintances.

"Still? Hell, son, I am the rounds. Heritage can't quit me. I'm like a safety blanket—except I write incident reports."

Kieran's smile didn't reach his eyes. He lifted his glass halfway—habit, not need.

Callahan leaned in, voice dropping into faux intimacy. "I still play golf with your old man every third Sunday. Rain or shine. Says he hasn't heard from you in a while."

"Yeah," Kieran said flatly. "He's still calling my kid by the wrong name. Figure silence is safer."

Jim winced like it personally inconvenienced him. "Families, huh?"

"No. Bigots."

Callahan tried to laugh, but it landed with all the grace of a thrown wrench. He shifted his weight, already scanning for a softer target.

"Yeah, well—" he said, tone skidding back toward casual, "—I heard you went regional. What happened? Piss off the wrong VP, or just get tired of the penthouse?"

Kieran's jaw flexed. "I've just been flying."

What Kieran didn't say—and what Jim damn well knew —was that he could've coasted. Could've let Callahan make a few calls. Get him fast-tracked into international widebody ops by twenty-eight. Sit on the board by forty. That was the pipeline, and Jim greased it for the sons of old friends like it was tradition.

But Kieran had sidestepped it. Deliberately. Kept his name off favors. Took the long way up. He wanted the bars on his shoulder to mean something.

Before he could say more, another voice cut in—smooth, warm, and corporate-polished.

"Jim, your Old Fashioned."

David Enright, Chief Operating Officer of Heritage Airlines, stepped into the conversation like he owned the floor. "Captain O'Hara." The nod was practiced, the smile just credible enough. "Always a pleasure," he added, as

Jim clapped him on the back like they were at a happy hour.

But Kieran knew better—this wasn't a cocktail party. It was a war room with hors d'oeuvres.

They'd only talked a couple weeks ago—cordial, controlled, all the right buzzwords. But even then, Kieran had clocked it: the good ol' boy cadence wrapped around a spreadsheet brain, the Midwestern humility that didn't hide how he treated Morgan like a box to check. He was the one who put her through the PAWG. The one who praised her in public and undermined her in every closed-door review. Smiled like a coach. Moved like a knife.

"Mr. Enright," Kieran said, nodding.

"David," he corrected, like that made him human. "Can I get you another? Rum and Coke, right?"

Kieran glanced down at his drink—ice melted, lime curling, untouched. "Just Coke," he said.

A moment passed. Just long enough.

Enright offered a tight smile. "Smart. Bottle to throttle, and all."

He said it like a joke, but it landed with the weight of a file being quietly opened. Without waiting for a response, he flagged a server to swap out Kieran's glass.

Jim chuckled. "He's always been a good boy, this one. At least when someone was watching."

Enright's eyes lingered on the glass, then moved back to Kieran with a quiet calculation. Kieran didn't smile. Didn't blink.

"Alright, fellas, I should make the rounds," Jim said, clapping Kieran on the back once more.

"Sure," Enright said. "Don't let us hold you back."

But Kieran could feel it—the shift. The quiet notch in Enright's brain that had just clicked into place.

"Do me a favor and give your dad a call," Jim called after him. "Don't be a stranger, kid!"

THEY STOOD in awkward silence for a few moments. Kieran was already drained.

Then came the voice.

"It's really good to see you here, O'Hara," Enright said, all silk tie and shark eyes, with that salt-of-the-earth drawl he wielded like a scalpel. "I was starting to think you'd gone full defector."

He let the word hang—just long enough to sting.

"Though I see Cami got to you first. Always did have a thing for her poster boys. God, the way she used to trot you out for media hits—like some prize stud for the breeding program." He smirked. "I think she's still in love with you. Thinks you're the only man who ever looked good in a press kit."

"Glad to know I still make a good mannequin."

Enright chuckled, but it didn't reach his eyes.

"Always so quick with it. Not so much with loyalty these days."

Kieran bit back a reply. He should've kept his mouth shut during that Zoom call—should've swallowed it when Enright dragged Morgan through that bullshit review. But whatever part of him still believed righteous anger fixed things—yeah, that had come out swinging. Raised voice. No filter. He'd made himself useful to the wrong person.

And now here it was. Consequence in a cufflink.

Enright took a slow sip of his drink, then leaned in just enough to pretend this was friendly.

"I've known Morgan since she was fresh out of college.

Back when she was still bright-eyed. Bushy-tailed. Thought she could change the world."

Kieran stayed silent.

Enright's mouth twisted into something that wasn't a smile.

"I know her better than she thinks. Her tells. What she forgets."

Kieran's hands went still at his sides.

Enright leaned in, voice low.

"Maybe remind her who still signs the paychecks."

The threat settled between them, heavy and obvious. Remind her. Like she needed reminding. Like he had pull. He thought Kieran could get to Morgan—calm her down, steer her back into being useful instead of dangerous.

Which meant he wasn't just watching her. He was watching them.

Kieran raised his eyebrows, voice dry as static.

"Sorry, you'll have to walk me through that. I'd hate to misunderstand."

But Enright didn't take the bait. No twitch. No smirk. Just a look—cold, flat, practiced. The kind they probably drilled into him at whatever Harvard-for-executives taught men to make threats without saying a word.

Kieran held his gaze anyway.

"I want you to remember what team you're on," Enright said after swirling his drink. "You were on top, O'Hara. You had it all. Prestige. Power. Respect. People listened when you talked. And now? You're skulking around like you're sorry for it."

Kieran didn't flinch. Didn't blink. He tilted his head, voice calm and flat.

"I've flown a few hundred people through the sky nearly every day for decades, knowing I was the only thing between them and a headline. That kind of pressure rewires you. You'd get it—if you'd ever flown."

He didn't miss the way Enright flinched. Everyone knew the COO kept a six-figure flight simulator in his office. A monument to the wings he never earned.

Enright opened his mouth then closed it. Just that flicker of irritation he couldn't hide. Kieran watched the man go, all stiff shoulders and pinched pride. No control. Just the quiet reality: some people fly, and some people circle the tower barking orders they'll never understand.

Laughter cracked behind him—sharp, derisive, corporate. Three young AeroVox execs, shiny suits, low morals.

"They want us to give a speech on safety," one said. "After the buffet."

"Oh, easy," another replied. "Tell 'em the 7X only kills boring passengers."

A third chimed in: "Or say it flies like a dream—as long as nobody sneezes near the avionics panel."

Kieran stared into his empty glass, memorizing every syllable. He didn't even need to write it down. This kind of rot etched itself into memory.

Then something shifted. A hush. A pivot in the energy.

He turned.

Morgan had walked in.

27

Morgan stepped into the ballroom like she had every right to be there—because she did. But the moment her eyes found Kieran across the room, she regretted everything and nothing all at once.

He looked at her like she'd personally ruined his life. That wasn't a polite, corporate smile. It wasn't *You look lovely tonight, Morgan.* It was *You are in so much trouble.*

Heat crawled up her neck, seared the tips of her ears. Her posture locked tight, like she was back in Catholic school and the nun had just caught her chewing gum.

His gaze dragged down her body like it had weight— measuring every inch of skin between the base of her neck and the small of her back. He didn't even try to look away. Just raised one eyebrow, slow and deliberate. *You wore that. On purpose.*

It wasn't admiration. It was calculation. Like he was already imagining how the silk would feel in his fist. *Not now. Not here. But later*—when it was just the two of them and she had nowhere to run. A promise, delivered without a word. And she felt it. Everywhere.

Morgan forced herself to keep walking—spine straight, head high, face burning. The room was full of Heritage executives. Board members. Elected officials. David Enright himself.

And all she could think was: *Don't let your eyes drop. Not here. Not with him looking at you like that.* She held her gaze steady. *You are not about to fall apart over a look—not with the COO watching and a Cabinet secretary on the guest list. Get it together.*

Still, she hated how easy it was. The way his attention made her feel like the dress was doing exactly what it was built for.

MORGAN MOVED through the ballroom with practiced ease, but every step was deliberate. Her heels echoed against marble, swallowed quickly by the polite hum of conversation and soft orchestral jazz playing near the ceiling.

The lights were warm, flattering, cruel. Every table she passed felt like a private island of power—billionaires in bespoke suits, political strategists with no soul behind their eyes, hedge fund managers dressed like senators and senators dressed like donors.

There were no accidents in the seating chart. No wasted guests.

This wasn't a gala. It was a portfolio. A yearly recalibration of wealth and policy. A quiet, glittering battlefield where the cost of fuel, the price of airfare, the existence of rural routes and essential air services—all of it—was quietly bartered over medium-rare filet mignon and bottom-shelf wine poured into crystal. The lives of flight attendants, mechanics, gate agents, and pilots would be shaped tonight. And no one here would feel the weight of it.

The Secretary of Transportation stood near the center of it all, laughing too easily, a glass of champagne in one hand and a cream envelope in the other.

Morgan had already heard the rumor. Heritage was flying his daughter's entire wedding party to Tahiti.

A "gift." No receipts.

No one would blink.

She smiled like she didn't see it.

Then a flash of red nails and warm perfume caught her from the side.

"Look at you," came the low, familiar voice, and Morgan turned—heart softening, breath catching.

Ava Thompkins.

Her mentor. Her first real advocate.

The first Black woman—and first woman, period—to become Deputy Director of the Chicago Command Center of Heritage Air.

Ava had taken Morgan under her wing when she was twenty-six and almost ready to quit. Held her hand through her first emergency reroute. Taught her how to write a board memo that could cut without drawing blood. Spent late nights with her in the break room, showing her how to survive in a room full of men who resented her presence before she spoke.

"You remember what I told you," Ava said now, pulling her into a hug that smelled like sandalwood and sunscreen.

"Don't let the cameras catch you blinking."

"I remember everything," Morgan whispered.

Ava stepped back, looking her over.

"You look like money, baby."

"I feel like bait."

"That's the job." A pause, a wink.

"Now go take your award and pretend you don't know what they're doing."

Then she was gone—vanishing back into the noise, into the bodies and blazers and fake smiles, like she'd never been there.

The podium was still across the room. Morgan inhaled. Held. Kept walking.

A hedge-fund-backed CEO from a rival airline caressed her elbow. "I keep telling my board to poach you," he said, too loud, too close.

She gave him a tight smile, and slipped her arm out of his grip like it was something sharp she didn't want to bleed on.

Then: Drew. Of course Drew. He appeared in front of her like a trick of the light—sharp suit, clean jaw, blond hair that always curled just a little too perfectly at the temples. He still looked like the world bent for him. Like a Skarsgård with a better tailor and worse intentions.

Six foot six. Built like a doorframe you couldn't walk around. She used to joke that he towered over everyone; now she couldn't unsee how much of that had been the point. When she'd tried to leave, his height hadn't just been a fact—it had been a barrier.

He'd never touched her in anger. He'd never needed to. The implication had always been enough. And even now, in a room full of powerful people, he still made her feel like the exit was something she'd have to earn.

"Morgan," he said, voice low, smug. "Wow. If I'd known you had that in your closet..."

She froze. Her heart stuttered, just once, but the sound of it cracked her composure. Her mouth went dry. Her breath came shallow.

The lights were too bright. The room felt too close.

She couldn't move. Couldn't respond.

Drew was still talking.

She couldn't hear the words—just the cadence, slick and familiar and soaked in a past she'd buried too deep to dig up now.

Her vision blurred at the edges.

Her body went still in that terrible, practiced way.

Fight. Flight. Freeze.

And then—heat, cologne, and stillness.

Kieran stepped into her periphery like a storm rolling in —dark suit, cleaner lines than should be legal, jaw set like he had already decided who needed to be removed. The heat of him. The scent of that understated cologne he wore —warm, woody, laced with something sharper underneath —cut through the noise like a scalpel.

Just standing there next to Drew, he made the other man look cheap. Sweaty. Juvenile. And just like that, the spiral broke.

Morgan blinked once. Her spine unlatched. Her breath came back in. Not calm. Not safe. But clear. Present.

Kieran didn't look at her. He didn't need to.

"Evening," he said to Drew, voice smooth as ice.

Drew blinked.

"This is a private conversation, O'Hara."

"No, it's not," Kieran said. "She didn't ask for it. She didn't want it. So you're done."

Morgan exhaled, the breath she hadn't realized she was holding rattling loose from her chest.

Kieran didn't touch her. Didn't look at her. Just held the line until Drew got the message and walked away, teeth clenched.

Only then did he look at her. Quietly. Gently.

"You okay?"

Morgan nodded once. It wasn't true. But it would be enough to get her to the podium.

The lights dimmed slightly. Someone called her name. Applause.

Time to speak.

Time to perform.

Time to survive.

28

From where he sat, Kieran could only see her in profile—spotlight kissing her cheekbone, posture straight, every inch of her the poised, impossible woman he'd been circling since she'd boarded his jet all those months ago.

He'd thought he was prepared. He wasn't.

She didn't open with jargon or statistics. She opened with a story.

A ten-year-old girl in a hangar after school, watching her father fix landing gear in a pair of coveralls stained with hydraulic fluid and hope. A man who never got to fly but made sure every plane he touched could.

Then—her stepfather. The man who taught her how to steer into wind, who paid for half her flight lessons by picking up extra shifts delivering cargo from Taipei to O'Hare. And the quiet family pride he carried, knowing his father once flew with the Tuskegee Airmen—Black military pilots who had to fight their own country's racism harder than they fought enemy planes, and did it anyway.

She didn't show emotion. Of course she didn't. But her

voice caught, just once, when she talked about what it meant to be given the chance to rise and the responsibility to pull others with her.

The scholarship program she launched last year for underrepresented kids who wanted to fly but couldn't afford ground school. The retention mentorships for first generation college grads. The quiet policy shifts she implemented inside the company—ones she never put her name on but always bled for.

Kieran swallowed hard. The back of his neck was hot.

The room was eating it up, of course. A few heads nodded like they understood. Like they'd been there. They hadn't.

He hadn't either if he was honest with himself. Not all of it—but enough to know she meant every word. Enough to know this wasn't a speech—it was a map of the climb. And none of these people had earned the right to hear it.

She ended it clean. Poised. That soft smile she used when she needed to look approachable without letting anyone too close.

The applause came in waves.

Kieran didn't clap right away. He just watched her, heart heavy and full, and thought: *This woman.*

This fucking woman.

And then he did clap—because anything less would've given him away.

29

Morgan descended the stage to a round of applause that felt just a little too loud, a little too clean—like the room had been waiting for her to finish so it could get back to the business of smiling with teeth.

She made it halfway across the ballroom before Ava materialized at her side, with the timing of a woman who had spent thirty years surviving rooms like this one.

"Beautiful speech, baby," Ava said, eyes scanning the crowd, not her. "You made it look easy."

Morgan let herself smile, just a little.

"Wasn't."

Ava took a sip of her wine, let the silence stretch.

"They love when you shine like that."

Her smile curved—just a touch too sharp.

"Right before the lights go out."

Morgan didn't flinch.

Ava's mouth tilted again—not quite a smile, not quite approval.

"Smile for them, baby," she murmured, wine glass tilting lazily in her hand. "You never know who's watching."

Her gaze slid, just once, toward a knot of people near the bar—where a young woman in a cocktail dress and a press badge was laughing a little too easily at some executive's joke. Ava didn't point. Didn't linger. She just moved on, leaving the warning hanging in the air.

Be careful.

Morgan didn't let any of it show. She just nodded, cool and even, as if Ava had complimented her dress and not laid bare the machine under the chandeliers. Then Ava was gone, and Morgan was alone again—surrounded, applauded, alone.

She barely had time to process the words before—

"Morgan Delgado?" A voice. Too close. Too intentional.

Morgan turned.

The woman was younger than she expected. Early twenties, maybe, with a press badge clipped to the strap of a cocktail dress like it belonged there.

"Sorry," the woman said quickly, not sorry at all. "Elena Chau. I'm with *The Current*. I know this isn't a press event, but I had a donor invite. I was hoping to speak with you— on the record, if you're willing."

Morgan's face didn't move. But her mind went surgical.

The Current. Aggressive. Credible. The kind of outlet that broke things open when the papers got scared.

"I'm not giving interviews tonight," Morgan said, voice pleasant but closed. "But please feel free get in touch with our PR team for anything specific."

"Of course," Elena replied, tone light.

"Maybe just a quote? About your speech? Or about the violent turbulence reports coming out of recent Heritage flights? I hear there's been internal movement."

There it was. The tell. The reason she was here.

Morgan tilted her head, just slightly.

"I think you know I can't comment on that."

"I had to ask," Elena said, with the smile of someone who already had half the story.

Then she was gone—pulled into a conversation with a VP from the National Transportation Research Council like this was all some kind of polite mixer.

Morgan stood still, heartbeat high in her throat, her skin too warm under the dress.

Ava's words rang in her ears.

MORGAN DIDN'T LEAVE the ballroom until almost midnight.

She'd spent the last three hours gritting through small talk with every board member who suddenly remembered her name.

She smiled at the Newark nerve center director like he hadn't tried to tank her reroute strategy in Q2.

She danced with the CEO—who'd only shown up for five minutes before flying to Abu Dhabi to meet with an oil exec about jet fuel pricing. His cologne cost more than a mechanic's monthly paycheck. She pretended not to notice.

And Kieran?

Kieran danced with several women. All smiles, all charm, all diplomatic as hell.

He danced with the Chief Marketing Officer three times. Once would've been enough. Twice was protocol. Three? Morgan filed it away. Said nothing.

Their eyes met across the room between dances—him loosening his collar, her pretending the ice in her glass was helping.

He smiled like he already knew how this night would end—and so did she.

Washington in late summer didn't breathe—it clung. The air outside the Smithsonian was heavy, thick with heat and the kind of humidity that wrapped around your neck like wool. The city was loud in its quiet: cicadas screaming in the trees, faint sirens echoing off limestone, the rhythmic thump of car doors closing as black cars rolled up and peeled off. The National Air and Space Museum glowed like a monument to hubris—spotlights washing the glass façade in gold, casting reflections of Saturn V rockets and capitalism onto the pavement. The Heritage banners from the gala still fluttered, a little limp now.

The crowd was thinning. Billionaires and lobbyists climbed into private town cars and SUVs, security details trailing them like shadows. The wealthy arrived with drivers. The truly rich pretended theirs weren't there.

A group of service staff stood off to the side, waiting to be told if they were cleared to leave or expected to reset the entire space for a morning breakfast briefing. Someone lit a cigarette behind a dumpster. The real night shift was just starting.

Kieran stood near the curb, jacket over his shoulder, collar open, wrist still marked from a champagne splash during his second dance with Cami. He checked his messages. There was only one from Morgan before she disappeared from the gala.

Meet me out front.

A pair of Real Housewives of D.C. types drifted by—flawless makeup, four-inch heels, and champagne confidence. They clocked Kieran instantly, eyes raking over him like he was something expensive and aged in a barrel. One of them smiled, slow.

"You coming to the Ambrosia afterparty, handsome?"

He returned the smile, warm and easy. "You girls have fun. Try not to get into too much trouble."

They giggled like he'd already kissed them on the cheek. Then—just as they walked off—the Suburban pulled up. Black-on-black. Windows tinted so dark it looked matte under the streetlights. No visible plates. The rear passenger door opened with a quiet click. It was dark inside.

He didn't hesitate. He stepped in. The door closed behind him. The cabin was dark—she'd already killed the lights.

Morgan sat before him in silence. Back straight, face unreadable, legs crossed like a weapon tucked beneath her dress. The slit still climbed high up her thigh. The partition was already up.

He didn't say a word. Neither did she. The only sounds were the low hum of the engine and the faint click of the locks. Street lamps cut through the dark interior in pulses of gold, slashing across the silk clinging to her body.

He didn't move at first. Just leaned in—breath warm on her neck—and kissed her. Soft. Slow. Almost chaste.

Almost.

Her breath caught. That barely-there kiss sent a shiver down her spine.

"You walked across that stage like you wanted to be punished later," he murmured. "Congratulations, Delgado. Later's here."

"Kieran..." Her voice cracked, breathy and raw. She was tired. Unraveled. Pliable. And she trusted him to take the reins.

"You knew what that dress would do to me."

He caught her wrist, stopping her just short—but not before her fingers grazed the hard line of him through his pants. He pulled her in, arm locking around her waist, body flush against his. She gasped. He tilted her chin up with one hand, lips brushing the spot beneath her earlobe.

The kiss there? Not soft. Not chaste.

His other hand slipped beneath the silk and tugged it down, baring one breast to the cold kiss of the A/C. Her nipple peaked instantly. He checked the front. Partition still up. Good. He palmed her breast, slow and firm, teasing until her quiet moans filled the cabin.

Neither of them knew how soundproof the car really was.

With one swift move, he flipped her over his knees. Thighs across his lap. Ass lifted. The slit in her dress fell open like a confession. No panties.

He exhaled a curse, low and rough.

She looked back at him—hair tousled, crown of head to the door, lips parted. There was fear in her eyes. But also hunger. Raw. Filthy. Addictive.

Kieran's eyes locked on hers. One hand hovered over the curve of her ass. She didn't speak.

"Let's talk about how many you've earned."

The smallest, defiant smirk. "Earned?"

His head tilted. "That look just added one."

She bit her lip. Looked away. He didn't.

"You think I don't take this seriously?"

A breathless laugh. Closer to a whimper. "Can I make a counteroffer?"

That smile—slow, lethal, full of teeth. "I'm reasonable. But if you're negotiating, come correct."

She didn't blink. Just moved. Deliberate. Legs parting. Back arching. Heels still on. Ass lifted like an offering. He could see everything. Slick. Wanting. A goddamn invitation.

His eyes dropped. Once.

Then his lips brushed her ear. "That's seven."

She groaned, forehead pressed to the leather.

"I need to hear it," he said. Low. Dangerous. "Where we're going. And if I'm allowed to keep going."

She didn't hesitate. "If I want you to stop, I'll say stop."

"Good girl."

He ran his left palm over her spine—then brought his right palm down on her ass with enough force to make her hipbones dig into his thighs.

A sharp cry punched out of her, muffled into her arm. The driver heard that. No way he didn't. Whether he knew what it meant? Another story.

Red bloomed across her skin. He ran his hand over the heat. Not to soothe. To claim.

Then came the second strike. Opposite cheek. She bit her lip. Hard.

He didn't raise his voice. Didn't need to.

Smack. "That's for making me sit there like a saint with blue balls, talking to a goddamn senator."

Smack. "That's for smiling like this wasn't your plan all along. Don't you dare play innocent."

Smack. His breath slowed. Even his palm was hot, lactic acid building in his bicep. "That's for mouthing off just now."

Smack. "That's for being shameless and enjoying this too much."

Smack. He leaned close, mouth at her ear. "That one?" A pause. "Just because I can."

Then—silence. Only her breath, shattered and trembling. A sob caught halfway to breaking. His hand slid over her again. Still not soothing. Still claiming.

"Still with me?"

She nodded. Barely. Tear-streaked. Dazed. Soaked.

"Good," he whispered. "Because I'm nowhere near finished."

He pulled her up until she was facing him, straddling his lap with her thighs on either side of his waist. The thick line of his cock strained against the fabric of his slacks, burning hot against her bare pussy, and she moaned—already grinding down, shameless and hungry for friction.

For a moment, he let her take the lead—let her pretend. She undid his belt with practiced ease, unzipped his pants like she owned him. But it was clear—immediately—that she didn't.

His hands turned rough, possessive. One locked onto her hip, the other twisted in her hair, yanking her head back until her neck arched just how he liked it.

And then he took control. Lifted her. Dropped her. She was already slick, her heat swallowing him inch by inch, tight enough to make him grit his teeth. No teasing, no easing in—she took him like she was made for it, her cunt gripping him like a fist, like she didn't need prep, didn't need time—just him, just this.

Every thrust dragged a broken sound from her throat, and he could feel her pulse around him, fluttering like she was already on the edge.

He looked down and noticed that he was nearly fully-dressed still, while her gown just bunched at her waist like an afterthought. Every downward grind dragged her bare ass against the rough fabric of his pants, the fresh welts he'd just given her likely flared sharp with each pass. He could see it in her face, in the way her mouth parted and her eyes unfocused—that the pain was a balm. That it cut through the static of the night: the fake conversations, the too-wide smiles, the exhausting theater of being likable, impressive, perfect.

He didn't know the details, but he felt the weight of it—the ghost of someone still clinging to her like rot. And whatever it was, it was gone now, stripped away under the rhythm of his body wrecking hers.

She had tried to take control, tried to shift her weight and ride him how she wanted, and he had just laughed—low, mean.

"No fucking way."

Then the tie was off his neck and wrapped around her wrists behind her back, knotted in seconds like he'd done it a hundred times. And that was it. He had taken over completely, fucking her with a focus so sharp it bordered on cruel. Using her like she was something he'd claimed—something that belonged to him and no one else.

He kept her dangling on the edge, desperate, unraveling —right where he wanted her.

"Ohh," she whispered like a prayer. "Kieran...I."

He watched her fall apart in his lap—mascara smudged, lips parted, every inch of her shaking like a live wire—and all he could think was *mine*.

All night she'd been putting on a show, walking through that room like a goddamn fever dream, letting every bastard with a glass in hand trip over their tongues just to get a smile. And now here she was—wrists bound, body open, begging for him.

"Look at you," he muttered, voice low and rough in her ear. "All that performance, all that effort...and you still ended up tied up and on your knees for me."

She whimpered, head dropping forward, breath stuttering.

"It's yours," she gasped. "It's just for you."

And that was it.

When he finally broke, it was like something inside him snapped. He slammed into her, hard, again and again, until she contorted beneath him, her legs split wide, trembling. She came again like the world was ending—violent, silent at first, then gasping, shaking, her body gripping him so tight it dragged him down with her.

He spilled into her in thick, endless waves, filling her up just as the Suburban began to slow. The car eased to a stop. The world outside went still.

Neither of them moved.

The partition stayed up, but it didn't matter—anyone paying attention would know something had happened. Something loud. Something dirty. Something real.

They didn't have long to catch their breath. The last thing they wanted was for the partition to drop and the driver to politely, yet unmistakably, kick them out.

He undid her bindings with one pull.

She slipped her dress back over her chest with practiced

speed, while he tugged on his now-wrinkled slacks, still breathing hard. The fog hadn't cleared—from their heads or the car. The air was thick, humid with sweat and the unmistakable scent of what they'd just done.

HE OPENED the car door and stepped onto a tree-lined block in Georgetown that looked like it had its own security clearance.

Gas lamps flickered like they'd been burning since the Eisenhower administration. Everything smelled like old stone, generational wealth, and the faint threat of surveillance.

Morgan followed him out, adjusting her dress—still rumpled, still clinging in all the wrong places. Her legs weren't fully cooperating, and she rubbed her wrists, the ghost of that silk tie still lingering even though it had mysteriously vanished.

Kieran looked equally wrecked, like he'd just descended from the top of the Washington Monument and left a prayer candle burning behind him.

"Wait, this is the place?" he asked, eyeing the gorgeous brick townhouse with wrought-iron railings and an entryway too symmetrical to trust.

"Yeah," she said, trying to sound casual. "It's my friend's. She's Foreign Service—on assignment in Madrid."

"Of course she is."

Morgan nodded down the block. "The Senate Majority Leader has a crash pad two doors down when Congress is in session. Secret Service does neighborhood watch."

Kieran let out a low whistle. "This street's seen things."

"Yeah. Hopefully not us in the back of that Suburban."

He snorted. The engine turned back on behind them, purring like it knew every detail.

Morgan's heel caught on the cobblestone. Kieran reached out, caught her waist, steadied her—then dropped his hand like her skin had a clearance level he didn't hold.

The driver didn't look. Didn't smirk. Didn't breathe. Just pulled away like discretion was part of the job description.

Morgan smoothed her dress. Kieran straightened his jacket. They stood side by side like two normal people who had not just desecrated a VIP company car.

She took one step forward—and promptly caught her heel on the cobblestones again.

Her balance gave out like a used brake pad. Six inches of designer stiletto plus what amounted to impromptu aerial yoga in the backseat had her legs staging a quiet rebellion.

This time, Kieran didn't just steady her.

He caught her. Scooped her.

Full-on bridal style, like it was nothing. Like she didn't weigh a damn thing.

"Oh my god," she muttered, mortified, grabbing at his jacket. "Put me down, I can walk—"

"You tried," he said, voice low and way too pleased with himself.

Her face flushed, instant and sharp. She buried it in his chest, the starched cotton of his shirt still smelling faintly of cologne and a hint of sin.

Kieran just kept walking, carrying her up the townhouse steps like it was his name on the mortgage and she was coming home from their reception dinner.

Morgan didn't fight it. She should have. But her thighs were shaking, her pride was shredded, and his heartbeat under her cheek was steady in a way that made her want to cry or moan or both.

At the top step, he paused.

"You good?" he murmured, like he didn't already know the answer.

She nodded without looking up.

He smiled to himself, let her scan her thumbprint on the door, then carried her inside.

She managed to mumble something about the layout—the bathroom's through the hall, the bedroom's on the left, towels are in the antique armoire she's not allowed to admit she hates.

Kieran listened, nodding, but didn't put her down. Didn't so much as let her toes brush the hardwood until he set her, gingerly, on the marble tile.

"Shower," he said, his voice in command mode—soft, no-nonsense. "Just hold on to me."

Morgan didn't argue. Her legs were still trembling, half from the heels, half from everything else.

He stepped them both under the spray, steady hands braced around her waist.

She pressed her cheek to his shoulder as the water ran over them, hot and too-bright, rinsing away sweat, makeup, and his own release—slick and unmistakable down the inside of her thigh.

He handled her like she was glass and holy. Washed every trace away with careful fingers and a low, quiet "okay?" every time she winced.

They stepped out, and he wrapped her in the fluffiest towel he'd ever touched.

She caught his eyes flick to her ass—green-blue bruises already blooming, finger-marks painted along her thighs like tiny, purple signatures.

His lips tightened. Not regret—something more primal, protective, like he wanted to apologize and brag at the same time.

He scooped her up again, didn't give her a chance to protest, and carried her to the bed.

"On your stomach," he said, voice gentler now.

Morgan sank down into the pillows, every muscle sighing in relief.

He curled around her. His hand ran up and down her spine, grounding, quiet. For a long moment, there was just breathing and the sound of rain starting on the old Georgetown windows.

He broke the silence first. "You know I'm serious about you, right?"

She stared at the wall. "I know."

He pressed a kiss to the back of her neck, then murmured, "Believe me, I've been trying not to fall for you. It's just not working."

That made her sigh. Still facing the wall, still too raw to turn around—but her fingers curled tighter around the sheet.

He shifted behind her, voice quieter now. "I know you're not there yet. I know there's stuff you don't say out loud. But I need you to know—I'm already in it. With you."

She hesitated, tension bunching in her shoulders.

"I need to take it slow, Kieran. I just...I need you to let me go at my own pace. I can't—" Her voice cracked, embarrassment rising. "I can't just jump. Not after everything."

He pressed a kiss to the back of her neck, a smile breaking through in his voice. "I'll wait," he said. "But I'm not putting this on ice. I'm not dialing it down. I'm here because I want you—and I'm not afraid of the time it takes to get it right."

Relief washed over her, softer than anything that had come before.

She let herself sink into his chest, the last of her armor dropping away.

They drifted into that sweet, exhausted silence—his palm spread warm over her bruised hip, her fingers tangled in his.

Outside, Georgetown slept.

Inside, the world finally let them breathe.

KIERAN WATCHED HER BREATHE, slow and steady now, tucked into his chest like the chaos of the night hadn't touched her. Like she hadn't been bruised by it, even though he'd seen the evidence written in violet fingerprints and green-blue shadows on her skin.

She was asleep.

He didn't move. Didn't dare.

Morgan fucking Delgado.

She was steel-willed and sharp-tongued, could reroute six aircraft in a storm and dismantle a boardroom full of cowards with one arched brow. He'd seen her take a flight control manager to pieces without raising her voice. She could break him in half and he'd thank her for the honor.

But curled up like this, bare-faced, boneless against him —she looked young. Not in a way that erased her power. In a way that made him want to go back in time and stand in front of her for every shitty thing life had thrown at her.

For every man who flinched at her strength and tried to cut her down to size. Especially that one.

Six years with that man who told her she was too much, too complicated, too intense. Six fucking years of being gaslit into thinking her softness was a liability, her instincts flawed, her ambition a threat.

Kieran wanted to find that man and make him understand what he'd done. Wanted to take a goddamn tire iron to the pedestal Drew had tried to build for himself inside her head.

Because the truth was, she wasn't too much.

She was everything.

And if she needed time, space, slow trust earned in inches instead of miles—he'd give her that. Not because he was some saint. But because Morgan Delgado was worth every second of learning how to love her right.

31

She let herself have the day. Just one.

The morning started with the smell of bacon and coffee and the rustle of a New Yorker magazine he read front to back while waiting for the toaster to finish. He cooked like someone who didn't think he was being watched, all relaxed lines and bare feet on tile.

She watched anyway. She wore one of his denim button-downs and took up space in his quiet like she'd been there forever—like the room had always been waiting for her to fill it. She kissed his shoulder without thinking.

He looked at her like she'd invented the sun.

Her phone buzzed. She flipped it facedown.

By noon they were sunk deep into the warm silence of a private couple's spa he'd insisted on. She let Kieran guide her into the steam room, watched the way sweat glistened along his collarbone. He didn't try anything—just sat close enough for her to feel the heat of him, his pinky brushing hers like a secret.

She didn't fall asleep during the massage. Not really. But she let her guard down enough to pretend.

More missed calls. One from the command center. One from Vee.

She didn't listen to either.

They did laundry in the afternoon, like idiots playing house. She folded his shirts like it meant something, like repetition could trick her body into thinking they had time. He pulled one of her panties out of a twisted sleeve—red, delicate, stitched like a secret—and held it up with both eyebrows raised.

"Can I keep this?"

It was her favorite Fleur du Mal pair. Moth wings and floral lace, engineered to seduce and survive—barely. Too intricate for a keepsake. Too expensive for a joke.

She didn't blink, taking it from him and putting it away.

"You wish."

He kissed her anyway. Fast and full and way too sure.

When he wasn't looking, she gave it a little spritz of her perfume and shoved it into the side pocket of his pilot bag.

Her phone buzzed again. She shoved it into the bottom of her suitcase.

By dinner, they'd drifted toward something even more dangerous—ease. A quiet corner table at a place down the street from the townhouse with low lights and red wine she didn't argue with.

He reached for her hand. She let him have it.

They didn't talk about the airline, the 7X, or what would happen when reality clawed its way back in.

She let herself laugh. And he watched her like he wanted to memorize the shape of it.

Her phone didn't stop vibrating.

But she'd already decided: if it was going to fall apart tomorrow, she would have today.

All of it.

32

The bags were packed. The sheets were wrecked. No more pillow talk, no more play—just sex and a frankly deranged competition over who could make each other come more.

He thought maybe they'd laughed enough to hold the dread at bay.

But Sunday didn't care. It showed up anyway, smug as hell.

And before the coffee even finished brewing, they were already fighting.

The first thing he noticed was how still she'd gotten. One minute, Morgan was curled beside him, warm and quiet under his shirt, her legs tangled in the sheets like she'd finally let herself rest.

Then came the buzz of her phone.

She checked it without thinking. And just like that, she was gone.

Not physically—yet. But her posture shifted, clean and sharp like the slide of a blade from its sheath.

She sat at the edge of the bed, phone to her ear, her

voice low and clipped. She was already dressing, already compartmentalizing. It was like watching a drawbridge rise.

He hated how fast she could disappear.

He sat up slowly, pulling on sweatpants, blinking sleep from his eyes.

Her voice was flat, surgical.

"They're grounding nothing. I already issued the call to Ops. It was reversed before I even—no. No one told me."

A pause.

"You said this would go through protocol. That's not what this looks like."

He watched her, heart thudding.

Something was wrong.

Worse than wrong.

She hung up and moved fast—found her blazer, checked her watch.

He hadn't even said good morning. Hadn't kissed her shoulder. Hadn't made the damn coffee.

"Morgan?" he said, gently.

She didn't look at him. Her fingers danced across her screen.

The words came out like bullets.

"There's another board meeting. Emergency. They're pushing a narrative—accusing me of scheming. Of leaking to the press."

He blinked.

"Wait, what? That's—what the hell are they even talking about?"

She turned toward him, blazer in hand, her expression a familiar mask of composure stretched too tight.

"Someone asked if I've been talking to a journalist. The implication was clear."

His pulse kicked.

"Have you?"

She gave him a look.

"Would I be this pissed if I had? My shit is ironclad. I haven't said a damn thing, and they know it. That's why they're inventing stories—because they can't find any real ones."

He nodded, chastised. Sat back on the bed while she paced.

He wanted to reach for her. Say something grounding.

But his own stomach was twisting.

He had something to say too. Had meant to say it last night, actually—before things got...unholy.

"I've been talking to someone," he said finally. "One of the union guys. He says maintenance reports started disappearing about a year ago. Like someone's scrubbing the system."

His voice faltered.

"I was going to tell you. I just—I don't know. I wanted one night where we weren't putting out fires."

She froze.

That pause? It was short. Maybe half a second. But long enough for the tension to stretch and catch.

She looked at him like she wasn't sure if he was an ally or an obstacle.

"Kieran," she said, low. "I asked you to dig, not advertise. You think no one's watching?"

He opened his mouth. And nothing came out.

He wanted to tell her he was out of his depth. That she was built for this kind of war and he wasn't. That after twenty-seven years of toeing the line and saluting the damn flag, the one time he spoke up—for her—he might've just made things worse.

That he didn't know who he was without the airline.

That the thought of Heritage putting him in a faulty cockpit—making him complicit in his own failure—was breaking him a little.

Instead, what came out was:

"Maybe we should slow down. Think it through."

Morgan stared at him, stone still.

She didn't yell. Didn't accuse.

But her voice turned cold.

"That phrase doesn't land well," she said, voice so even it made his chest ache. "Don't use it with me."

He cursed himself.

Of course it didn't land well. It sounded just like the shit Drew used to say—think it through, use your logic, you're being too emotional.

As if she ever made a move without thinking it through six different ways.

As if she hadn't survived by out-thinking everyone around her.

And now he'd played himself straight into that script.

She turned and disappeared into the bathroom, the sound of the shower roaring like static in his ears.

He stood there, rooted. Let it all play again in his head—and still couldn't find the version where he said the right thing.

When she came out, she was fully armored. Makeup flawless. Hair pulled back. Business casual that still looked unfairly hot.

She didn't glance at him as she took her suitcase from beside the door and slung it up with a flick of her wrist.

She was already on the phone—low voice, clipped, efficient.

Probably her lawyer.

Definitely not him.

When she hung up, she finally looked at him.

"I need to go," she said. "Let's talk later."

He moved toward her, instinctive. Just wanted to press a kiss to her temple, let her know he was still here. That he hadn't stopped wanting her, not even for a second.

She dodged—barely, but enough.

The door closed behind her with a whisper.

Not a slam.

That would've been easier.

33

He showered. Got dressed. Pulled on his uniform the way he always did, each piece going on without a second thought. White shirt, navy pants, wings pinned over his heart.

She usually stayed to watch. Always liked seeing him put it on.

This morning though, the room was so empty it felt like it was laughing at him.

The housekeeper came by around nine. He held the door for her and thanked her like he always did. She smiled and said good morning.

He smiled back and meant it, but it felt thin.

The ride to the airport was quiet. He took the DC Metro, shoulders hunched against the sway of the train. People crammed in around him with their backpacks and headphones and tired faces.

He was just another body in the crowd, another uniform headed to work.

He stepped off at Dulles International Airport Station, keyed-up in a way he hadn't been in years.

He'd been flying long enough to trust it.

Something was coming.

He didn't know what, but he could feel it.

He killed time in the crew lounge. Sipped burnt coffee. Texted Ren some street art that made him think of them. After that, he couldn't focus on much of anything.

Other pilots came and went, nodding at him in passing.

He must have looked normal enough from the outside.

He was halfway through a second cup when he heard his name.

"Captain O'Hara? Room Four."

He looked up.

The supervisor didn't smile. No explanation, no pretense. Just nodded toward the hallway like a priest pointing to confession.

Room Four was an FAA station.

You didn't end up there unless something was wrong.

Testing. Paperwork. Occasionally a pilot crying behind closed doors.

He'd seen enough to know the difference between routine and targeted.

He set his coffee down, the mug suddenly heavy, and followed.

The room was cold and windowless, a space built to make you feel small.

The compliance officer barely looked up when Kieran walked in. Just unsealed the test kit and placed it on the table like they were about to dissect him.

"Random alcohol screening," the officer said. "Per FAA protocol."

Kieran stayed still.

"Spot check?"

"Names are pulled at random."

He didn't even try to hide the skepticism in his face. He'd been flying for twenty-seven years. He knew what random looked like. This wasn't it.

Not after the past few weeks. Not after he'd spoken up—calling out Enright.

"You'll need to blow twice," the officer said, sliding over a clipboard. "And sign."

He read the form.

One box checked: *Reasonable Suspicion.*

Not *Random*. Not *Post-incident.*

Suspicion.

"You want to tell me what I'm being suspected of?"

"I don't make the notes, Captain. I just file the results."

Of course.

He hadn't had a drink in years. Not since Ren was thirteen and he'd nearly missed a visitation weekend with whiskey still clinging to his breath.

He'd fixed that.

Therapy, accountability, and AA.

But none of that mattered here.

He took the test—slow, deliberate. Blew until the machine beeped.

"Clear," the officer said. "Both samples."

That was it. No apology. No context.

Just a nod toward the door, like he'd been dismissed from his own name.

Out in the hallway, someone glanced up—another crew member. Younger. They locked eyes for half a second before the kid looked away, expression tight with something between pity and curiosity.

That was the look that stuck. The kind that spread.

He could already hear it starting in the backchannels, the texts, the crew lounge whispers: *Captain O'Hara? Pulled for testing. Weird, right? Thought he was one of the straight arrows. Didn't he used to fly long-haul?*

His hands were steady. His chest wasn't.

He pulled out his phone. Typed a message to Morgan.

Need to talk. Got pulled for a test. Said I passed but—

He deleted it. He didn't want to drag her into this. Not when she had her own battles. Not like this.

But something was coming.

He could feel it, quiet and deliberate, moving under the surface like an undertow.

34

T he boardroom was too quiet when Morgan walked in on Tuesday morning—an eerie, calculated stillness, like a storm had already passed and no one dared to name the wreckage.

Four lawyers sat at the table, all in varying stages of fake concern and performative professionalism. General Counsel was there, looking freshly botoxed and slightly annoyed. Two VPs who never had the spine to say anything directly to her face. And of course, David Enright, who smiled like this was just another breakfast meeting and not an ambush.

Morgan's pulse was steady, but only because she had brought the one woman who could outmaneuver them all.

Sloane Campbell entered like she owned the building. Six feet tall in heels, long legs cutting across the carpet like a blade, and a trench coat that should've had its own billing credit. Born to Jamaican parents, raised in Queens, and built to win fights. Hair slicked into a bun so sharp it could slice egos. Very little makeup except for some bb cream and a matte red lip that warned everyone in the room: you're already losing.

She didn't bother sitting right away. Just looked around, slow and deliberate, like she was giving them all a chance to embarrass themselves before she opened her mouth.

"I'm Sloane Campbell, counsel for Ms. Delgado," she said, voice smooth as molasses and sharp as glass. "And before we go any further, I'd strongly advise everyone in this room to think very carefully about what they say next."

Someone tried to speak—some mid-level legal drone who probably thought he could bluff his way through this.

Sloane cut him off with a raised hand.

"No. We're not doing that."

Morgan sat, silent, composed, letting Sloane drive. She didn't have to fake calm—Sloane was calm, and it was contagious.

"I've reviewed the internal communications," Sloane continued. "And the accusations being floated here? Defamatory. Unsubstantiated. And legally actionable if repeated or recorded.

My client has followed every relevant protocol outlined in the company's operations manual. She documented her decisions, escalated concerns through internal channels, and acted in accordance with both FAA regulations and Heritage's own chain of command."

She let that hang, turning to the General Counsel with the faintest smile.

"So unless someone in this room can produce—right now—documented evidence of a code of conduct violation, a breach of confidentiality with verifiable timestamps, and a direct link between my client and the alleged press leak...I'd recommend we all take a breath and move very carefully."

No one said a word.

Sloane finally sat, crossing her legs, calm as Sunday morning.

"You cannot fire my client today," she said. "Not legally. Not quietly. Not without consequences you are absolutely unprepared for."

The silence was delicious. Even Enright didn't smirk this time. One of the other lawyers looked like they might faint.

"Consider this your warning," Sloane added, voice quiet but deadly.

"What happens next will be in writing. I expect a formal retraction of all defamatory statements made in the past three days and written confirmation of my client's continued employment in good standing. You'll have it to me by end of day."

She stood, smoothed her blazer, and glanced at Morgan.

"We're done here."

Morgan rose, jaw set, eyes unreadable.

They walked out together—heels and confidence echoing off the glass and steel.

And not one person in that room dared to stop them.

THE RIDE BACK WAS QUIET. Downtown blurred past in glass and gridlock. The drive to O'Hare always felt longer when she was dreading the destination. Forty minutes, easy—more if the Kennedy was acting up. Long enough to spiral. Long enough to sit in silence and pretend it was strategy.

Morgan sat pressed against the door, hands folded in her lap, staring out the window like the skyline had answers.

Sloane didn't say anything. Not right away. She gave her the kind of silence only the people who really knew you had the guts to sit with.

Morgan's throat was tight. Not with fear. Not even with rage. Just that sinking, cold weight in her chest that came with being reminded—again—that winning didn't mean you were safe.

"Thank you," she said quietly.

Sloane didn't look over.

"You're welcome."

They drove a few more blocks. The light changed. Horns somewhere in the distance.

"They were ready to fire me," Morgan said, like she was still trying to believe it.

Sloane finally turned her head.

"Yes."

Morgan exhaled.

"You were nice to warn them."

A ghost of a smile crossed Sloane's mouth.

"I'm nicer in the morning."

That almost made Morgan laugh. Almost.

"I need to ground the 7X."

Now Sloane looked at her fully. Calm. Composed. But with a softness that didn't quite reach her voice.

"Morgan, I can protect your job. I can keep them from smearing your name, from retaliating in obvious ways. But I can't pull an aircraft off the line. That's FAA. Or someone on the inside with leverage."

"I am on the inside."

"For now."

That landed like a pin dropped in a cathedral.

Sloane reached for her phone, thumbed something into her notes.

Then: "I'll send language for a formal memo, if you want to log concerns about the 7X. Keep your paper trail clean."

"Already is."

Sloane nodded, like that was the only answer she would've accepted.

Outside the window, the skyline gave way to highway ramps, concrete overpasses, and the beige sprawl of airport hotels. Heritage Command Center wasn't far now—just beyond the maze.

"Just know," Sloane said quietly, "I can buy you time. That's all this was."

Morgan blinked slowly, eyes fixed on nothing.

"I know."

"You don't have to fix it all today."

Morgan gave a tired, bitter half-smile.

"If I don't, someone else will fuck it up worse."

The car pulled to a stop in front of her building.

She still had work after all.

Sloane didn't follow her out.

Morgan stepped onto the curb, wind tugging her blazer open, and turned just enough to meet Sloane's eyes through the open door.

"Again, thank you," she said again.

Sloane just gave her a look that said *Don't waste it.*

Then the door shut, and the car was gone.

THE ELEVATOR DOORS parted with a mechanical sigh, and what met her wasn't silence, exactly—

It was the absence of life.

Her badge blinked green. Still functional. For now.

Heritage's nerve center never slept. It murmured, it ticked, it breathed in data and exhaled urgency.

But now? Now it was a mausoleum dressed in LED lighting.

No radio chatter. No keyboard percussion. No clipped back-and-forths from dispatch.

Just a hush so precise it felt engineered.

Heads turned to her. Not out of recognition. Out of protocol.

A few nodded, the way one might nod at a figure in a portrait they don't quite remember.

Most just watched.

Her name had arrived before her body did. It had passed through the cables, leaked from phones, clung to doorframes.

Dead woman walking. They didn't say it. They didn't have to.

She adjusted her blazer with hands that remembered the weight of consequence, stepped forward like the floor wasn't made of eggshells and old loyalties.

Passed teams she'd built from scratch. Walked past conference rooms where she'd made her bones and slept upright in storm seasons. Past desks she'd once laughed at until she wheezed.

No laughter now.

Just the buzz of the overhead fluorescents, sharp as a blade.

Keep walking.

And then—

The rupture.

She was twenty-three again. Standing in that same hallway, but the walls were taller and the ceiling seemed farther away. She was smaller then. Brighter. Palms sweaty with ambition.

Back then, power had no scent. But aviation had. It smelled like jet fuel and fluorescent toner and hot coffee left too long on the burner. It felt sacred. Like a code she was lucky enough to decipher. Every flight plan was a hymn. Every takeoff, an act of faith.

Ava Thompkins had been there—composed, immaculate, a monument in a navy sheath dress. The kind of woman who spoke in directives that sounded like destiny.

Morgan had followed like scripture.

She learned fast. Learned how to hear the soul in a runway report. Learned the choreography of Ops.

She'd wanted to remake this place in her image. She used to dream of filling this place with women who looked like her. Girls with sharp minds and sharper tongues. Who didn't apologize for taking up space. She wanted them to see the miracle under the metal. She wanted to hand them the keys to it.

But that was then.

Now the hallway reeked of toner and betrayal.

And just like that, the silence cracked.

The noise came rushing back—radios hissing, voices rising, keyboards resuming their mechanical staccato like someone had hit "unpause" on the simulation.

People turned back to their screens with the urgency of the guilty.

Her deputy, Tim, was holding down the fort.

He looked up. Met her eyes for a second too long—and then looked away like he'd stolen something.

"Status update?" she said.

Neutral. Commanding. Controlled.

He didn't answer. Didn't even flinch. He just kept talking to one of the flight operators, bent low over a workstation lit by six glowing screens. Performing urgency like it was a moral shield. Murmuring about weather patterns over Denver like her presence wasn't tectonic. Like she hadn't asked a damn thing. Like she wasn't standing ten feet away. Like she was already gone.

SHE DIDN'T NEED COFFEE. She needed air.

The break room reeked of burnt toast and bad intentions.

She went for the water tap, bracing a hand against the counter. Pretended not to notice how the room went pin-drop silent the second she walked in.

Then—

Enright.

His voice, slick as oil: "Tough day, huh?"

She turned.

He was already blocking the doorway, smiling like charisma could cover rot. Tim stood beside him—shoulders tense, guilt carved deep into his face. Wouldn't meet her eyes. That told her everything.

"We're making some realignments at the executive level," Enright said.

"Tim here's stepping in to ensure continuity. He'll report directly to me. You'll stay on payroll while we...finalize your transition plan."

She didn't move. Didn't blink.

"Nothing personal," Enright said, almost sweet. "Just a strategic reassignment."

Tim got called back to the floor—reroute issue. The kind they never gave him. The kind that always landed on her desk. Typical.

Enright took a step closer.

"Course, strategy's never exactly been your strong suit, has it, Morgan?"

She said nothing.

He leaned against the counter like they were catching up over drinks.

"You think I didn't notice?" he said, voice low and smug. "The sudden transparency. The cleaned-up logs. Union noise getting louder overnight. Please. I've seen this movie before."

Another step forward.

She didn't flinch. Wouldn't give him the show.

"But you?" he sneered. "You're not even good at it. Just another idiot who thought screwing the right guy would get her what she wants."

Blood pounded in her ears.

There it was. Barefaced, deliberate. Pretending her love life had anything—*anything*—to do with grounding dangerous planes.

It didn't. But men like Enright didn't need logic. They just needed a knife—and somewhere soft to stick it.

Her body screamed: run, fight, freeze. She made herself still. Detached. Yoga breath. Don't react.

"That's what gets me," he said. "I thought you were smarter. But you let another one crawl into your bed and into your head, and now you're out here playing whistle-blower Barbie—like you're gonna bring down a fleet with mood lighting and encrypted emails."

He smiled. Slow. Rotten.

"Do yourself a favor, Delgado. Pick a hustle. Sex or strategy. You're not built to pull off both."

Her stomach twisted.

He didn't stop.

"Oh, and you really thought no one would connect the dots? That O'Hara, who kept caping for you in meetings, wasn't part of whatever half-assed rebellion you're running?"

He looked her up and down, already measuring the space she'd leave behind.

"You're not a threat, Morgan. You're a liability with a lipstick budget."

Her throat burned.

Not with tears—those dried up years ago. This was something older. Hotter. Angrier.

"You're a coward," she said.

Then she walked out.

SHE DIDN'T CRY in the break room. She didn't cry in the elevator, or when her badge scanner blinked green like it hadn't just been weaponized against her.

But now—now she was in the women's restroom on the second floor, one hand braced on the cool tile wall, the other gripping the edge of the sink like it might save her.

The tears came quietly at first. Just a sting behind her eyes, like smoke.

But then her throat caught on itself, her chest spasmed, and it broke loose—an ugly, gasping sob that bent her double.

She kept the water running. Reflex. Disguise. Learned young.

Not because she was ashamed. Because she knew what came next if she didn't pull it together.

They'd try to erase her. And they wouldn't stop with her.

Enright's voice echoed in her skull, coiled and slick.

"You really thought no one would connect the dots?

That O'Hara...wasn't part of whatever half-assed rebellion you're running?"

The tears stopped like a switch had been flipped. She grabbed a paper towel. Dabbed her face. Looked herself in the mirror—not at the damage, but at what was still intact.

Her mouth was a flat line. Her eyes were cold steel. She pulled out her phone. The call connected on the third ring.

"Kieran," she said as soon as he picked up, her voice tighter than she meant it to be. "Where are you?"

There was a pause—too long.

Then: "I'm home."

Something about the way he said it made her spine straighten.

"In Traverse?"

"Yeah."

Her stomach dropped.

The air in the room shifted—cooler, thinner.

"I thought you were flying today."

"Yeah, well."

His voice was a quiet scrape.

"Not anymore."

Her hand tightened around the edge of the sink. The faucet was still running behind her. She didn't turn it off.

"They grounded you," she said.

It wasn't a question.

"Pulled me from rotation. 'Pending review.' They're not saying why, but come on. I've been in this too long not to recognize the leash when they put it on."

She pressed her palm flat to the counter, heart pounding in her throat.

Of course they had. Of course Enright hadn't been bluffing.

"I'm sorry," she said, and hated how her voice cracked halfway through.

"Don't."

He cut her off, gentle but firm.

"Don't do that. You did the right thing. They're just pissed they didn't get to bury it first."

She sank down onto the floor. The tile wall was cold at her back.

"They're coming for both of us."

"I know."

"I told him he was a coward," she muttered. "Should've said more. Should've dragged Enright by his veneers."

It earned the smallest exhale on the other end of the line. Almost a laugh.

"I'm fine, Morgan. Really."

"No, you're not," she snapped, more truth than she meant to give. "This is the one thing. The one thing that's always been yours. And they're trying to take it from you."

Silence. But not the safe kind.

She imagined him standing in his kitchen, surrounded by warm wood cabinetry and sunlight he couldn't feel. Dogs at his heels. Lost. Untethered.

When he spoke again, his voice was almost inaudible.

"I don't know what to do."

Her chest clenched.

"You don't have to know," she said. "Just don't go quiet on me."

The words hit the air, heavy.

Then—self-recrimination, fast and raw—

"I mean it," she added, voice rough. "And I won't either. Not this time."

There was a pause. She heard the breath he took before answering.

"I won't go quiet," he said. "Promise."

Then quieter: "But you have to do something for me too."

She closed her eyes.

"What?"

"Keep burning. Make them hurt."

The silence that followed wasn't empty—it was full of something sharp and warm and dangerous. The kind of silence that turned into action.

"I'll try," she said.

A shuddering breath, muffled through the line.

"Text me your lawyer's info," she added.

"Done."

They didn't hang up right away. Neither moved to end it. They just stayed—connected by breath, by signal, by the invisible thread stretched taut between two people who had everything to lose and finally understood the stakes.

35

The headlines bled chaos.

Heritage flights canceled nationwide.

DELAY. DELAY. CANCELED.

Hurricane Calvin slamming the Eastern Seaboard like a wrecking ball.

Morgan closed her laptop. Reopened it. Refreshed her inbox like the outcome might change if she glared hard enough. Emails kept vanishing—one by one—like someone was yanking bricks out from under a house they still expected her to defend.

Technically, she was still the director of the command center. That's what the company line said now. Post-Sloane. Post-retractions. Post-"misunderstandings."

In reality? Her title was a husk. Her authority scattered and buried under murky reclassifications. No briefings. No priority alerts. Just a glorified figurehead with an expired badge and enough NDA clauses to tie her hands behind her back.

Still, she hadn't stopped. She blocked shady aircraft movements. Delayed reckless dispatches. Stayed connected through loyalty and backchannels, trying to patch a sinking ship with whatever she had left.

And then the call came.

Tim. Panicked. Out of breath.

"Morgan. Please. I know you're not technically...but it's bad. You've seen the news? Everything's backed up. Ops is scrambled. People are re-routing like it's musical chairs and the chairs are all on fire."

She didn't answer. He kept going.

"We've got a 737 that shouldn't be flying over Indiana, a regional that almost clipped a weather cell it wasn't even supposed to be near, and half the senior dispatchers are frozen like we're in an actual war zone. I need you. Please, please, Morgan. I'll do anything."

That last part hung in the air. She almost said no. Almost reminded him they'd gutted her job, stripped her authority, handed the reins to men who couldn't even spell reroute.

Almost.

But the wiring was too deep—built into her bones, her breath, the electric hum of her nerves. Help anyway. Hold it together anyway. Even when they stepped on your neck while asking. Especially then.

"I'll be there in thirty," she said.

And she was.

The command center had never looked so relieved. They didn't say it out loud, but it rippled through the room the second she walked in. Shoulders loosened. Eyes flicked up and back down, with the kind of reverence usually reserved for miracles.

Morgan didn't smile. She didn't bask. She sat down at the main console and got to work.

Triage first. Stabilize the grid. Move the pieces.

She rebuilt crew rotations. Pulled planes off dangerous patterns. Called emergency reroutes on three transcontinental flights and a charter that never should've left the gate. She did it all without breaking rhythm. Because it had to be done. Because no one else could.

Hours passed. Six, then twelve. Someone brought her a bottled water. She forgot to open it. Someone offered food. She waved them off.

Her hands wouldn't stop. There were keys under her fingers, planes in the sky, lives on the line.

Meanwhile, her phone wouldn't stop vibrating. Vee had been blowing it up for the past two hours—texts, missed calls, voice memos laced with swearing. At one point, Morgan thought she heard her name being screamed all the way from the hangar.

And then, silence. That should've been the warning.

Fifteen minutes later, Vee stormed into the command center like she was about to fight someone—or everyone.

"Where the hell is she?" she snapped at Tim, who barely managed to stammer something useless before Vee spotted her.

Morgan didn't look up. Just said, calm as a cut: "Vee, not now."

"Oh, now. Definitely now." Vee stalked forward, fury wrapped in engine grease. "You haven't eaten. You haven't peed. Three dispatchers told me you're pale as death, and I can see your hands shaking from across the damn room. This is an intervention."

"Vee," Morgan said again, lower, sharper.

"I'm not joking. You're going to keel over, and then what? Let Enright tell everyone you cracked under pressure? Let this place devour you after everything you've done?"

Finally, Morgan looked up. Her eyes were bloodshot. Her jaw was set.

"Leave," she said. One syllable, flat and immovable—the voice she used when there was no more negotiating, when the plane was already stalling and she'd already decided how it was going to land.

Vee froze. She wasn't scared—Vee didn't scare—but she knew that tone. She'd heard it once before, years ago, back in aviation magnet high school, when some idiot in shop class had called her a "dyke" loud enough for everyone to hear. Morgan hadn't even hesitated. She'd said one word, in that same dead-cold tone—"Apologize"—then jumped a guy twice her size while still wearing Cookie Monster pajama pants and half a bag of hot Cheetos shoved into her hoodie.

This was that voice. The voice that ended conversations —and sometimes careers.

Morgan turned back to the monitor, dismissing Vee like an air current.

Vee didn't move for a full five seconds. Then she exhaled hard, muttered, "I swear to God, Delgado," and backed off. But not without pulling out her phone.

36

His phone buzzed while he stared blankly at the news ticker crawling across the bottom of the TV: HERITAGE AIRLINES CANCELS OVER 400 FLIGHTS DUE TO EASTERN STORM CHAOS. UNION RUMORS SURFACE AMID OPERATIONAL BREAKDOWN

He didn't check the caller ID until after he picked up.

A woman's voice, sharp and dry, cut through the background noise—the high-pitched whine of a torque wrench, the clank of a dropped socket, distant shouting over engine tests.

"Yeah, you don't know me. I'm Vee. Hangar ops. I'm Morgan's mechanic. And this is not a social call."

That woke him up fast.

"I'm listening."

"She came in around one this morning. Saved the whole damn command center like it was nothing. Everyone's thrilled. They're calling her a miracle. But she hasn't eaten. No water. Looks like she's running on sheer spite and nicotine patches—except she doesn't even smoke."

Kieran stood. The dogs stirred at his feet.

"Is she okay?"

"Of course not. She's vertical. That's about it. For now. But I know the look. I know the timeline. She's about to fall —and she's too proud to let anyone catch her. She'll work until she drops, then apologize for bleeding on the carpet."

"Why are you telling me this?"

"Because she won't listen to me. And if I call her family to run intervention, that might be the end of our friendship."

Vee's voice flattened.

"We don't involve families in our shit. Too messy. Too many opinions. Too many ways to make it worse."

He exhaled hard through his nose.

"Jesus."

"Right?" Vee said, dry. "I'm calling because I'm hoping you're someone she won't knee in the nuts for dragging her out of here. If she passes out in front of a bunch of Heritage snakes? They'll use it."

His mouth tightened.

"Do I need a badge?"

"I sent your name to a floor tech. Visitor pass at the south entrance. Don't screw this up."

"Thank you," he said, then added, "It'll take me five hours to drive—there's not a single damn flight out of Traverse."

"I'm not doing this for you, sweetheart," she snapped. "This is my ride-or-die we're talking about."

In the background, he heard shouting—her voice again, full volume:

"—don't talk to me about protocol, you paper-pushing coward. Half these delays are on YOU and your little spread-sheet cult—"

Then she was back on the line, unfazed.

"You still there? Get in the car. Bring a water bottle. She's gonna hate it. You can drop your dogs off with me at the hangar when you get here."

Kieran blinked.

"How'd you know I have dogs?"

"You sound like a dog person."

He squinted, suspicious.

"Also, Morgan told me."

"You're serious?"

"Do I sound like I'm kidding?"

The line went dead.

The day had been long. Brutal, even.

Twelve flight diversions. A statement from the CEO. Three union complaints. An FAA follow-up already in her inbox.

She'd barely eaten. Her second coffee had gone cold. Her third was aspirational at best.

But she was still standing.

Still straight-backed, perfectly dressed. Hair smooth, eyes sharp, voice just brisk enough to be respected.

"Anything else?" she asked.

Tim shook his head.

"Alright, everyone, go home. Make sure whoever's taking your shift has a direct line to you. Get some sleep."

They left. She stayed.

The lights in ops ran fluorescent and punishing. She leaned against the desk.

Just for a second. Just long enough for the edges of her vision to go dark.

K ieran was already running down the hallway toward the war room when he heard it.

Not a crash. Not a cry. Just a sound too soft for the brain to register—but the gut knew.

He sprinted.

Found her on the floor, gripping the leg of the briefing table like it was the only thing keeping her tethered to earth.

Her breath came uneven, shallow. Blood dribbled from her hairline. The table edge had caught her on the way down.

"Hey—hey—" He was at her side in seconds.

"Don't—" Her voice was low, frayed. "Don't call anyone."

He froze.

"You need—"

"I just need to go to the hospital," she whispered. "Don't make a scene. Don't tell ops. Don't let anyone see."

And then he understood.

Not the pain. Not the injury. The shame.

The first one of her kind to ever hold this job—collapsed on the ops floor? They'd devour her.

The vultures would circle, all teeth behind polished smiles.

Too much responsibility. Too much stress. We support diversity, of course, but maybe this role is better suited to someone with more stamina.

Her voice cracked.

"Please. Just get me out of here."

He didn't hesitate again.

"Okay," he said, soft. "I've got you."

No medics. No radios. No emergency call.

Just her blazer in one arm and her weight in the other.

He didn't speak. Didn't check her vitals. Not until they were clear—down the back corridor, where no one went after hours.

She hadn't collapsed from weakness. She'd collapsed from holding it all together for too damn long.

From being steel in a place still waiting for her to break.

And all she asked for was the dignity to fall in peace.

So he gave her that.

39

The ER parking lot buzzed under harsh halogen lights, slick with rain. He parked crooked, hazards on. Didn't even kill the engine.

Morgan was still slumped in the passenger seat, barely conscious. Her blazer was folded under her head, her lips pale, jaw clenched tight like even now she didn't want to look vulnerable.

Kieran rested his forehead against the steering wheel.

One breath. Then another.

And then he moved.

He popped the glove box open with muscle memory.

Dug through it, heart hammering, blood still on his sleeve. Found the old wedding band.

It had been there for years. He didn't keep it out of hope for his past, but because it meant something. Commitment. Failure. Growth. All of it. And he wasn't the kind of man to throw that away lightly.

It was simple: gold, unadorned.

He slipped it on. Then looked at her.

Her hands were cold. One curled loosely in her lap, the

other resting against her ribs like she was holding herself together through sheer will. On her right ring finger, the diamond glinted—sharp, defiant, unmistakably hers.

He remembered her telling him about it last weekend, offhand, like it wasn't a big deal: "Promotion ring. Bought it for myself. Men buy toys, I buy diamonds."

He hesitated.

Then, gently—carefully—he slid it off.

Held it in his palm for a moment, feeling the weight of it. The weight of her. Then he moved it to her left hand. Pressed it into place like it had always belonged there.

There.

Now he was just a husband bringing his wife in after a fall. No one would stop him from following her gurney through the swinging doors.

He leaned back for a second, hand still wrapped around hers. Looked down at the two rings. His and hers. Old and new. Promise and power.

Then he turned off the engine, took a deep breath, and got ready to lie like hell.

THEY WHEELED her in without a second glance at him.

He kept his head down, hand resting lightly on the gurney rail, walking beside her like it was instinct. Like he belonged.

He said he was her husband. That was enough.

They got her vitals—blood pressure low, heart rate too high, oxygen normal. The nurse clipped a pulse ox to her finger and asked about allergies.

None.

The CT scan came next. Fast, cold, efficient. They slid

her into the machine while he stood outside the glass, hands in his pockets, watching her lie still in a tube meant to catch disaster before it bloomed. He could see the shape of her skull on the screen—her brilliant, overworked, impossible brain turned grayscale and fragile.

Back in the ER bay, she didn't flinch when the nurse touched the bruise at her hairline.

The doctor came in a few minutes later. No nonsense. Mid-forties, no makeup, scrubs under a coat that had seen at least two shifts too many.

"Hairline fracture," she said, tapping the scan on a tablet. "Right parietal. No displacement, no bleed. That we can see."

Morgan started to push herself up.

"So I can go—"

"You're not going anywhere," the doctor said. "You've got a crack in your skull, not a hangnail. We're monitoring for delayed swelling."

Morgan didn't argue. Not really. But Kieran saw the exact second she started mentally rescheduling half the Eastern Seaboard in her head.

He didn't move from the chair. Not when the nurse returned, clipboard in hand, eyes flicking between him and Morgan.

"Sir, do you mind stepping out for a second?" she asked politely.

Kieran hesitated, looked at Morgan. She gave him a faint nod.

"It's fine."

He stepped into the hallway. The cold hit him differently there—stale, metallic.

He pulled out his phone and texted Vee.

Still here. No bleed. Skull fracture. Monitoring her overnight.

Sent.

Inside, he could hear the nurse's voice through the thin curtain.

"Can you tell me how the injury happened?"

Morgan: "I fainted. Long shift. No food. Stupid."

A pause. Then quieter: "Do you feel safe at home?"

He felt that question like a punch. Heard her answer just as clearly.

"Yes."

No hesitation. Calm. Final.

The curtain shifted a moment later as the nurse slipped past him.

No comment. No glance. Just one professional to another, doing her job.

When he stepped back in, Morgan didn't look at him. She just closed her eyes and leaned toward the window like she didn't want to burn the energy to center herself anymore.

THE NEURO CHECKS started after midnight.

Same nurse, same flashlight, same clipboard.

"What's your name?"

"Morgan Delgado."

"Where are you?"

"Hospital."

"Do you know the date?"

"Don't test me."

Kieran kept answering the things she didn't bother with.

No seizures. No blood thinners. No other recent head trauma.

Yes, she fainted. No, she wasn't drinking. Yes, she skipped meals. No, she never stops.

The nurse made a note. Gave him a look that said: *So she's always like this.*

He just nodded.

They let the lights dim after that, but not for long.

Every two hours, like clockwork, the check-ins came. Same questions. Same protocol. Wake her up, make sure the brain's still talking.

By three in the morning, her answers were down to syllables. Her voice was rough. Her body still. After the last round, she turned her head toward him, barely moving her lips.

"Am I allowed to sleep yet, or do I need to recite the alphabet backward first?"

"You're still not funny," he said.

She gave him the smallest flicker of a smile. Then nothing.

Her gaze drifted to his hand. Then to her own. She saw the rings.

Didn't speak. Didn't take it off.

He didn't explain. She didn't ask.

40

It was just after four the morning. The hospital had barely caught its breath. Fluorescent lights hummed.

The hallway outside Morgan's room was still—that brittle kind of quiet that only comes after the machinery of emergency winds down and the consequences start to settle in.

Kieran hadn't moved from the chair. Not when the nurses rotated. Not when his phone buzzed again.

He kept his eyes on Morgan, now asleep, finally too exhausted to keep pretending she was fine.

Then the elevator dinged. At first, he didn't look up. Probably a nurse. Maybe a new shift.

Then the voices hit—loud, fast, too many at once.

And then they came. All of them.

The first wave crashed in—younger voices arguing about coffee orders and whose car was blocking the fire lane. Two guys still dressed like they'd barely stumbled out of the club, a woman in scrubs juggling a tray of Dunkin'.

The Filipino side, it seemed.

The next wave came in harder—cousins from Humboldt

Park, the girls from next door, Yarelis and Kiara, their mother right behind them, sharp-voiced and moving fast.

And then him. Shaved head under a White Sox cap and tattoos crawling up his neck. Two more men trailed him, heavyset, watchful—not cousins, not neighbors. Muscle.

Kieran stayed still, kept his body loose, even as his instincts pricked up sharp.

Another figure broke through the noise—a Black man in his late twenties, maybe early thirties, moving with a different kind of authority. Calm in a way only pilots learned to be. Leather jacket with a private charter logo.

A crocodile-embossed duffel bag slung over his shoulder —shiny, cherry red, the kind of expensive, high-fashion nonsense that was so clearly Morgan's it practically announced itself.

A silk scarf dangled from the zipper like a final, petty flourish.

Kieran placed him the second he saw the walk, the set of his shoulders: The younger version frozen in a cockpit photo at Morgan's house, grinning between her and her stepfather.

The man scanned Kieran, fast and clinical.

Before Kieran could get a word out, Morgan stirred in the bed, her voice rough but clear:

"Amari? Oh my god, you didn't have to come. Who else is here?"

"Everyone," Amari said, deadpan, like it should've been obvious.

Morgan let her head fall back and winced.

"What did you expect?" Amari added. "You land in a hospital in Cook County and you think Irene wouldn't hear about it?"

Then he turned to Kieran, sharp-eyed and direct:

"You with her?"

Kieran nodded once, throat tight.

"Yeah."

Amari nodded back, once.

"Amari. Her brother. Stepbrother, technically," he added, like he was used to skipping the confused looks.

Without another word, he shoved the duffel into Kieran's hands—heavier than it looked—then turned toward the nurses' station, already asking for room details.

And then came the final two. The hallway shifted—a quiet ripple, like the whole hospital remembered itself.

Her mother swept in first, moving like she owned the place. Black hair pulled back tight, not a strand out of place. Lipstick sharp enough to cut. Warm-toned skin catching the harsh light and turning it soft. A raincoat still cinched tight around her petite frame, less for the weather, more like armor.

And behind her—her husband. Tall. Solid. Pilot's shoulders. Deep brown skin. Quiet, steady eyes. The kind of man who didn't need to raise his voice to be heard—not in a cockpit, not in a room, not even here. The one who taught Morgan how to hold her own against egos twice her size. The one who taught her how to fly.

Kieran saw it now—the blueprint. The calm. The command. The same bones Amari carried, younger and sharper, but unmistakable all the same.

No one had to introduce them.

Kieran knew.

And they didn't ask who he was either. They saw him sitting there. Saw Morgan's hand curled near his. Saw the rings. They didn't say a word. They were here for her.

Kieran—sitting in the quiet eye of it all—understood something he hadn't before.

Morgan had never been alone. Not once. Not even close.

He thought about how the world loved to talk about women like her—ambitious, successful, single—like it was a sad story.

Like it ended in cold apartments and echoing kitchens. Like choosing yourself meant giving up everyone else. But Morgan had never been orbiting alone. She was the orbit.

KIERAN STEPPED into the hallway to refill Morgan's water bottle and walked straight into a gauntlet. A pair of cousins were already stationed there.

He recognized Kiara immediately—the twenty-five-year-old cousin from Humboldt Park, still in her CTA uniform, all bright-eyed and ready to start something. She clocked him without hesitation, manicured finger aimed straight at his chest.

"Yeah, that's him. I've seen him at her place."

Next to her, the bald, tatted man stood with his arms crossed. His eyes sharpened on Kieran, zero friendliness.

"You a pilot too?" he asked, suspicious like he already knew the answer—and already hated it.

"Yeah," Kieran said.

The crowd around him winced. It wasn't small. It was the kind of wince that traveled from the neck to the toes.

Strike one.

"I'm not him," Kieran added, voice flat.

He didn't cuss—no, not here—but the way he said *him* carried enough weight to leave a dent. The bald man stared him down like he was trying to decide how much trouble he could get away with in a hospital hallway.

Kieran didn't blink.

He wasn't here to puff his chest.

From the corner of his eye, he caught two men slouched on plastic chairs nearby shift forward, just enough to matter. Waiting. Watching. Reading the bald man's posture like a weather report.

The whole pack of them—quiet types with old scars and silent tells, men who didn't bluff because they didn't need to.

A few had that particular stillness you only earned by surviving things you never spoke about.

Kieran knew men like them.

Had shaken their hands at backyard cookouts on Ren's side of the family.

You didn't ask where they'd been. You didn't ask what they'd done. You just knew when respect had to be earned —and when you'd better come correct or not come at all.

Tension hung heavy enough to cut until Morgan's mother appeared, still speaking in easy, rolling Tagalog to a knot of nurses. Her husband followed behind her, hands in jacket pockets.

She stepped into the silence like a woman walking into her own living room—already in charge. She looked at the bald man first, her voice mild enough to sound grandmotherly if you weren't listening too hard.

"Sebastian," she said, warm and cutting at the same time, "thank you for coming all this way, but sometimes people just take a fall—and it's exactly what it looks like."

There it was—no raised voice, no pointed finger—just a gentle, lethal reminder: *Stand down.*

"And if it's not too much trouble," she added, as if it had just occurred to her, "your car's blocking the ambulance lane."

Sebastian gave a tiny nod—the kind you gave when

there wasn't another option—and turned away, his associates trailing behind him.

Only then did Morgan's mother finally turn her attention to Kieran. The look she gave him was surgical—measuring, not unkind, but thorough.

Kieran had walked into a lot of tough rooms in his life.

Arbitration panels. Funeral homes. Living rooms where you could still smell the fight that had blown through the night before. None of them hit him quite like this. He needed to be solid. Nothing else would cut it.

The woman who stepped forward was smaller than he expected—but everything about her posture said she didn't need size to make herself known.

Skinny hand, crushing grip. The kind of handshake that checked your wiring.

"I'm Irene Greene," she said. "Morgan's mother."

The resemblance slammed into Kieran like a freight train. The way they both stood. The way they looked at you like they already knew the worst thing you'd ever done and were deciding whether they could live with it. It made him a little delighted, a little scared shitless. He was seeing the blueprint, and realizing Morgan didn't just come from good stock—she came from unyielding stock.

Behind her, a man nodded—easy, warm, with rough palms that spoke of real work.

"Elijah Greene," he said.

"How old are you?" Irene asked.

No chitchat. No easing in.

"Forty-nine," he said.

He didn't stumble over it. Wouldn't give the audience formed around him the satisfaction.

She glanced sideways at Elijah.

He shrugged like, *This is your rodeo, hon.*

"Are you her boyfriend?"

"If that's what she wants me to be," he said.

Not cocky. Not meek. Just true.

She crossed her arms. It was like a gate slamming down.

"She doesn't like us in her business. Drew made sure of that. He cut her off from us, and she still thinks she let it happen."

There was an edge to her voice that made the whole room pay attention.

"So now she holds us at arm's length."

He sighed.

"Feels stupid to have to say it out loud, but—she's her own person. Always has been. I'm just lucky she lets me be close. It's not my place to tell her how to be with her own people."

Irene nodded like she'd heard it all before.

"I was a nurse in Chicago for thirty years," she said, flicking a hand toward the hospital walls like they were an old purse she didn't care to explain.

"Small town. Big mouths. If one of mine ends up here, I hear about it."

Kieran didn't waste energy pretending otherwise.

Somebody had crossed a line for her—and he respected the hell out of it.

Her eyes dropped to his left hand. The ring. Still there. She didn't have to ask. She already knew why he was wearing it, why security hadn't made him rot in the waiting room. Not judging. Just cataloguing.

"You've been married," she said.

"Yes," Kieran answered. "Divorced."

Behind her, some cousin nobody asked for let out a long, messy "ooh" like they were judging a talent show.

Irene didn't even blink.

She cut her eyes at them, clean and lethal, and they clammed up so fast you could hear it.

Kieran almost smiled.

It was pure Morgan.

"We can be a lot," she said, with a smile that could open you up or tear you apart.

"Morgan is very private. Especially after everything. But we raised her to be smart. Careful."

Kieran nodded once.

She tilted her head, studying him like he was a piece of machinery she was deciding whether to trust with her daughter's life.

"If she let you bring her here," she said slowly, "I'll assume she knows what she's doing."

A pause. Just long enough to sting.

"I just hope you know what you're doing."

Kieran met her gaze without hesitation.

"I do," he said.

Another breathless pause.

Then Irene gave a small nod. Just enough.

"Good," she said, voice soft but still sharp.

It wasn't until they turned away that he felt the adrenaline start to drain.

MORGAN DIDN'T SAY much after the neuro cleared her.

Just gave one sharp nod like it was a boardroom vote and not her own body being discussed.

She took the discharge papers without flinching, eyes already scanning for loopholes she could exploit.

Kieran could see her cataloging: what meds would let

her stay functional, what hours could be bent, what "no screens" really meant in practice.

She wasn't trying to be reckless. She was trying not to need anything. Which was worse.

The nurse reviewed her aftercare instructions, direct and brisk. Morgan answered every question before it was finished being asked.

Vitals were good. Pain was manageable.

Her voice was steadier than it had been, and that worried him more than if she'd slurred.

Outside the curtain, the volume had dropped.

Family packing up, low murmurs in English, Spanish, and Tagalog, the soft clatter of someone consolidating a bag of snacks and chargers.

Morgan's mother stepped in, followed by her tía from next door, who finally introduced herself as Valentina and batted her lashes at him.

Kieran barely had time to shift to his feet before he caught the look from her mother—we need a moment.

He nodded and stepped out without being told twice. Leaned against the wall across the hall, arms crossed, jaw tight.

Behind the closed curtain, the voices didn't rise, but they didn't need to. He caught the cadence—sharp, familiar, surgical. The kind of conversation that started in concern and landed somewhere just short of indictment.

He knew that tone. He'd been raised on that tone. Not yelling. Not cruelty. Just the kind of love that left indentations where no one could see.

Morgan tried to argue—he could hear it. Low and clipped. That tone she used when she was gaining ground—measured, unbothered, laced with just enough condescension to make you doubt yourself.

Then silence. Then something shorter. Probably that look. The one she used in the war room to end conversations. But they didn't back down. They doubled it. Matched her measure for measure.

He didn't have to see it to know. He could feel the pause. The quiet surrender. Not defeat—just that moment when pride buckled under the weight of love and exhaustion.

Ten minutes later, the curtain pulled back.

Her mom came out first, face carved from stone. Valentina followed, adjusting her scarf and giving him a single glance—one that said: *She's all yours. Don't fuck it up.*

Morgan didn't come out right away. When she did, she didn't storm or skulk. She moved like the conversation hadn't happened at all—shoulders back, chin set, steps measured like a clock wound too tight.

And because she was Morgan fucking Delgado, even her collapse looked curated—linen, silk, and a mouth that dared you to point it out. Lips glossed and stubborn. Only the taped-up gauze at the crook of her elbow—and the fat Band-Aid skimming her hairline—gave her away. She didn't look cowed. She didn't even look angry anymore. She looked—unmoored. Like someone had finally said the thing she couldn't bear to name.

And now she had to carry it around where everyone could see it.

"I've been ordered to leave the city," she said, slinging her bag over her shoulder.

She said it like it was a court summons. Pissed. Tight. Like she'd rather peel her own skin off than admit it felt like a relief.

"They don't trust me not to go back to work."

He didn't smile. Didn't joke. Just nodded once.

"Traverse is quiet," he said.

Morgan stared out the window, mouth twitching like she was swallowing glass. When she finally spoke, her voice cracked around the edges of it.

"Good," she said. "I'm tired of being seen."

41

They were somewhere in southwest Michigan, nothing but highway and sky, her family safely one-hundred-and-twenty miles behind them—finally out of range, out of earshot, out of reach.

Morgan sat with one leg tucked under her, watching pines and half-empty rest stops blur past like an exhale, resisting the urge to touch the butterfly bandage beneath her curls.

Morgan twisted the promotion ring around her left finger once, but didn't take it off.

Kieran's hand stayed loose on the wheel, the old wedding band still gleaming against his knuckle like it had every right to be there. Neither of them said anything about it.

Daisy and Scout were sound asleep in the back. There hadn't been much fanfare when they met her—just a few sniffs, a circle or two around her legs, and then a quiet, almost bored sort of acceptance. Like they'd already known her scent, picked it up off Kieran's skin or the fabric of his shirts months ago, and had just been waiting for her to catch up.

It was the first time in a while she didn't feel like she was being watched. No monitors. No corporate surveillance. No maternal side-eyes. Just the hum of the road and Kieran's hand on the wheel, steady at ten o'clock.

He drove the way he flew—decisive, smooth, unbothered by turbulence. His left forearm flexed every time he adjusted, veins cutting sharp beneath the sleeve of his henley, disappearing into tattoos she still hadn't had the time—or audacity—to trace with her tongue. She watched the tendons shift, the muscles pull, the skin tighten across bone, and briefly imagined the steering wheel wasn't the only thing under that hand. That kind of pressure, that kind of control, applied to her with the same calm authority— nothing frantic, just deliberate.

Her mouth went a little dry.

Kieran glanced over. "You okay?"

She blinked.

"Hmm? Yeah. Just..." She let the words trail off.

He raised an eyebrow but didn't push.

She turned back to the window and let the silence stretch another mile before saying, "The neurologist cleared me for sex. As long as it's not...too vigorous."

She didn't look at him directly, but from the corner of her eye, she felt the shift. His hand tightened on the wheel —just enough for those veins to rise, sharp as truth through ink. He swore under his breath, and she stretched like a cat —slow, deliberate, her voice lazy with provocation: "I don't think he realized how subjective that is."

They pulled off near a sign for dunes and bluffside trails. Kieran parked like a man caught between two authorities: the neurologist, who mandated two-hour breaks on the long drive, and his dick, currently making a strong argument of its own.

Morgan stepped out of the truck barefoot, her Jimmy Choos discarded unceremoniously on the passenger side floor. Low block heels. Bone-colored leather. Gold buckles at the ankle. Elegant. Understated. The kind of shoe that said: *Yes, I'm recovering from a neurological incident—but I still know a resort collection when I see one.*

Her feet sank into cool, packed sand as she walked toward the lip of the bluff. It smelled like the tail end of summer, sun-warmed dunes and lake salt. Her blouse was unbuttoned one notch too far, and the breeze flirted with the silk at her collarbones. She felt sticky and wild and uncontainable. Her hair was a mess. Her lip gloss was a joke.

She turned back toward him, the man who had refused to touch her like his hands had been registered as deadly weapons. He wasn't far—leaning against the hood of the truck, arms crossed, jaw tight. Watching her with that look again. Like she might shatter. Like she hadn't just told him she wanted him. Like he was protecting her from himself.

"Don't look at me like that," she said, voice low.

"Like what?"

"Like I'm going to snap in half if you kiss me wrong."

He sighed.

"Morgan. You were bleeding in my truck last night."

"Not currently bleeding."

"Jesus."

She hated him a little for being decent. Hated the carefulness in his voice, the restraint stitched into his shoulders. Hated how much it turned her on.

Maybe it was the concussion. Or maybe nearly dying just makes you want to get absolutely railed in the woods.

She read that somewhere. Probably WebMD. Probably bullshit.

Her heart beat like it was still catching up to the adrenaline. She could feel it in her thighs, her sternum, the base of her skull. Every nerve ending prickled with want.

She turned away from him before she did something irreversible. Walked toward the sand dunes with her shoulders squared and her teeth clenched, like she could outpace the pull of her own body.

The wind carried the sound of waves somewhere below the bluff, crashing just out of sight.

She didn't look back. If he followed, she wasn't sure what would happen. But it wouldn't be calm. It wouldn't be polite. And it sure as hell wouldn't be safe.

When she finally turned around, he was already there. Close. Silent. Solid.

She didn't get a word out before he kissed her.

He didn't touch her face. Not her chin, not her jaw, not the scalp under her thick waves like he usually did—the thing that undid her, every time. His hands stayed low. Controlled. Intentionally distant from what was still healing.

She felt the frustration rise, immediate and electric. Her body moved on instinct, pressing into him, chasing the pressure he wasn't giving. Her arms slid up his chest, trying to pull him closer, trying to make him lose that calm.

He didn't budge.

His left arm came up around her shoulders, holding her close. Not loose. Not soft. Restrictive. She twisted into it instinctively, the angle making her lean back into the crook of his elbow, almost resting on it. Her arms were pressed tight to her sides. She could squirm, but only so much.

His right arm wrapped around her waist, pulling her chest flush against him. Locked her there.

Then—one shift of his stance, and he dipped her. She felt the world tilt. Not a fall, not a stumble—just that moment of total suspension, like the ground had given her up and his arms were the only thing holding her in place.

She stilled. Breathless. Trapped. Anchored.

And only then—when she finally stopped twisting, when her body gave in to stillness—he kissed her deeper. No hesitation. No caution. Just pressure and heat and precision. Mouths open, tongues sliding, lips catching—biting, tasting. Barely breathing. His grip stayed firm, one arm at her waist, the other behind her shoulders, keeping her exactly where he wanted her.

Then—

Barking. Loud. Joyful. Unapologetic.

Daisy bounded over first, tail wagging so hard her whole body moved with it. Scout followed, less elegant, more chaotic, straight into the scene like he was returning from war.

Morgan pulled back instantly, breath still ragged, and pushed Kieran off like he was the one interrupting something sacred.

"Oh my goodness, look who woke from their naptime!" she said, already dropping to her knees.

Daisy whined and licked her face. Scout barreled into her and flopped over, showing his belly.

Kieran stood there, heart pounding, looking like he was trying to remember his own name while she buried her hands in fur and cooed like she hadn't just been about to straddle him in the sand.

"Unreal," he muttered.

Morgan glanced up.

"They missed me."

"They met you two hours ago."

She didn't respond. She was too busy hugging Daisy like she didn't have a healing skull fracture and lip gloss smeared halfway across her cheek.

She felt happiest like this—kiss-drunk, dirt-smudged, and surrounded by creatures who loved her instantly.

He'd just have to wait his turn.

42

The gravel driveway wound through the trees like an afterthought, each crunch of the tires echoing in the stillness of the forest.

Morgan rolled down her window halfway, inhaling the smell of pine, cold dirt, and the sharp tang of lake water.

The house revealed itself only at the last second—a cabin tucked low against the tree line, dark brown siding weathered into something close to gray, solar panels angled like stubborn shoulders toward the weak afternoon sun.

Before Kieran even cut the ignition, Scout and Daisy launched themselves out, their heads shoving past her seat, tails battering her shoulder in their scramble for freedom.

They tumbled into the yard like furry missiles, immediately dropping to do their business with the urgency of long-suffering passengers. Then, as if on cue, they trotted off to do what Morgan quickly understood was their self-appointed perimeter check—circling the lot, sniffing at imaginary intruders, leaving paw prints in the mud.

Kieran reached into the back and grabbed her cherry-red Briggs & Riley duffel—the only real pop of color against the battered North Face backpack he slung over his own shoulder.

He carried hers without a second thought, like it didn't weigh anything.

"Just—uh, sorry in advance about the dog toys," he muttered, looking almost bashful as he shouldered the bag.

Morgan smiled to herself, stepping out onto the gravel. The air tasted like pine sap.

The house wasn't big—just stubbornly solid, with a heavy wood door and a porch littered with old dog beds and the skeletal remains of summer plants.

Inside, it was a different world.

The inside hit her like a wall—warm and a little stale, the way cabins always were when the windows stayed shut too long. No air conditioning, of course.

He moved through the room without ceremony, dragging open windows and propping the screen door.

Within minutes, the cool lake air poured through, sweeping away the leftover heat and carrying in the smell of pine, earth, and clean water.

The interior was a love letter to practicality—knotty pine walls, sturdy furniture, ancient plaid curtains—but it was alive with small signs of affection.

Blankets thrown over couches. A mug half-forgotten on a side table. A rubber chicken toy with one leg missing under an armchair.

And the books—God, the books.

They swallowed a whole wall and then some, erupting out of custom-built shelves, stacked in tilting towers on the floor, lined up in neat hopeless rows across the fireplace mantle.

Aviation manuals, feminist theory, fat YA fantasy novels with cracked spines.

A copy of *Beloved* jammed between *Stick and Rudder* and *An Indigenous Peoples' History of the United States*. Dog-eared, annotated, loved.

Morgan ran her fingertips along a stack as they passed, awe warming her chest.

This wasn't curated. This wasn't Instagrammable. This was real.

Kieran threw their bags by the door, already kicking off his boots.

"Couch is, uh, dangerous," he said gruffly. "Sucks you in. Be warned."

She didn't even hesitate. She dropped onto it, sinking so deep she almost disappeared into the cushions.

Kieran followed without a word, dropping down beside her with a grunt and a lazy sprawl that brushed his thigh against hers like it was the most natural thing in the world.

Morgan let herself lean in, breathing in the faint smell of his soap and the cooler air slipping through the open windows. She felt him shift—no hesitation—just lifting his arm and settling it around her shoulders like he was built for it. She fit against his side easily, like this wasn't the first time, like some part of her body already knew what it was doing.

The dogs thudded inside a moment later, circling before collapsing into satisfied piles on the rug.

Morgan stretched her legs out, eyes catching the frames on the far wall—three of them, spaced with the kind of care that said Kieran had hung them himself, probably with a level and three rounds of swearing.

The first was a photo of a baby—all chubby fists and furious squint—swaddled in an oversized green blanket like a burrito.

Kieran was holding holding them up, maybe twenty-five

if she had to guess, auburn hair without the grays, grin easy and devastating.

Jesus Christ.

He'd been stupid hot. Like bail-money-required hot.

But it wasn't the cheekbones that wrecked her.

It was the way he looked at that baby. Like joy was the only thing in the world worth surviving for.

Next was a newer shot—Ren again, cap and gown crooked, grinning like they'd just gotten away with something. Kieran hovered just out of frame, hand steady on their shoulder. Proud. Whole.

The last frame was different. Older. Faded.

Two boys standing shoulder-to-shoulder by a rusted-out pickup, maybe twelve and ten. One was Kieran—same sharp jaw, same mess of freckles. The younger kid looked like someone had just been dared to do something dangerous, and he was already halfway there.

Kieran followed her gaze from across the room.

"That's Conor," he said simply. "Two years younger. Got his license before I did. Hotshot."

Morgan glanced at him, catching the tightness in his jaw, the way his fingers flexed once against his jeans before going still again.

"He fought hard," Kieran said, voice careful. "Longer than anybody knew he could."

Morgan knew what he meant. The kind of pressure that told boys to be strong or be nothing. To carry it alone or not at all.

It crushed them young. It crushed them quiet.

White men have the highest suicide rates in the United States. Everybody knew this. Not enough talked about it.

She didn't say anything. She just held him—steady, certain—like he didn't have to carry it tonight.

Kieran stiffened for half a second, then let his weight tip into her, slow and exhausted.

TIME BENT in a way it only did when you were too tired to chase it and too happy to care. Hours slipped between the pines, slid across the water, curled into the soft corners of the cabin.

By the second morning, she realized the Wi-Fi wasn't just unplugged—it had been surgically removed. She found the router cord in a kitchen drawer, neatly coiled and labeled in his handwriting: *Relax. It's not forever.*

She let him confiscate her phone too—not because he asked, but because she wanted him to. Wanted the excuse to stop answering emails, to stop explaining herself to anyone. He dropped it into a ceramic bowl by the door like he was checking a weapon.

It wasn't weird. It wasn't isolation the way she'd lived it before—the dull-edged kind, full of silence and second-guessing. This was different. This was her choosing to be quiet for once.

And anyway, it wasn't like she was cut off.

Kieran got drafted—against his will and with absolutely no warning—into a thirty-person Greene-Delgado-Marasigan group chat that treated emotional check-ins and dog pictures like federally mandated activities.

The next day, they went to the beach. The lake was too cold to swim, but they walked the shore barefoot, skipping stones, doing corny shit she used to roll her eyes at—before she realized she needed it.

They kayaked. He packed a cooler. She rolled her eyes

again and took pictures of him like he was a park ranger
thirst trap.

He cooked every night. She walked the dogs every
morning while he worked out in the detached garage gym
that looked like a CrossFit cult compound.

Daisy slept by her side like she'd always belonged there.

Only one thing ruined the illusion.

Scout had a habit of stealing one of her shoes while she
brushed her teeth. Cute, at first. Until the morning she
stepped outside and found the remains of her Stuart
Weitzman slides—nude leather, delicate gold trim—
shredded across the porch like a hate crime.

She didn't scream. Didn't cry. Just stared at the wreckage
like she was ID'ing a body.

Kieran had the good sense to apologize with his whole
chest.

"He's still got puppy brain," he offered weakly, holding
up what used to be the insole. "I'll buy you another pair."

She didn't look at him.

"They were a seasonal exclusive. You can't buy another
pair."

That night, she began sketching out a concept for
custom "luxury shoe safes." She didn't joke about it. Because
loving a man with dogs was one thing. But if this was going
to work, she was going to need climate-controlled, lockable
footwear storage.

Somewhere around midnight, the sound of power tools
started humming in the garage.

By Thursday, all was forgiven.

She was brushing Scout's coat with one of Kieran's old
beard combs. No one questioned it.

Friday night, she met the Not Book Club Book Club.

Six retired or semi-retired aviation guys, all of them big

feelings and big forearms, sitting around a patio with beers and annotated copies of *The Will to Change* and *Caste* next to smoked ribs and a bluetooth speaker playing Fleetwood Mac.

They were sharp, hilarious, surprisingly intersectional.

She expected to feel out of place. She didn't.

They liked her. One of them cried a little. Another offered her a part-time consulting job she had no intention of taking but appreciated anyway.

On Saturday, Ren came up from Detroit.

They were taller than she expected. Taller than Kieran by a couple inches. Sharp. Reserved. Hair half-buzzed, half-curly, eyebrows too powerful to be legal.

She clocked the suspicion in their eyes the second they met.

Morgan stepped into the kitchen in Kieran's sweats, with a half-healed scar just visible beneath her hairline. Ren was already posted up against the counter, spooning peanut butter straight from the jar like it was a protest.

The chipped black nail polish said they hadn't had the energy. The frayed hoodie said they didn't care who noticed.

Morgan registered the posture, the stare, the clear radius of emotional barbed wire.

Ren gave a once over of her face, the clothes, and the air of someone who didn't believe in rest and learned to schedule mental breakdowns like meetings.

"Let me guess," Ren said, not even looking up. "You're the woman my dad swears he's 'just working with.'"

Morgan lifted an eyebrow. "You're the reason he suddenly knows what 'dissociate' means."

Ren didn't smile. But they didn't blink, either. "Cute. You rehearse that?"

"I don't rehearse," Morgan said, reaching for a mug. "I brief."

Ren took another bite, still watching her like it was a TSA screening.

"So?" they asked. "Are you?"

Morgan didn't miss a step. "Sleeping with your dad?"

Ren grimaced. "Ew! No. Dating. And you're supposed to be the polished one?"

Morgan exhaled through her nose. No flinch. "I clean up well. Doesn't mean I'm not winging half of it."

Their grip on the spoon relaxed—barely.

"You know saying that out loud doesn't make it less true. Or less of a problem."

"You want vulnerability or a PowerPoint? Pick one."

That earned her something. Not a smile, but a visible loosening of the jaw. A détente, however temporary.

Ren set the spoon down. "You look like you give TED talks as a hobby and cry in locked bathrooms."

Morgan didn't blink. "You look like you overcommit to impossible causes and ghost anyone who tries to text you twice."

Ren's mouth twitched.

"We should never hang out."

"God, no."

Morgan took a sip of coffee.

Ren nodded, slowly.

"I'm not pretending I'm chill about strangers around him. I'm protective. It's pathological. But fair."

"Noted." Morgan glanced out the window.

Ren didn't respond for a long stretch, scrolling through social media on their phone.

"He told me what you're up against," they said eventually.

Morgan didn't answer, but something in her posture flickered. A crack of acknowledgment.

"You scared?" Ren asked, tone light but too direct to be casual.

Morgan gave a tired, sharp-edged smirk. "You mean, besides meeting the one person whose opinion actually matters to him?"

Their eyes met. Mutual side-eye. Mutual respect.

"Not bad," Ren said. "For a tragically straight, hashtag girlboss."

Morgan raised her mug. "Not bad for a Huey-P.-Newton-in-crimson-Doc-Martens dupe."

Ren snorted, shoulders dropping half an inch. Not warmth, exactly—but recognition.

No hugs. No high-fives. Just a silent agreement as they retreated to their separate corners of the kitchen, like two cats who'd hissed it out and decided the couch was big enough for now.

THE STARS WERE JUST STARTING to show when Morgan set the plates down on the outdoor table, her movements lazy and precise, like she'd been doing it for years.

She wore Kieran's flannel over a tank top, sleeves rolled, hair tucked behind one ear.

The dogs tore around the yard in their glow-in-the-dark vests like chaos with paws, crashing through bushes and kicking up little bursts of firefly light.

Kieran stood at the grill, tongs in hand, while Ren

hovered nearby, arguing about whether or not sweet corn belonged in barbecue.

They'd made ribs—messy, sticky, the kind that required paper towels and moral flexibility.

There was a bowl of salad greens Morgan had prepped earlier from Ren's community garden, and a cobbler cooling on the windowsill like they were in a damn folk song.

String lights buzzed overhead. The air was warm with just enough bite to remind them summer didn't last.

For the first time in weeks, maybe longer, Kieran felt like things had settled. Like peace wasn't a punishment.

They ate until the silence turned companionable, until the only sounds were chewing, soft jazz from Ren's phone speaker, and Scout snuffling under the table like he was casing the joint.

Morgan leaned back in her chair, wine glass in hand, eyes half-lidded, legs stretched out under the table.

"Okay," she murmured, "that was borderline obscene."

Ren, also slightly wine-softened, nodded solemnly. "I would die for that corn."

Kieran smiled. Took a slow breath.

The moment was perfect. Which, of course, meant it was time to break it.

He reached down to the side table, pulled out the laptop and her phone—fully charged, notifications already buzzing.

Morgan didn't notice at first. She was watching the dogs.

Ren caught it first, eyebrows lifting as Kieran opened the laptop and set it in front of him.

"Seriously?" Morgan asked, not even turning.

Kieran hesitated. "Even God rested on the seventh day," he said. "But on the eighth, He checked His email."

Morgan sighed. "You're lucky I'm full."

"I waited as long as I could," he said, quieter now.

She turned. Really looked. Saw the tightness around his eyes. The weight behind it.

Ren sat up straighter and cleared his throat.

She shot a look at the kid. Even they knew something was up.

Kieran didn't answer. He pushed the laptop toward Morgan.

She unlocked it.

Her phone lit up a second later—buzz after buzz after buzz. Push alerts. Twitter mentions. A message from Sloane. Two from Vee. Several emails from Elena Chau, the journalist from the gala.

She stared at the screen. No words yet. Just absorbing.

Her name wasn't in the headlines. Not directly. But the phrasing was enough:

"Airline Insider Blamed for Severe Routing Errors Amid Turbulence Surge"

"Heritage Exec Under Scrutiny—Union Reps Call for Accountability"

"FOX: 'DEI priorities putting passenger safety at risk?'"

In the group chats, they weren't subtle:

"It's her, right?"

"Morgan Delgado rerouted that flight last month. She's the one."

And somewhere on Reddit: "The nerve center director is trending in all the wrong ways."

Morgan's hand hovered over the wine glass, but didn't pick it up.

The stars were still out. The string lights still buzzed. Scout let out a soft bark somewhere in the dark, chasing something he couldn't catch.

Morgan finally blinked.

"So," she said, voice low and even. "They're doing this now."

Kieran nodded.

Dinner ended with quiet cleanup and a half-hearted attempt at dessert. Morgan barely touched the cobbler.

At the door, Ren shifted from foot to foot, keys in one hand, hoodie sleeves stretched down past their knuckles. The dogs circled their ankles like tiny bodyguards.

"Hey," they said, voice pitched lower, like they didn't want to wake whatever raw thing was still breathing in the room. "Sorry for going in on you this morning."

A breath caught in Morgan's chest. Not quite a laugh, but close. She exhaled through her nose and gave a nod. "Get home safe."

Ren stepped forward, one arm looping around her in a stiff, brief hug that felt more like a truce than comfort.

Then they were gone—out into the dark with a muttered goodbye, Scout following them to the porch like a silent, glowing escort.

Inside, everything was still.

Morgan didn't say a word as she padded back down the hall. Didn't speak as she crossed the threshold into Kieran's bedroom and sat on the edge of the bed with her phone in hand like it was a scalpel. She just scrolled, eyes flicking, thumb moving like a machine.

He didn't follow right away. Gave her space. Let the quiet settle until the only sound was the low whir of the fan and the faint hum of rage behind every tap of her screen.

And when he finally stepped into the doorway, he saw it all—the weight in her shoulders, the taut line of her jaw, the color drained from her face but not her fire. Just sat there, scrolling like her thumb was a loaded trigger.

Headlines. Tweets. DEI grifter. Diversity optics hire. Corporate puppet. Every post more venomous than the last.

He watched the color shift in her. That quiet rage. The kind that didn't need yelling to level a room. Her whole body wound tight like a wire about to snap.

Then she looked up.

"You didn't tell me this was blowing up."

Her voice wasn't raised. That was worse. She didn't raise her voice when she was angry—she tightened it, sharpened it, made it cut.

Kieran didn't blink. He stepped in, slow and sure, like every inch between them was a decision.

"No," he said. "I didn't."

"You knew. And you kept it from me."

He didn't back down. Didn't soften his voice or reach for the easy out. He looked her dead in the eye.

"I did. I knew. And I made the call."

Silence. Just her breathing, measured but clipped.

She was already doing the calculus—of trust, of control, of betrayal.

"You weren't okay, Morgan. You said you were, but I watched your hands shake every morning while you made coffee. I watched you pretend your head didn't hurt when the sun hit the window too hard. I wasn't going to stand there and watch you crash."

He kept his voice low. Steady. Not for her comfort—but because the truth didn't need volume to land.

"Your mom knew. Your aunt. Vee. They all said the same thing I did: 'Let her rest. Hold the line.' So I did."

Morgan opened her mouth, but he raised a hand—not to silence her, but to make her listen.

"This wasn't about keeping you in the dark. It was about

giving you a week to be human again. Just one week where no one needed you to fix everything."

He let the last words settle. She didn't interrupt. That was something.

"You're the most capable person I've ever met. But you're still a person. And when you were too tired to protect yourself, I stepped in. I stood between you and this shitstorm. And I'd do it again."

Morgan didn't answer. Just sat there for a long moment, her thumb brushing the edge of her diamond ring without pulling it off.

The resignation settled in her bones—quiet, inevitable. The illusion was over. The week was over. The world was waiting.

She looked up, voice low. "I need to pack."

Kieran nodded once. Didn't try to stop her.

Later that night, they lay side by side in the bed—the dogs sprawled at their feet, the fan humming overhead. Close enough to touch, but neither of them reaching.

In the dim light, he caught it—the way her diamond ring had migrated back to her right hand.

Not a fight. Not a declaration. Just a quiet, necessary shift.

He turned his face into the pillow and closed his eyes.

43

By the time Morgan returned to Chicago, the air had shifted. It was still her city—her streets, her skyline—but everything felt sharper now, brittle and glassy. The kind of quiet that settled after an explosion, when you were still blinking dust from your eyes, too stunned to know whether to run or start picking up the pieces.

She didn't go back to Heritage Command Center. Sloane had warned her not to.

"They'll try to provoke you. Don't let them see your face until you're paid."

She listened. Barely. Her phone stayed off. Email went to auto-reply. She lived in her own house like it was a bunker, curtains drawn, laptop closed.

She wasn't fired. Not officially. Not yet. But the silence from Heritage—the calculated, weaponized absence of communication—told her exactly where she stood.

Sloane, on the other hand, was in full war mode. She stormed Morgan's living room in heels that clacked like gavel strikes, silk blouse untucked and phone glued to her hand as she rewrote every inch of Morgan's exit paperwork. By the time she was done, Morgan's severance looked like a corporate hostage negotiation: salary, benefits, non-disparagement clauses, backpay from her last performance review —plus a quiet little line item titled "personal security expenses."

"You're not resigning," Sloane said, circling the coffee table like a panther. "You're extracting."

At the same time, Vee was on the tarmac in a hard hat and fire in her chest. The mechanics' union staged a walkout —officially for pay, but Vee wasn't pretending it was only about money. It was a demand for truth. For accountability. For Morgan.

"You want safe planes and a safe industry?" Vee said on a livestream, her voice calm and surgical. "Then you listen to the people who make them fly. And you pay us like it."

In the background, someone held a cardboard sign that read: WE STAND WITH MORGAN. STOCK OPTIONS WON'T TIGHTEN A BOLT.

It should have felt like vindication. Instead, it felt like a eulogy.

The internet was worse. In the pilot forums, it was open season. On PPRuNe, someone Morgan had managed years ago—a man she once defended in a staffing meeting— posted:

"She couldn't read a METAR if it bit her in the ass, and that's who's running ops? No wonder flights are getting tossed like salad."

Another replied:

"Only turbulence she's used to is in the bedroom, amirite?"

She didn't even get through the Reddit threads. The headlines were enough:

"Heritage's DEI darling crashes and burns."

"Fast-tracked and fast-tracked, if you know what I mean."

Then came the quotes. Anonymous at first, but unmistakable. And then, finally, Drew—on record, in a sleazy industry blog that only existed to court rumor and ruin.

"She was always hungry for power. That's what turned her on. She didn't want partnership—she wanted worship."

She read it once. Then again. She closed the last tab. Sat back. Let the silence swallow her whole.

It was over. Not the story. Her. The industry had already moved on, carving her name into its cautionary tale list in invisible ink. She wasn't in the headlines—but everyone who mattered knew. Ops directors. Union reps. Pilots she'd never meet.

She wasn't just done at Heritage. She was done in aviation.

Her body stayed in the chair, but her mind floated somewhere else. Detached. Distant. Like back then—when Drew would climb on top of her and she'd stare at the ceiling, counting the cracks, pretending she was anywhere else.

It felt like that now. Like being touched without consent. Like grief with no tears left.

She was done before they even fired her. She just had to make it official.

44

Kieran had never been good at sitting still.

While Morgan battened down the hatches, he started digging. Quietly. Methodically. He called in every favor that mattered, starting with the guys from Not Book Club Book Club.

Chuck—the one who smelled like hickory smoke and always took notes in a spiral notebook—happened to be the vice president of the International Pilots Union. Within forty-eight hours, Kieran had him drafting a formal letter of concern.

The letter didn't name names. But it referenced the Meridian 7X by model and incident number. It listed discrepancies, delays, cabin pressurization alarms, and unreported maintenance failures.

"We are documenting a pattern of safety anomalies consistent with systemic manufacturer negligence."

The union press secretary sent it to the board. To the FAA. To the press. Quietly. Carefully. But directly.

Meanwhile, Sloane handled the FAA's investigation into the alcohol test—Kieran's own little slice of scandal, which

Enright had orchestrated like a poorly written soap opera subplot. The lab cleared him. No ambiguity. No room for spin. Zero substances. Zero violations. Just politics.

Sloane forwarded the results with a one-line note: "We're done here."

He didn't celebrate. Didn't even exhale. Just clicked "Forward," attached the full FAA clearance, and sent it to his lawyer with a subject line that read:

Heritage Airlines – Reputational Defamation Case Prep.

And in the body:

"I don't need the money. I want to come after the bottom line. They questioned my integrity, and that's the only currency I've got. Let's make it cost them."

Then he turned his attention to Drew.

He traced the leak backward—timestamps, metadata, sloppy anonymity that only felt clever to the kind of man who still used Facebook for professional networking. The gossip, the smears, the carefully worded quotes from an "anonymous union source" that just happened to match Drew's exact phrasing in old emails.

It all led to the same person.

And this time, Kieran didn't bring it to Morgan.

KIERAN PARKED in front of a garage in Cicero, Illinois with no name, no listed hours, and exactly one working light flickering above the bay door like it was doing its best. The kind of place you didn't Google—just heard about through someone's cousin who used to fix alternators and occasionally people.

He stepped inside, envelope tucked under his arm.

The smell hit first: motor oil, blunt wraps, and fried food

no one had ordered. A couple guys sat around a beat-up card table, watching grainy TV. One wore a Cubs jacket over a Bad Bunny tee. Another was sharpening something—not a knife, just...something.

One of them looked up.

"You lost, man?"

Kieran blinked. "No. I'm looking for Sebastian."

They stared. A long, meaningful silence. Then:

"Aw hell no. You come all the way down here with your little folder thinkin' what—what, we're gonna do a hit for you?"

The others cracked up. One clutched his chest like it physically hurt.

"Damn, bro. You think we're The Sopranos?"

Kieran flushed. "That's not—"

"You see this? White boy thinks we do favors like we're in a TV show."

He opened his mouth to defend himself, thought better of it, and just said, "Okay. Fair. That's fair."

A voice cut through the laughter—smoother, closer.

"Damn, y'all are loud," the man said, stepping in from the hallway like he'd been waiting for his cue.

Sebastian.

He didn't match the room. Where the others wore hoodies, grease-stained tees, and work boots Sebastian looked like he'd just come from closing on a two-flat. Slate-blue button-down tucked into charcoal slacks. Bald, early forties, with killer's eyes—sharp, patient, waiting. The same hard grit that ran through Morgan's blood was stamped into his face too: high cheekbones, squared-off jaw, and that resting look that dared you to waste his time.

At the hospital, he'd shown up in sweats and a White Sox cap, looking more like a man who was ready to bust kneecaps until he got answers. He'd been the one to drive Morgan's Humboldt Park relatives to the ER. He was also in the family group chat—and had heart-reacted to Kieran's last dog picture.

His forearms—rolled sleeves, of course—bore three names in script. His daughters. Below them, a black-and-grey portrait of an older woman smiling in a church pew: their grandmother. Morgan's father's mother.

Sebastian nodded once. "Kieran."

Kieran nodded back. "Sebastian."

"Can we talk?"

Sebastian jerked his chin toward the back.

"Yeah. Let's talk."

The "office" was a back room with a folding table, three mismatched chairs, and a mini fridge plastered in faded bumper stickers: IF YOU TALK TO COPS, DON'T TALK TO US.

Kieran sat and placed the envelope on the table. No one reached for it.

"Inside's everything he's been saying. About her. Forum posts, blogs, private Discord leaks. All of it."

Silence.

"I'm not asking you to break anyone's legs."

Sebastian raised an eyebrow. "Hypothetically. How far do you want this to go?"

Kieran sighed. "I just need him scared. Shaken. So he stops harassing her."

"And you don't want her to know."

"No," Kieran said. "I want her to wonder."

Sebastian cracked his knuckles like they were just sorting out Saturday carpool—whose turn to drive, whose turn to handle the dirty work.

"Then you're leaving town today."

Kieran caught the subtext. "I'd been planning to go up to Detroit anyways. My kid's got a full protest slate coming up. Might even hit the news."

Sebastian nodded, slow and approving. "Perfect. Be helpful. Be supportive. Be somewhere else."

"I'll be in the background. Holding signs. Passing out water bottles. Peak wholesome dad energy."

"Good," Sebastian said, tone bone-dry as he fed the envelope into an industrial shredder without even glancing inside. Paper hissed and disappeared. "Now get out before the guys start thinking I'm flipping for the Feds."

Kieran stood.

No handshake. Just a nod—the kind you give when a door's opened behind you, and you know it's not going to close again.

Outside, he sat in his car for a moment. Buckled his seatbelt.

Then started the engine and drove—quiet, steady. Like a man who'd done what needed doing, and wasn't looking back.

M organ didn't leave a note. Just the e-mail.

Subject: Resignation – Effective Immediately
Effective immediately, I resign my position with Heritage Airlines. Per the terms of my contract, I expect full severance and all accrued benefits to be processed within the standard timeframe. I will not be making further comment.
CC: Sloane Campbell, Esq.

No SIGN-OFF. No postscript. No name at the bottom. They knew who it was from.

She clicked send. Nothing happened. No alert. No fanfare. Just the cursor blinking in a now-silent inbox.

Sloane sat across from her, still in heels, phone in one hand and a glass of something stiff in the other. She didn't ask if Morgan was okay. She'd known the answer for days.

MORGAN DIDN'T GET out of bed much after that. Not really. She moved when she had to—water, bathroom, a protein bar when her hands stopped shaking long enough to open the wrapper. The curtains stayed closed. The inbox piled up, silent and heavy as dirt. She let it.

His text message came sixty seconds after she hit send on her resignation. She hadn't even taken her finger off the mouse.

I'm heading to Detroit. There's something I need to take care of. I'll explain soon. Please take care of yourself.

She read it once. Then again. The words didn't get better.

Not *I'm here*. Not *I saw what they did and I've got you.* Just distance, gift-wrapped as care.

She stared at the screen until the letters blurred. Then she typed:

You couldn't have picked a worse moment to disappear. Let's take some space. I'll reach out when I'm no longer being dissected on national television.

She hit send. Then she blocked him.

Not out of anger. Out of survival.

Because when everything cracked open, he made himself elsewhere. And that—more than the firestorm, more than the headlines—was what finally pulled her under.

THE THIRD NIGHT blurred into morning, or maybe it was the other way around. Time had lost its structure. No clocks, no calendar—just the throb behind her eyes and the sour taste of survival.

Her phone hadn't buzzed. Not since she blocked him. Not since she'd deleted the last dozen news alerts.

The world could end, and she wouldn't know until the ceiling collapsed. She reached for the charger, not out of hope, just habit.

That's when it came. Her phone buzzed. Not a call. Just a single text.

From Ava. No greeting. No explanation. Just a link.

She stared at it for a long time. Thumb hovering. Then tapped.

FLIGHT RISK: Inside the Meridian 7X Scandal Heritage Tried to Hide

By Elena Chau, for *The Current*

Her breath caught. Not from surprise. From recognition.

Cabin pressurization failures. Buried maintenance reports. Manufacturer memos. Redacted internal safety audits—now unredacted. Screenshots. Flight logs. Test data with falsified signatures.

And near the end, nestled like a landmine:

"Sources say the recent resignation of a high-ranking executive may have signaled internal dissent. Requests for comment were declined."

Not a quote. Not even a name. But it was enough. It made her look like a prophet or a coward. And neither was true.

She didn't need a byline to know whose fingerprints were on it. The cadence. The clean threading of dots that shouldn't connect but now did.

That was Ava. Always Ava. Ava, who'd spent a decade consulting after her so-called retirement. Ava, who built

Morgan from the ground up—and then used her as a distraction while she set the fuse.

While the company flailed, eyes locked on the wrong fire, Ava walked through the smoke with a box of matches and a file full of names.

It hit all at once—the things she should've seen.

Never flinch first. Never explain. Never bleed where they can see it.

Ava's rules. Ava's voice in her head, steady as gospel, even now.

The visitor badge she'd signed off on for Ava weeks ago without thinking, the box of paczki left like an offering she never got to accept. Marisa's voice in her ear: someone else had been digging, someone whose fingerprints were too old to trace. Ava at the gala, smiling like a woman who already knew the ending and had the receipts tucked in her clutch.

All of it layered over her now—too late, too loud, too clear.

Morgan sat up, sweating. Her limbs shaky like she hadn't moved in years. The blinking router light watched her like a witness.

She dialed. Ava picked up on the second ring.

Calm. Cold.

"You used me," Morgan said. No hello. No breath.

"Not used," Ava replied. "Deployed."

"I didn't agree to be your goddamn sacrificial lamb."

"You weren't. You were the cover. Elena and I were the strike."

Morgan's throat went tight.

"You should've told me."

"I couldn't risk it. Not with you that close to breaking. If you knew, they would've smelled it on you."

"You built me," she said. "Then left me to burn."

A pause. Then:

"And now you're free."

Morgan looked around her room. The plates, the clothes, the mess of a life paused mid-collapse.

"No," she said. "I'm scorched fucking earth."

And she hung up.

46

Seventy-two hours. No calls. No texts. Not even from Sloane. Just silence.

The article had detonated across the internet. Every cockpit WhatsApp thread, every pilot forum worth its salt—buzzing. Deafening. Theories flying faster than a charter jet on an empty leg.

Most assumed it had to be Morgan Delgado. Who else could've pulled the black box receipts?

But none of the aviation trades would touch her side of it. Heritage had lawyers locked and loaded. AeroVox went nuclear with a sweeping defamation suit.

Sloane hit back with one of her own—strategic and scorched earth—to keep Morgan's name off the record and out of the mud. And just so no one forgot whose name they were trying to bury, Sloane had her hacker crew running a proprietary surveillance loop that made federal watchdogs look like dial-up.

Every hour on the hour, their system scraped the internet for Morgan Delgado linked to any legitimate media outlet. If her name showed up in even mildly defamatory company, the algorithm flagged it, parsed tone and subtext, and fired off a cease-and-desist so precise it could pass the bar.

It didn't guess. It knew. It could sniff out a thinkpiece buried in a meme and spot a euphemism faster than an HR rep covering a manager's ass.

They weren't just protecting Morgan—they were building a legal moat around her name deep enough to drown entire careers.

Retractions hit inboxes faster than the gossip could circulate. Aviation journalism, a clique small enough to fit in one Delta Sky Club lounge, got the message: mention Morgan Delgado, and her lawyer would end you before your SEO finished indexing.

But outside the institutions—on Reddit, TikTok, and burner Twitter—the speculation never let up.

They called Morgan a whistleblower. A traitor. A bitter ex. A power-hungry bitch. Just not right.

Heritage's comms team burped out a rinse cycle of bleached corporate non-denials. AeroVox followed with two paragraphs of boilerplate safety jargon that might as well have been lifted from a Reagan-era crash site playbook.

Then there was Enright, sweating on CNBC, his voice cracking as he stumbled through lies about "isolated systems anomalies."

Sloane watched him in silence, sipping her tea like it was blood.

When the camera cut back to the anchor, she smiled for the first time all week.

Vee, though?

Vee wasn't quiet. She was fire. She was jet fuel. She was done.

When word hit the floor that the Meridian 7X had been

cleared for flights again, Vee walked off the line mid-shift. No announcement. No grandstanding. Just dropped her wrench and peeled off her gloves like they were evidence from a crime scene.

Her silence moved faster than rumor, louder than any protest chant.

One shop turned. Then another.

Midway. O'Hare. Detroit. St. Louis was already rumbling.

She was backlit by halogen and rage when a camera caught her outside the hangar.

"If they won't ground the jets, we'll ground ourselves."

1.4 million views in under fifteen minutes. Three trending hashtags. One unbothered Vee.

Her phone blew up. Offers. Threats. Union brass. Reporters. Her ex.

And still, Vee found time to show up at Morgan's door with a matcha ube latte and a crowbar in case anyone tried it.

Morgan opened the door in sweatpants and an old flight school tee. No bra. No words.

"You look like shit," Vee said, stepping in.

"You're glowing," Morgan said flatly.

"Revolution agrees with me."

Vee dropped the matcha on the table and sat on the couch like it was hers.

"You could maybe say thank you for shutting down three airports."

Morgan blinked slowly.

"Thank you."

"Anything for you, babe," Vee added, eyes flicking toward the headlines on Morgan's muted TV.

Vee snatched the remote.

"Okay, that's enough CNN for the rest of your natural life."

Click. Flip. Flip.

"We're watching MILF Fight Club."

Morgan blinked.

"That's not—"

"Too late. I've committed. These women are all wearing four layers of foundation and brass knuckles, and honestly? I support them."

Onscreen, someone named Tawny elbowed a former Miss Ohio into a buffet table.

Morgan almost smiled. Almost.

47

They made it through an entire season of *MILF Fight Club* before the world came knocking again.

Morgan stayed mostly horizontal, a blanket half-tangled around her legs, a forgotten mug of tea cooling on the coffee table. Vee was sprawled across the armchair like she owned it, live-texting someone about Tawny's betrayal in episode six.

They were queueing up Season Two—new cast, higher stakes, twice the spray tans—when the door banged open without ceremony.

Sloane, trench coat swinging like a warning shot, phone still in her hand.

"You're being subpoenaed," she said, like she was handing over takeout.

"Hello to you too," Vee muttered, not even glancing up from her phone.

Morgan sat up slowly. Eyes rimmed red. Bones aching. Soul scorched.

There was no terror left. No fight-or-flight spark. No fear pounding under her ribs. She had already survived everything that could kill her—and most of what couldn't. Now there was only the hollow calm that came after a crash. The world could demand anything it wanted. It couldn't take what she didn't have left.

She nodded once, steady and silent.

"Fine," she said.

That was Sunday.

By Monday morning, Sloane was back, tapping her Cartier watch like it was a detonator. She moved through Morgan's kitchen like she paid the damn mortgage.

"You've got a Senate hearing in forty-eight hours and you're still in compression socks?"

Morgan didn't bother looking up from her laptop.

"I'm reviewing flight path anomalies."

"No, babe. You're spiraling in a spreadsheet. Cute hobby. But today, we're doing optics."

She tossed a legal pad onto the table like it was evidence in court.

"Committee chair's ex–Air Force. Hates mess. Hates emotion. You'll sit there like the Penn-trained tactical nuke you are and bore them into respect. You flinch, you joke, you cry—they win. Wear something that says: yes, I survived corporate assassination attempts and still moisturize."

Morgan snapped the laptop shut with surgical finality, spine straightening like a verdict.

"Did you come here to coach me or dress me?"

Sloane grinned—unbothered, dangerous.

"Why not both?"

They walked into the closet.

"My god, woman," Sloane said, flipping through rows of power suits arranged by mood, "this is a Bergdorf Goodman wet dream."

She held up heels that could kill a man without leaving

a trace and enough structured blazers to run a D.C. brunch circuit. Twice.

Vee, still in her coveralls, leaned against the doorway holding out two iced coffees like a peace treaty.

"You've been living the braless good life. That ends today."

Morgan raised an eyebrow.

"Is this my makeover montage? *Clueless*-style? Who's Cher?"

"Me, obviously," Sloane said.

"Please. You're more like the woman Cher would leave Josh for," Vee said, eyes flicking over her.

Sloane didn't flinch. Just smirked.

"What was that?"

"Nothing," Vee said, setting the coffees down with a thud.

"Morgan needs to look hot for C-SPAN."

Sloane pulled a navy suit from the rack like she was unsheathing a blade.

"This says, 'I read your whole case file and didn't blink.'"

Vee lifted a silk cream blouse like a mic drop.

"And this says, 'Interrupt me and die.'"

Morgan rolled her eyes but stepped into the center of the room like a good soldier.

"You're both insufferable."

"You're welcome," they said in perfect, smug harmony.

They dressed her like she was going to war—because she was.

Hair slicked back in a lethal knot. Makeup matte, sharp, and merciless. The navy suit tailored for bloodsport. No jewelry except a thin gold chain that had belonged to her father—a tether to the man who taught her to love planes and fight fair.

Vee adjusted the collar, caught her eye in the mirror.

"You look like you run the country."

Morgan smirked, all cool fire.

"Maybe I should."

Sloane crossed her arms.

"Let's get through Wednesday. Then we can stage the coup."

48

The congressional hearing room smelled like wood polish, stale coffee, and the ghosts of unchallenged power. Oak-paneled walls rose like a cathedral around them, carved with the arrogance of centuries. The overhead lights were too bright, that sterile LED sharpness that turned skin waxy and every wrinkle into a map of compromise. But the old brass sconces along the walls still hummed with heat, and they gave off that scent—like warm metal and antique dust—that reminded Kieran of church pews and forgotten attics.

It was freezing in the room, the kind of artificial chill designed to keep people sharp or uncomfortable, depending on how much you belonged there.

The floor creaked as men in tailored suits shuffled into their designated spots, laughing like they were still at Yale, clutching their notes and their egos. Somewhere behind him, a staffer chuckled at a joke about "the TikTok plane." Someone smelled expensive. Bleu de Chanel, maybe. Another reeked of Old Spice and entitlement.

Kieran sat still. Back straight, jaw tight, hands on his

thighs. His union pin caught the light. His dress uniform was pressed so clean you could've performed surgery on it.

But inside, he was unraveling. Slow and silent and terrible.

Chuck sat stiffly beside him, suit jacket straining at the shoulders, tie askew like he'd lost the will to fix it somewhere between security and the waiting room.

Behind them, a line of pilots filled the pew-like benches, dress uniforms sharp, union pins glinting like silent warnings. Their presence wasn't loud. It didn't need to be. It was solidarity made flesh.

Kieran didn't dare turn to look at them—not yet. If he did, he might lose whatever fragile composure he still had.

He had blown it. The one moment Morgan needed him to show up with clarity, he choked. His silence had cut deeper than any words could've, and now—now she had to clean it up. Alone. On the record.

And then she walked in. Like storm clouds parting. Like thunder in heels.

Morgan Delgado entered the room as if it belonged to her. And maybe it did. Sloane flanked her left, all legs and legal firepower. Vee on her right, in a navy International Brotherhood of Aircraft Technicians bomber jacket faded from use, Local 313 patch on the sleeve, zipped halfway like a warning; her stare said she'd rewired a plane and would gladly do the same to a senator.

Morgan's presence sucked all the air out of the room. The lights caught the sheen of her tailored navy pantsuit, the gleam of a subtle gold chain over her collarbone that Kieran swore hadn't been there before.

He didn't blink when Morgan took her seat at the witness table. He couldn't. There was something about the way she moved now—like she'd gone from woman to weapon in the span of twenty feet.

Her face was unreadable, but her eyes—those eyes were full of fire on a low simmer.

He watched her swallow once, slow and tight, like the pressure had settled just behind her throat. She reached for the glass of water on the table—not shaking, not hurried. A single sip. Enough to cut through the recycled air. Her fingers stayed wrapped around the glass like she was holding something back.

A breath. A scream. The whole truth.

Sloane sat beside her, cool and elegant in that terrifying way lawyers can be when they know they're the smartest person in the room. Their shoulders touched once, barely, and that was all it took. A glance. A nod.

They weren't whispering. They didn't need to.

Morgan didn't need armor. She was the goddamn shield.

And across from her? A dais full of men pretending not to be afraid.

The Kentucky congressman leaned in, microphone close, fake sincerity dripping from his voice like molasses.

"Ms. Delgado, would you care to explain how your department—on your watch—failed to flag a string of mechanical reports that eventually led to the grounding of sixteen Meridian 7X aircraft? Seems like someone fell asleep at the switch."

His tone was mild, but his words were loaded. Dog whistles wrapped in protocol.

Your department. On *your* watch.

What he meant was *you. A woman. Not white. Alone now.*

Kieran clenched his jaw. His boot tapped once under the bench. Chuck noticed, but didn't say anything.

Morgan lifted her chin. Just a fraction. Then she leaned

forward into the mic with the kind of stillness that made people instinctively shut the hell up.

"I'd be happy to," she said.

Her voice didn't waver. It didn't rise, didn't perform. It landed. Clear. Precise. A Chicago drawl wrapped in razor wire.

"What this committee is referring to—those unflagged reports—were, in fact, compiled. They were submitted. They were escalated internally and archived under a restricted operations code used specifically by the executive safety board of Heritage Airlines, which, I will remind you, has yet to appear before this chamber today."

Silence.

She shifted her gaze across the row of congressmen, slow and pointed. Kieran had seen that look once before—during the reroute crisis in the command center and Morgan rebuilt the system like she was doing origami under a countdown clock.

"The issue here," she continued, "is not a lapse in procedure. It is a lapse in accountability at the highest levels. This isn't a case of missed memos. It's a case of buried documentation. And I was pushed out of my role shortly after I escalated those concerns to the board."

Someone coughed. Another checked their watch.

The Kentucky guy tried again.

"Well now, Ms. Delgado, surely you're not suggesting Heritage Airlines engaged in—what—intentional cover-up? Isn't it more likely this was a bureaucratic tangle?"

"No," she said.

Just that. *No.*

The room stilled.

She glanced back at Sloane, who gave her the barest nod.

Kieran watched her chest rise and fall—steady, not shaken. Her mouth twitched at the corner. Not a smile. Something harder. Resigned. Like she'd already fought the real war behind closed doors, and now this public flogging was just the encore.

She was answering to men who didn't care about safety. They didn't want truth. They wanted soundbites and villain edits. They wanted to be seen grilling her on cable news so their donors could sip whiskey and grunt about how corporate America was under siege by "diversity hires."

Morgan was just a more palatable sacrifice than the CEO.

And the worst part? She knew it.

You could see it in the way she held herself—like a statue that had decided to outlast the storm.

"My department," she said slowly, "did not fail. The system was designed to make it look like we did. So you could ask the wrong questions in this hearing. So you could sit up here and stage a morality play without ever subpoenaing the real architects of this failure."

Another congressman—a younger one, eager to make a name for himself—started to interrupt.

Morgan didn't look at him. She looked at Kieran.

A single glance. One second, maybe less.

But it hit him like a freight train going off-schedule and straight through his ribcage.

The rest of the chamber dissolved. Cameras, lights, talking points—all of it dropped away like static cutting out mid-sentence.

Her eyes didn't plead. They demanded.

I know you see me. I need you to see all of it.

He didn't move. Didn't nod. Just met her gaze with the

quiet desperation of a man who'd seen God, fumbled the prayer, and was still trying to remember the words.

He wanted to cross the room. Wanted to throw himself between her and the blast radius. But he couldn't. Not yet.

This was her fire to walk through.

One of the older congressmen leaned back with a theatrical sigh, as if Morgan had personally inconvenienced his legacy.

"Thank you, Ms. Delgado," he said, voice oily. "You're dismissed."

The word hung in the air like a slap. *Dismissed.*

Morgan didn't flinch. She gathered her notes with the kind of grace that made you realize how much was actually holding her together.

As she stood, Sloane was already by her side, eyes locked on the committee with all the warmth of an open flame. Vee rose too, arms crossed, chin high, her union jacket like a dare. Together they walked out—not hurried, not bowed. Just done giving oxygen to the performance.

Kieran watched them go. Watched her go.

Then came the Heritage lawyer. Smug. Measured. Clean-shaven like that made him innocent. He talked in tight, practiced loops about "procedural gray zones," "data irregularities," and "evolving safety frameworks."

Kieran didn't hear a word of it. Just noted what wasn't said.

Not once did the man say "pilot." Not once did he say "passenger." Not once did he say "dead."

He wasn't testifying. He was laundering liability.

The CEO, of course, had somehow slipped the subpoena entirely—something about international travel, or a health complication, or maybe just the magic of being a multimillionaire with the right friends in the right subcommittees.

But David Enright had shown up. Two seats behind the general counsel, just far enough to avoid questions and just close enough to be seen. He wore a pleasant, PR-friendly smile—the kind that looked good in photos and meant absolutely nothing.

Chuck leaned over.

"You're up," he said, quiet.

There was a ripple of movement as Kieran stood—subtle, but unmistakable.

Heads turned.

The rhythm of the room shifted.

A good-looking white guy in uniform had approached the dais, and suddenly, everyone remembered how to pay attention.

More camera flashes. Warmer smiles.

Kieran O'Hara cleaned up well, and the photographers knew it.

He sat at the long table in front of the congressional subcommittee in his crisp navy suit and union pin, the kind that looked boring until the light hit it right and the lapels did something a little lethal.

His tie was modest.

The room had gotten warmer, noticeably so.

The chill that had followed Morgan Delgado into these hearings—the polite skepticism, the over-articulated professionalism, the questions loaded with accusation—seemed to have evaporated.

The old men on the committee were all smiling now, all "we appreciate you being here, Captain O'Hara."

One even reached across the table to shake his hand.

A few looked like they were seeing an old war buddy or their better-looking son-in-law.

The projection was thick enough to cut with a butterknife.

He thanked them, of course. Because that's what you do.

He gave his name, his role with the pilots' union, confirmed that he'd logged nearly three decades in commercial aviation, and he launched into what was supposed to be a short, neutral statement.

He spoke plainly, as he always did, about safety. About how he and the other signatories on his letter represented hundreds of pilots, and how they all had the same concern: the Meridian 7X aircraft wasn't right. Not technically unsafe, maybe. But not safe, either. Not by any standard a pilot could live with. And he should have stopped there. That was the plan. But something in his gut turned.

Maybe it was the cameras clicking too often. Maybe it was the way they leaned in when he talked, the indulgent attention they never gave Morgan. Maybe it was the fact that Morgan, who had given more to Heritage than anyone in that room ever would, had been hung out to dry while these men tripped over themselves to kiss his ass.

He thought of the way she looked at him—in that room, under those lights, right before they dismissed her like she was debris instead of a damn commander. And that was it.

He set his notes down and looked at the committee.

"With all due respect, gentlemen," he said, voice low and steady, "you already have the power to ground these planes. You don't need another study. You don't need another internal memo. You just need to act."

The room shifted. Chuck coughed and shifted in his seat. A few members blinked, the ones who didn't expect the pilot in the nice suit to speak without asking permission.

"Workers across Heritage—mechanics, operations staff, pilots—have been raising the alarm for months. And the response has been silence. Or worse—retaliation. We've been treated like we're making noise for the sake of it. We're not. We're saying: this is urgent."

He paused. Let it settle.

"And I know I don't have as much to lose by saying this as some of my colleagues do. Maybe it's the graying hair. Maybe it's the accent you all find comforting. Or maybe it's just that I'm not the woman who ran a command center like a goddamn symphony and still got left to take the fall.

Either way, the message has been the same. If something goes wrong—it's on you. You can't say you weren't warned."

That's when the gavel came down. Hard.

"Captain O'Hara—"

But he didn't flinch. Just nodded—like a man closing a sermon for a congregation that knew the crops were dying and still refused to pray for rain.

"Also I do find it curious," he added, voice calm, gesturing to the general direction of Heritage execs behind him, "that the man who ran interference on our safety warnings—David Enright—isn't the one sitting at this table.

But I suppose that's how cowards delegate."

"Captain O'Hara," one of the congressmen snapped, tone sharp with embarrassment, "we need to move on. Please conclude your remarks."

Another cleared his throat, trying to reset the room.

Kieran looked into the lens of the camera across the room. His voice softened just enough to cut deeper, the steel still underneath.

"Just one more thing: we owe it to the people who keep the airline running. Folks who show up every day, even when the people in charge don't have their backs. We owe them clarity. We owe them honesty.

And we owe the ones who spoke up something more than just silence."

That last sentence wasn't for the committee. That was for her. And he hoped she'd hear it.

He didn't say her name. Didn't have to.

But somewhere in the building, he hoped she knew: he saw her. He believed her.

And if given the chance, he wasn't going to disappear on her again. Not when it mattered.

Not ever.

49

M organ didn't remember the moment it was officially over. There was no single headline. No champagne pop. No cathartic montage where the villains got what they deserved and the survivors walked into the sunset.

Just emails. Statements. Headlines that felt both too loud and not loud enough. Her name trending beside words like "whistleblower" and "hero" and "diversity hire" depending on the source.

The FAA opened their investigation first—dry, exacting, merciless. The NTSB followed. They pulled black boxes, subpoenaed maintenance logs, and dragged Heritage's executive safety board into the light like corpses from a lake.

Within weeks, the dominos fell. The CEO cited "unexpected health concerns" and quietly disappeared to a country without extradition treaties. Enright tried to smile his way through it, and still ended up escorted out of a back door without his tie.

Heritage stock nosedived. The board resigned. Some voluntarily. Some in disgrace.

And on social media? Feral chaos.

"Y'all. #RegionalPilotDaddy stood up for his boss and union brothers, we're not okay."

Morgan saw the clip once—Kieran at the hearing, jaw tight, voice even, eyes hard—and immediately closed the app. She wasn't ready to feel what that stirred up. Not yet.

And then came the thank-yous. From pilots. From ops folks. From a group of mechanics in Vee's shop who started calling her "Command Mom." Flowers showed up on her doorstep with no card.

Still, she couldn't sleep through the night. Her jaw ached from clenching. Some mornings, she woke up already crying and didn't know why.

Her therapist's number was still saved under Dr. S. in her phone. She'd stopped going three years ago. Said she was "fine" and "too busy" and "healed enough." But after the hearings, she booked an appointment without hesitation. No ceremony. Just picked a Wednesday, 9 a.m., and walked back into that office like someone re-entering orbit.

Morgan told her everything. Slowly. Haltingly.

She didn't cry until the second session, when she tried to explain the silence—the one that happened after she won. The part where everyone kept saying you must be so proud and she kept nodding like that was the truth.

Ava and Elena published a follow-up exposé a week later. The receipts were brutal. The timeline, airtight.

Sloane was already orchestrating two class-action lawsuits and hinting at more. Heritage didn't just bleed—it hemorrhaged. Shareholders scrambled. PR firms spun.

And Morgan? She sat on her couch, wrapped in a blanket, watching the scroll of breaking news until her eyes blurred.

There was a profile in *The New Yorker*. Elegant. Sharp. Carefully sanitized. She hated it.

It described her as "steely" and "composed" and "a rare mind under pressure." It didn't mention how often she threw up during the investigation. Or that she couldn't listen to the sound of jet engines anymore without her heart slamming against her ribs.

People told her she was brave. That she was a role model. That she'd changed aviation. She just felt tired.

There were still days she didn't pick up the phone. Messages from Sloane, from Vee, from her mom and her brother and her cousins. Not because she didn't care. Because she didn't have the words. Because being strong for this long meant she had to break somewhere private.

And Kieran—

Well. They hadn't spoken since the hearing. Not directly. Not really.

She missed him like a pulled muscle—tight, tender, impossible to ignore when she tried to move forward.

Her therapist asked if she planned on calling him. She said no. Said it like a reflex. Like touching a hot stove. The truth was, she didn't know how to talk to someone who had hesitated at the edge of a cliff while she freefell.

Still, after the appointment, she scrolled to his name once—thumb hovering over "unblock" like it was a tripwire.

And then, just as quietly, she did it. No text. No call. Just opened the door.

If he wanted to show up, he could figure out how.

Then came the news: Drew had taken a fall. Three stories down. Onto a tarmac. No jet bridge. No working cameras. No witnesses. Too clean to be chance. The kind of aftermath that closed its own file.

Something cracked open. And beneath it, something

darker bloomed. Rage. Relief. That old fear crawling up her spine and finding nothing left to cling to.

She didn't know if she wanted to cry, or scream, or fuck. But she knew exactly who she wanted.

And she couldn't tell if that made her a monster. Or just finally safe.

50

4 months later

Before flying to D.C., Kieran made sure the dog sitter had keys, that Ren's fridge was stocked, and that the sidewalk salt was still in the garage where it belonged. Small things. Real things. The kind you hold onto when everything else feels untethered.

He hadn't slept well. He never did before these things. Not because of nerves—he didn't have those anymore—but because he'd learned that bureaucratic grief didn't come with adrenaline.

He was flying again—different airline, different routes. The work felt cleaner. Less compromised.

A month back, his local voted him into the safety committee. He hadn't run for it. Just kept showing up. Told the truth when it mattered. Apparently, that was enough. It came with exhaustion. Paperwork. Dry rooms and dry eyes.

And men like Jim Callahan, his father's perpetual golf buddy, and Associate Administrator for Aviation Safety at the FAA.

The bastard was already there when Kieran arrived. Tan. Smiling. A golf tan in January—that's how you knew he was up to no good.

Callahan clapped him on the shoulder like they were frat brothers or teammates, not two men who saw the industry from opposite ends of the moral spectrum.

"Heard you made a splash last time, O'Hara. Network can't stop running the clip. You really went all in, huh?"

Kieran gave him a nod. Tight-lipped. Didn't trust himself to speak yet.

Callahan didn't need encouragement. "Did you hear? The Aviation Advisory Standards Council is looking at Enright for a consultant role. Supposedly to advise on operational risk and crisis response."

Kieran blinked. "That a joke?"

"Nah," Callahan said, real easy. "That's how the game works. Getting dragged by Congress makes you qualified to advise on avoiding it next time."

That was the thing about Callahan. He wasn't even trying to be cruel. He just thought this was the weather.

"You had it good, O'Hara," he went on, voice low like he was sharing a fond memory instead of an indictment. "That blonde girl from Grosse Pointe in college? Sweet. Normal. White-picket-fence type. Then Naomi—well, she acted like she was too good for you, and you let her. Your dad always said you'd spiral once she left. He wasn't wrong."

He gave a humorless little laugh. "And now this Delgado thing? Jesus. You looked like a lovesick puppy on national television."

Kieran smiled. Slow. Feral.

"Naomi *was* too good for me," he said. "We're friends now. Took me years to earn that. And I was lucky she gave me the time to try."

Callahan scoffed. "So this new one's got you all bent outta shape?"

"That new one," Kieran said, stepping just slightly into Callahan's space, "saved lives. And I still love her, yeah. You got something to say about that, Jim?"

Callahan hesitated. Just for a second.

Kieran didn't blink. "Keep the names of the women I care about out of your fucking mouth. I see you. I see all of you. You're not going anywhere—and neither are we. That's how the game works, right?"

And then he turned, because there it was—her.

A. Morgan Delgado.

Tailored. Still. Entirely too composed. Watching. Then came the sound of her heels, echoing after the silence like a dare.

She didn't say anything. Didn't need to.

And Kieran—something low in him went hot and tense all at once. She looked incredible. Not just sharp—alive. There was color in her face again. Her posture wasn't survival anymore—it was power. Like she'd finally stepped out of something that had been crushing her for years.

It hit him harder than he expected.

He'd missed her. Missed the way she moved, the weight of her silence, the way a room bent around her like it knew. And now she was here.

And he couldn't do a damn thing but stand there, hands at his sides, and take it.

They filed into the FAA meeting room like it was church. Grim. The kind of gathering where everything mattered, but nothing felt urgent. Review this. Note that. Revisit protocols that wouldn't save anyone until five more boards and one more crash signed off on them.

Kieran spoke once. Morgan spoke twice. Their voices steady. Their eye contact unwavering.

By the time it ended, his eyes had glazed over. He wasn't sure why he'd volunteered to rep the union—just felt like a waste of a layover now.

People trickled out. Callahan was already nodding along to some Delta rep's pitch for steak and top-shelf scotch.

Soon, Kieran was the last one in the room. Or so he thought.

"Captain O'Hara," she said—cool, crisp, no trace of hesitation. "You dropped this."

She handed him a manila folder. Plain. Standard-issue. Bureaucracy in paper form. Inside? A room key.

No note. No flourish. Just precision. And the faintest curve of her mouth as she walked away.

51

Kieran showed up after dark. He hadn't been sure when to go. The card hadn't said. Just a room number, the name of the hotel, and nothing else.

Very Morgan. Specific in her omissions. Sharp in her silences.

He'd spiraled for a bit—paced, re-showered, typed out a check-in to Ren he didn't send—before finally pulling on his jacket and stepping out into the D.C. night.

The hotel was called The Vestry. The name matched the clean lettering on the brass plaque out front, tucked discreetly into the stone of what had clearly once been a church. Gothic arches. Stained glass windows darkened to jewel tones. The kind of building that didn't just ask for reverence—it demanded it. It was expensive. Seductive. Absolutely her.

Everyone who worked there looked like they'd stepped off a runway in Paris or out of an underground speakeasy in Berlin. The whole place smelled like bergamot and candle wax.

Dark walls. Gold accents. People in tailored black whispering about reservations.

It was...not subtle. It was the kind of hotel where everything was too dark, too quiet, and too expensive to be innocent.

He found the elevator. Rode it in silence.

Room 506.

He stood outside the door for a full thirty seconds before knocking. Because he was polite. Because he didn't want to assume. No answer. He slid the keycard in.

The room looked like it used to host liturgies. Not literally—but the layout had that kind of gravity.

The bed was the centerpiece, raised slightly like an altar, framed by black velvet curtains that pooled on the floor. Four tall posts stood at each corner, dark wood polished to a sinful shine. The walls were a soft, matte charcoal, broken up by gold sconces and shadow. There was no art. Just the bones of the space. Arched doorways. Crown molding like filigree. A high ceiling that caught the light and held it.

The lighting was low—warm, indirect, intentional. The kind that made everything feel like dusk, no matter the time of day.

He crossed the room and drew back the curtain to reveal a private balcony. It was unseasonably warm—low fifties, maybe. Strange for January in D.C.

Morgan was out there, still in the suit she'd worn to the meeting. Silhouetted by city lights. One leg crossed over the other. Hair pinned up. That curve of her neck visible even in shadow—sharp, familiar, lethal.

She was on FaceTime.

"—I don't know, okay?" Vee was saying. "She looked at me like she wanted to kill me or kiss me and honestly? I'd take either. It's Sloane, Morgan."

Then Vee saw him over Morgan's shoulder. Her face twisted immediately.

"Oh my god. Ew. No. Morgan, hang up. Hang. Up. I do not want to witness this."

Morgan muttered, "You're so dramatic," and ended the call.

She didn't say hello. She didn't stand. Just looked over her shoulder toward him, slow and deliberate, and said, "You came."

He could barely breathe. "Course I did."

She looked back into the city lights and waited.

Like this wasn't a seduction. Like it was a ceremony.

He dropped his bag and jacket on the table and walked towards her.

She sat in a narrow patio chair on the balcony, hands folded in her lap, her phone face-down beneath one palm.

He came up behind her, slow and silent. Standing over her, he bent low—hands gripping the armrests on either side, caging her in place. It earned a hitched breath.

He leaned in, face hovering just above the soft curve of her neck. The scent of her made his breath catch—and other parts of him react instantly. His lips stopped just shy of her skin. The heat between them tightened her grip and made her shift in her seat.

"I've missed you," he said. "I still want you. But I'm not moving until you tell me to."

Morgan looked at him. Really looked at him. Like she was checking if this version of him was made of more than just guilt and apologies.

Then—

She reached up. Undid the clasp at her throat.

Her voice was quiet. Steady.

"Then move."

And he did. Slowly.

He lowered his mouth to the spot he'd been hovering over, slow and certain. And when his lips finally met her skin, he damn near forgot how to breathe.

He didn't rush. He didn't need to. Just his mouth working its way along her neck—first one side, then the other—soft kisses like he was making up for lost time.

She started to lean back, legs open, still dressed sharp in that suit, and dragging those manicured nails through his hair like she was trying to guide him closer, deeper, like that would satisfy the ache.

She squirmed. She was still in the chair, and he was still standing behind it. He hadn't even moved his hands. Just his mouth—his mouth was doing all the work, undoing her piece by piece.

He kissed behind her ears, then lower, below her collarbone, now bare from the way she shifted to give him more.

She got greedy.

That's when he moved—just one hand, resting it high on her chest, right above her collarbone. Simple. Steady. Like he belonged there, like she'd been waiting for him without even knowing it.

It wasn't the size of his hand that wrecked her—it was the weight. The quiet possession of it. The way it sank into her, just enough to pull a gasp from her lips, quick and helpless.

He smiled against her skin, then leaned in and kissed her, full and unhurried.

It wasn't gentle. It wasn't sweet. It was long and consuming and bruising, the kind of kiss that stripped you bare from the inside out.

Her tongue curled against his, and just when she tried to

turn and face him—like she wanted to shift the dynamic—
he stopped her.

He took both of her wrists in his free hand, pressed them
firm against her chest, and kept her there. Kept her
grounded with the other hand at the base of her neck,
holding her exactly where he wanted her—right there,
undone, tasting like everything he'd ever missed.

She let out a low sound—half frustration, half surrender
—that unfurled into a sigh.

It wasn't tender. It wasn't patient. It was months of
hunger poured into one moment, reckless and unrelenting.

Somewhere in the middle of it, he lost track of himself—
might've even blacked out, because when he came back to
his senses, she was already undone in his arms.

Her breath was ragged, lips swollen and shining at the
corners, her eyes half-closed like she wasn't quite sure
where she was anymore.

He moved around her slow, steady, like a man stalking
something sacred, never letting his eyes leave hers.

When he dropped to his knees, it wasn't some kind of
theater.

It was instinct.

She sat in that chair like she'd been born to rule, and he
didn't mind one bit.

"Hold the armrests," he said, voice low.

She obeyed without hesitation, the corners of her mouth
twitching with mischief, even though her pupils were blown
wide like the night sky had just cracked open behind her
eyes.

He worked the buttons of her blouse one by one, slow,
pressing a kiss to each patch of skin.

She started to slip her arms free, but he caught her wrist

and pressed it down to the patio chair's armrest, a quiet smile tugging at the corner of his mouth.

She glared at him, sharp and scorching, but didn't move again—just kept her hands where he'd put them.

He nearly lost it, holding back a laugh that threatened to crack the mood wide open.

He finished with the last button, and there she was— blouse hanging open, chest bare but for the moss green lace he eased down with both care and intention.

It was the kind of bra that looked like it cost too much and was made to be ruined.

A cool breeze off the rooftop curled in around them, catching at the delicate fabric and forming goosebumps on her skin.

She sat back in the chair, a vision that'd burn itself into him: hands clamped around the cold metal arms, blazer hanging open like a curtain drawn for the main act, the fabric parting to show the most perfect round tits that made him feel every bit of want he'd ever known.

He kissed her down the center of her stomach, steady and deliberate, until he got to the slacks.

He undid the button and slid them down along with her underwear, baring her to him completely.

"Kieran," she gasped, looking down at him like she might unravel.

"Stay still," he said, voice low and full of heat.

Not a request. A promise.

He drew in a deep breath, pulling her scent into his lungs like he needed it to live. There was something wild and clean and purely her in it—like sun-warmed sheets— but tangled up with something headier, sweeter.

It hit him low and hard, a quiet kind of intoxication.

He was suddenly convinced he would have never started drinking if he knew this was what it meant to be drunk.

He leaned in, slow and certain, and laid one long, deliberate lick with the flat of his tongue. She jolted like she'd touched a live wire, hips rocking back and a sound tearing out of her that had no business being that filthy.

The rooftop patio might've had high walls and a proper railing, but it wasn't soundproof. Not even close.

He didn't tease. Not tonight. Not with the way she was already trembling under his hands. He went after it with purpose, tongue circling her with that same calm determination—the kind of steady rhythm that made you believe in things. He moved slow, sure, and when she broke apart, shaking and gasping against his mouth, he held her there, let her ride it out.

Her whimpers came soft, tight in her throat, like she was trying to bite them down out of politeness, out of respect for the discreet air of this place.

But there was no hiding it—not really. Not when she was already spilling over, all salt and sweetness and every soft part of her given over to him completely.

When he finally came up for air, the taste of her still lingering on his tongue, he found her trembling—chest rising in shallow gasps, one hand clenched hard around the armrest like it was the only thing keeping her tethered to the Earth.

Her knuckles blanched, jaw slack, and still—she hadn't moved. Not an inch. Obedient to the last word he'd spoken. It knocked the wind out of him, the way she gave in and held back all at once.

He leaned in, caught one perfect nipple in his mouth, and suckled slow.

She threw her head back with a sound that curled through him like smoke.

"Oh—God," she gasped. "I need you. Right now. All of you."

He didn't say a word.

Just smiled against her skin, warm and pleased, then shifted to her other nipple, dragging his teeth just enough to make her writhe.

"But you're doing so damn well," he murmured, voice low, steady.

Praise, pure and plainspoken.

He looked up. And God, she was a sight—eyes glassy, lips parted, trying to hold herself still, glowing with need and pride like the brilliant overachiever she was. A woman who knew how to run a whole damn fleet but right now was unraveling just for him.

He didn't rush. Kept his mouth on her, kept coaxing every reaction like he was learning her by heart.

One hand slipped down between her thighs, and when he eased a finger inside, she was already so ready for him she took him in with no resistance—like her body had been waiting, calling him home. He stroked slow and deep, then added a second finger, curling just right until she gasped and arched off the seat. Her whole body tightened around his touch, those beautiful walls fluttering as she clenched down, chasing whatever edge he was holding just out of reach.

"Jesus, Morgan," he muttered, voice thick. "Look at you taking me so well."

He glanced down where his fingers worked inside her, his thumb idly circling.

She was flushed all over, beautiful in that raw, aching way that made his chest tight.

He tugged her nipple from his mouth, watching her shiver.

And still, his fingers moved—deep, slow, curling like he was coaxing secrets from inside her. Like he could shape her body into saying things she didn't dare speak aloud.

He stayed there, relentless and sure, until he felt her hips start to stutter, start to shake.

Then he shifted, dragged his mouth back down between her thighs, and gave her one long, anchoring lick over her swollen bud—measured, sure, meant.

That's when she messed up.

Or maybe she didn't.

She reached for her own breast, fingertips teasing the peaked flesh, playing with herself like she didn't already have all of him on her.

He caught it the moment he came up for air.

Brushed her hand away, not rough, but firm.

"You don't know when to stop, do you, Morgan?" he asked low, voice coiled with heat. "No sense of when to just be still."

"And you're always...fucking with me," she whispered, her voice catching like a match being struck.

Her eyes locked on his, wild and full of defiance.

He tilted his head, half amusement, half promise.

"Oh. You think this is me fucking with you?"

He stood.

Stepped into her space with the kind of calm that made the air go heavy.

His fingers found the back of her head, tangled in her hair, and pulled—not cruel, but unyielding.

Her chin tipped up, neck arched like a bow pulled tight, eyes blown wide and glassy.

She was still sitting.

The look in her eyes was almost unearthly.

Like she was floating inches above her own body, drunk on him, on this.

Her pupils wide as night, swallowing all the light, face slack with pleasure and something that looked like surrender.

She reached for him like it was a decision she'd been turning over for days, and when her fingers undid the button of his jeans, it wasn't rebellion—it was certainty.

She tugged them down, boxers too, until he stood bare before her, thick and ready.

She didn't hesitate.

Her hand wrapped around him, slick with the wetness beading at the tip, and she stroked him slow, sure, like she meant to memorize every inch.

He clenched his jaw, fighting for composure, as she leaned in and took him into her mouth.

He was still gripping her hair, knuckles white, but she moved how she pleased—hungry, taking him deeper with each pass of her lips.

Her tongue worked deliberate, teasing, and when he hit the back of her throat, she didn't stop.

She pushed forward, let herself choke on him, tears slipping down her cheeks, painting black trails through her mascara.

He let her have that moment—let her own it—before he tightened his grip and pulled her off.

Her mouth left him with a wet pop, and she looked up at him, eyes shining, wrecked and ruined under the night sky.

"You do what you want, huh?" he said, breath sharp. "You don't ask. You just take."

Something burned behind her gaze.

A challenge.

A promise.

She licked her lips, slow and deliberate, and they caught the bedroom light like glossed honey.

He cursed low under his breath—more gravel than voice—and hauled her off the chair without ceremony.

In a few long strides, he dragged her to the bed and tossed her across it like she weighed nothing at all.

She barely had time to catch her breath before he was on her—knee swinging over her hip, body pinning hers down.

He caught both her wrists in one hand and slammed them above her head, holding her there.

But she wasn't built for surrender.

Her hips came up, grinding against the line of him with a purpose that made his jaw clench.

He didn't stop her—hell no—but his free hand came down, the edge of his palm pressing firm into the hollow at her collarbone.

She gasped, back arching just so, and that sound—sharp, involuntary—traveled straight through his cock.

Then he saw it.

The bed—four-poster, old wood, heavy—was dressed up with curtain ropes.

Thick, twisted, and soft to the touch.

Beautiful and intentional.

They weren't just there for show.

Whoever designed this room wanted it to look tasteful while doubling as something else entirely.

It hit him then.

She picked this room.

This bed.

Even her planning was seduction—sharp, clean, and two steps ahead of him.

She didn't just think about the moment.

She carved it, set the scene, baited the hook.

And damn if he didn't fall for it, again and again.

She was perfect.

Strategic in a way that could scare a man—if he didn't already want her to ruin him.

He looked down at her, breath tight in his chest.

She was all flushed skin and fire.

He took one of the ropes and dragged it gently over the soft skin of her forearm.

"Morgan," he asked, voice low, rasp dragging at the edges, "Is this what you want? Want to be tied up like this for me?"

She closed her eyes for a moment, a soft moan coming out of her.

"Yes."

His hand traced down her thigh.

"Want to be used like this?"

Her answer came without hesitation, heat curled around every syllable: "Fuck yes."

He smiled—slow and wolfish—and stripped her bare the rest of the way out of her top and that damn bra that looked like concept art.

Then, methodically, he tied her down.

One rope per limb, each knot practiced and sure, until she was laid out like an offering, every inch of her his to touch, to taste, to claim.

And he did.

He knelt between her thighs and worshipped—mouth, tongue, hands—until she came again, writhing against the ropes, cursing him like a woman unmade.

"Please, just fuck me already," she gasped, voice wrecked and glorious.

He moved up, kissed her hard, letting her taste herself.

She bit his lip, playful but pointed.

His fingers tangled in her hair, yanked just enough to remind her who she'd given herself to.

"Oh, you know better than that," he growled—low, amused, possessive.

He'd meant to tease her longer. He wanted to.

But restraint broke under the weight of her.

He entered her in one relentless thrust, buried deep, driven by need that had nowhere left to go but into her.

He didn't stop—couldn't—even with her knees pressed against his shoulders, every inch of her open, taken.

Each stroke purposeful, brutal, the thick head of him dragging right over that spot that made her sob his name.

She struggled against the restraints with a kind of desperation, her body trembling in ripples beneath his, the tears streaming unchecked down her cheeks as the silk bit gently into her skin.

And he—God, he came so hard it knocked the lights out behind his eyes, the world slipping into black around the edges.

When he came back to himself, he found her beneath him, slack and glowing, drifting like tidewater over the mattress, her breath ragged, her eyes half-lidded with a kind of stunned grace.

The sharp, calculating gleam she always carried in her gaze—gone.

For once, her mind was still.

He pressed his face into her sweat-damp hair, drawing breath into his lungs, skin slick and warm beneath his palms.

He kissed her then—her cheeks, her jaw, her lips, her

eyelids—the way a man might kiss the ground after walking through fire.

"You did so good, Morgan," he murmured, words tumbling against her mouth, her nose, the smooth curve of her forehead.

He tasted the salt of her tears at the corners of her eyes, wiped them away with his tongue, gentle as rain.

Then, with the same care he used to tie her up he began to loosen the knots.

One by one.

Slowly.

Intentionally.

His thumbs rubbed circles over the marks left behind, callused hands tender against her wrists.

"You okay?" he asked, low and sure.

She nodded.

"Right wrist is fine," she said.

And he'd done it right—just snug enough. There'd be bruises. But he saw the way her eyes seemed to light up at the thought. Muttered something about wearing long sleeves. Good thing it was full on winter back home.

After that, they didn't speak right away.

Kieran moved first. Quietly. Deliberately.

He found a hand towel in the bathroom, soaked it in warm water, and came back to her.

Morgan was curled up at the edge of the bed, knees drawn slightly inward, hair tousled, mouth still parted like she was catching her breath.

He knelt in front of her and wiped her down with slow strokes. Then he cleaned himself off. Tossed the towel aside.

No dramatics. No assumptions.

The patio door was still open, letting in the cool night air. It slipped across their skin like a benediction.

They collapsed into the bed, not with urgency this time, but with gravity. With choice.

They lay on their sides, facing each other.

She curled into him, tucked her face against his chest, arms wrapped around his neck like she was anchoring both of them. They could feel each other's heartbeat.

"Morgan," he said, and the voice was different now. Not the low command of earlier. This one was quieter. Unsure. Careful.

"I'm sorry. I fucked up. I disappeared when you needed me. I thought I was protecting you by staying out of the way —trying to handle things on my own. But that wasn't strength. That was disrespectful."

She nodded once, against his skin.

"It was."

He exhaled through his nose, forehead pressed to hers now.

"You deserve better than that," he said. "Someone who shows up at the right time. Every time."

"I do."

There was a pause. A long one. The kind that stretched between what he meant and what he feared.

"I wouldn't blame you," he said, voice low, "if you decided I wasn't worth trying again. I've still got a lot to unlearn."

She pulled back just enough to look at him.

"I don't do projects," she said.

His shoulders fell. Just slightly.

The light dimmed behind his eyes.

But she didn't stop.

"And I don't think you are one."

His eyes flicked to hers.

"You're allowed to fuck up. I just—I don't want to live

like I'm always waiting for the fall. That's not love. That's fear. And I'm done building my life around what might go wrong."

"I don't want to love you like I'm afraid, either," he said, eyes wide. "I just want to keep showing up. As many times as it takes."

She blinked once, slow—like she was letting the words settle in her bones before deciding whether to believe them.

"Then get used to showing up. Because I don't do anything halfway."

When she said it, she didn't flinch.

When he heard it, he looked like a man who'd just been given a second name.

His smile was stunned, soft, almost boyish—like it had taken decades to earn.

"Jesus," he murmured, voice cracking. "What the hell did we get ourselves into?"

Morgan laughed—shoulders shaking, mouth at his collarbone.

She held him tighter.

"Something good, I think," she said. "Finally."

52

One year later, Morgan Delgado had a new closet big enough to hold her entire shoe collection—and her secrets. Kieran built it for her. Temperature-controlled, dog-proof, lit like a boutique on the Champs-Élysées.

They'd left Humboldt Park. She loved her family. But she didn't need to keep seeing Drew's ghost in her kitchen.

They talked about him once. Brief. Just enough.

"I know what you did," she said.

Kieran nodded.

"I didn't call," she added. "I didn't know what to say."

"You didn't have to."

That was it. No apologies. No excuses. Just truth. She turned off the stove and said, "We're painting the bedroom matte charcoal."

The new neighborhood was quiet. Leafy. Boring in the best way. Kieran let her choose the house—no questions asked. It was a hundred-and-thirty-year-old brownstone with a turret you could sit in and watch the Chicago skyline burn gold at dusk.

The floors creaked, the doors groaned, and Morgan loved it like a secret.

The dogs adjusted faster than they did. Daisy claimed every sunspot. Scout learned the new doorbell in a day.

She went into real therapy—EMDR, trauma work, unlearning the hustle-scars she'd once called resilience. It was brutal. It was boring. It was exactly what she needed.

She consulted off the record. No LinkedIn updates. No press releases. She showed up, listened, left before anyone could slap her name on a slide deck. It was satisfying in a low-stakes, high-control kind of way.

Then came the wedding.

Cathedral, of course—too many family members who would've rioted otherwise. Her stepdad walked her down the aisle. He didn't say anything; just squeezed her hand so tight it almost hurt. She didn't cry until halfway down—until she felt his hand tremble against hers. Pride. Worry. Love. All the things he'd never been good at naming.

She leaned into him and kept walking.

Morgan wore Elie Saab—a gown stitched out of moonlight and intention. The bodice was sculpted silver lace, cinched sharp at the waist with boning so fine it looked like a whispered threat. Tiny sheer panels peeked between the embroidery, hinting at structure beneath the softness. The skirt fell in gauzy layers that moved like mist around her ankles, each step shifting the light like a tide.

Her heels, of course, were Louboutins, spiked and gleaming like weapons.

The closer she got to the altar, the more Kieran looked at her like he was witnessing something holy.

Honestly? That would've been enough.

But then came the rest.

Ren showed up in a black sequined suit jacket with

nothing underneath, silver chains winking at their throat. Their new boyfriend—some sweet, physics grad student with glasses—hovered close behind them, looking like he couldn't believe his luck.

Naomi and her husband flew in from Jakarta, landing just in time. Naomi hugged Morgan like they were old friends in a new life, slipping a tiny carved bird into her hand.

Vee cried by the second hymn. Sloane's speech allegedly turned two aunties gay. (Confirmed via group chat by midnight.)

Sebastian danced his daughters into exhaustion, spinning them until their matching dresses puffed out like parade floats.

The karaoke machine showed up after dinner—because of course it did—and Amari handed Morgan a mic with the kind of grin that promised violence. She tried to refuse. She really did.

But he just said, loud enough for the whole room to hear, "Come on. One more for the Dead Reckoning?"

The crowd hooted. Morgan groaned. Flipped him off without any real heat.

They sang anyway. It was good. Good enough that the whole reception hall went quiet by the second verse. Good enough that a few older uncles cried into their gin and tonics.

Kieran was still staring, slack-jawed, when Morgan's mom sidled up beside him, drink in hand, and leaned in close like she was about to tell him state secrets.

"They had a band once, you know," she said, voice low, amused. "Brother-sister act. Almost got signed. Had a manager and everything."

Kieran blinked, glancing between her and the two idiots onstage laughing into their mics.

Irene just smiled, took a slow sip of her wine, and added, "Honestly? Thank God it didn't happen. Can you imagine Morgan with a record deal at nineteen? Would've either ruled the world or burned it down."

She clinked her glass lightly against his and wandered off into the crowd, leaving him stunned and a little bit in love with all of them.

THEY HONEYMOONED IN TRAVERSE. No WiFi. No alarms. Just the old cabin, tucked into the trees, the porch sagging like an old sigh.

The first morning, Morgan woke tangled in linen sheets. Kieran's hand heavy on her thigh. The dogs snoring on the floor like they'd never lived anywhere else.

She read half a novel on the porch, socked feet curled against the railing. Kieran grilled fish he'd caught that morning—proud, messy, barefoot.

They slept more than they talked. Ate like teenagers. Fucked like they had nothing left to prove. At night, they lay in bed listening to the wind in the pines, whispering promises they hadn't yet found the words for.

It wasn't grand. It was better. It was theirs.

Life settled.

Until one day, an email: LUMA Air. No fanfare. Just a name.

She didn't open it right away. But she already knew.

She wasn't surviving anymore. She was rising.

53

Morgan Delgado stepped off the plane in Copenhagen and immediately noted the difference: everything was too clean, too orderly.

The airport gleamed like a showroom—no scuff marks, no barely-working lights, no announcements crackling in from a stressed gate agent whose mic was always just a little too close. It was Scandinavian austerity with high-speed Wi-Fi. Neat lines. Symmetry. So many blonde people she started scanning for contrast like she was doing color correction in her head.

She had said yes to the invite from LUMA Air for "exploratory talks," even though she knew damn well she was already half in the bag.

The real reason? She'd been quietly obsessed with Freja Lindström for years. First woman CEO of a major European airline in the early aughts, back before she broke off and founded LUMA—a radical boutique startup that operated more like a cooperative than a corporate nightmare.

Freja was everything legacy aviation wasn't: elegant,

unbothered, actually giving a damn about the planet, and—Morgan noted clinically, like the professional she was—hot in that tall, Nordic, glacial-goddess way that made even Morgan's shoes feel self-conscious.

Their meeting started polite. Coffee, rooftop terrace, overlooking a city that didn't believe in public trash.

And then Freja said it—just dropped it like it was casual:

"We've admired your work for years. Since the beginning, actually. We're doing well—legacy carriers are flailing, the future is in boutique, progressive aviation. LUMA is expanding to the U.S., and Chicago's on our shortlist."

Morgan's pulse kicked. Hard. She knew what was coming, and it still landed like a punch lined with glitter.

"We want you to run it. CEO, U.S. Division."

Morgan blinked. Her body lit up like someone had plugged her spine into a power grid. She could feel every beat of her heart in her neck, her wrists, behind her eyes.

It was too much. It was perfect.

Her entire career—everything she'd fought for, been punished for, survived—condensed into this one elegant offer in a city that smelled like sea air and trust funds.

And Freja—cool, composed, fan-of-you-too Freja—wasn't hiring her despite the scandal. She was hiring her because of it.

"LUMA doesn't fear the media," she said simply. "We're ESG-forward, union-cooperative, and we market in truth. Your survival of public crucifixion makes you untouchable. Your knowledge and your integrity are the brand."

Morgan wanted to cry. Or punch something. Or laugh like a maniac.

Her whole body thrummed with disbelief—the stunned, slightly dissociative joy of getting offered the job, that job, in an industry that had tried to grind her into dust.

But then Freja got quiet. Her expression didn't change, but the shift was palpable.

"One thing I want to be transparent about," she said. "This wouldn't have changed the offer, but...Ava's the reason your name ended up in front of the hiring committee. She made the case. Strongly."

And just like that, Morgan's stomach dropped. Spiral: activated.

She wrapped the meeting quickly. Thanked Freja. Pretended she wasn't already halfway in love with the company.

LUMA was everything she'd once dreamed of—diverse, progressive, built to last. A company that could make money without gutting its conscience, wrapped in branding so sharp it could cut glass.

She went back to her hotel, stared at the ceiling for two hours, and finally did something she hadn't done in four years. She called Ava.

"What the hell are you doing?" Morgan snapped.

Ava didn't miss a beat.

"It was always for you. And yeah, I wanted to burn Heritage too. They took the best years of my life, but you? You're the best person for this job. I'm not asking for forgiveness. Take it or don't."

Morgan exhaled. Long and bitter.

"Yeah. I know."

She hung up.

She hated the idea of running into Ava again.

Then again, this industry was smaller than people realized. Even Enright had failed up—he was now tucked safely inside the FAA.

～

BACK HOME, the offer letter sat on the kitchen table like it had always belonged there.

The house had settled into itself—dark walls, low lighting, floor-to-ceiling bookshelves stuffed with aviation manuals and banned books. Candles that smelled like black tea and bergamot burned low.

Half the furniture looked antique, the other half looked like it might have been chosen for aesthetic but also...functional purposes.

Vee, curled into a brown leather divan in a cropped sweater and too many rings, let her gaze sweep the room.

"Is it just me, or is there a suspicious number of beautifully crafted silk ropes in here?" she said, deadpan.

"Like—decorative. But also...not not functional."

Sloane didn't even look up from the contract.

"Yes. Morgan's house is giving 'dark academia dominatrix.' Focus."

She was deep in the legalese, red pen in hand. Morgan hovered, restless.

Kieran moved through the kitchen like a man born to sauté—something warm and buttery curling through the air.

Daisy and Scout lay at everyone's feet like furry sentinels, perfectly still.

Morgan's finger hovered over the trackpad. Her breath hitched. Shallow. Fast. Her hand trembled once—small, human—and then steadied.

She clicked.

When she looked up, Kieran was already watching her.

No smile, no words.

Just that steady, quiet gaze—like he'd been waiting for years to see her choose herself.

The gray was winning now, threading through his hair

where the auburn used to catch the light. Less fire, maybe.
But more gravity. More of the man she'd chosen to wait for.

The email sent with a soft swoosh.

The room exhaled.

Even the dogs sighed.

Vee nudged one of them with her foot.

"You've seen some shit, haven't you."

Morgan smiled.

Yeah. They all had.

But this time, they'd lived.

EPILOGUE

Kieran adjusted his grip on the yoke, eyes flicking from the glide slope to the altimeter, fingers steady despite the wind shear flirting just outside the pattern. The FO was calling out checklists like clockwork. Just another routine descent into O'Hare. Except nothing about this flight felt routine.

Ping.

ACARS.

[NOC MSG: DELGADO, A.M.]

"Gate change to B19. Might want to line up for 28L instead— gives you a smoother ride and a longer stretch to slow down, Captain."

He blinked.

How the hell was she still in ACARS? She was CEO now, sure—but that didn't explain how she could drop a reroute like she still worked ops.

Unless...

Of course. She'd kept her sandbox login. The one for the test environment for LUMA's new comms interface. God-tier privileges. No one ever revoked them. No one ever would. Kieran didn't answer her back. Didn't need to. His jaw ticked—once, twice.

He read it again. She knew exactly what she was doing.

Longer stretch. Smoother ride. Time to slow down.

Runway 28L would buy him extra seconds in the flare—seconds to curse her name through gritted teeth while every inch of his body remembered how she'd looked spread for him just last night.

Gate B19 was a pain in the ass from the originally assigned runway. But this wasn't about taxi times or fuel burn. Not really.

This was her voice in his ear, her breath at his neck, while she sat five floors above ground in that glass box pretending this was about operational efficiency—and not about leaving him with tactical blue balls mid-landing.

"You want me to switch runways?" the FO asked, glancing over. Kieran's voice was calm. Always calm.

"Yeah. Request 28L. Traffic's light enough. And we've got a gate shift."

The FO relayed the request. Tower approved it. And Kieran adjusted his approach, the new runway sliding into alignment like it had always been part of the plan. He couldn't stop thinking about her voice in his ear. About the last time they were in the same room. About the sound she made when he—

Focus.

He landed like a goddamn dream. The kind of landing they teach new hires to emulate. Kissed the centerline. Minimal reversers. Taxi like butter. But inside, he was coiled so tight it was a miracle he didn't crack the tiller. They reached the gate. Blocks in. Beacon off. Flight complete.

He stood up from the seat, stretched his back, and grabbed his phone from the side pocket of his bag.

Text from her waiting. No words. Just: *Nice landing.*

He didn't respond. He hit call. She picked up on the first ring.

"Captain O'Hara," she said, voice silk-wrapped smug. "Didn't think you'd be able to read ACARS with all that blood rushing south."

"You want to play games, Morgan?" he said, voice low, the kind of low that made FO's rethink career choices. "You want to flirt over dispatch channels while I'm landing 180,000 pounds of metal?"

She didn't answer. He could hear her smiling.

"You're lucky I'm a professional."

"Lucky," she said softly. "Sure."

He leaned against the cockpit door, grip tight on the phone.

"When I see you next, you're going to remember that I can land a plane with one hand—" he paused, letting the weight of that hit, "—and use the other to teach you a lesson."

Silence on the line. Then her quiet inhale.

"Fifteen minutes," he said. "Meet me at the stairwell by the old maintenance annex. The one with the broken light."

And then he hung up. Because she'd know exactly where he meant. Their unofficial ceasefire zone. Neutral ground.

Kieran got there first. Leaned against the cinderblock wall, arms crossed, tie undone, uniform shirt rolled to the elbows like he didn't just land a full cabin and walk off the plane with a hard-on and a vendetta.

His forearm flexed as he shifted, the ink of his sleeve tattoo catching the low, flickering light. Bold black and grayscale work crept from wrist to bicep, visible now on his right arm—the one she always watched while he flew.

Compass rose. Storm waves. A new pair of wings tucked in there somewhere, half-hidden.

The flickering overhead light still hadn't been fixed.

He heard her heels before he saw her. The rhythm of someone who didn't need to run to command attention. Then—there she was. Black trousers, crisp shirt, and sharp as hell. No blazer. No badge. Just her. Morgan Delgado. Formidable. Fucking radiant. A menace.

"You're late," he said, voice rough.

"I was watching the playback," she said, stepping closer. "Smooth flare, Captain. You always perform that well under pressure?"

He arched a brow. "You want to test me?"

She was already standing in front of him, eyes dark, mouth just barely curled in that try me smirk. But beneath it —he saw it. The softness. The hesitation. The tiny flicker of vulnerability she tried to bury under snark and heels. And just like that, his anger dissolved into something heavier. Hotter. Older. He reached out, brushed his knuckles along her jaw.

"You really think you can pull shit like that and I won't come find you?"

"I was being efficient," she murmured.

He huffed. "You pick the worst ways to get my attention."

She shrugged, unapologetic. "Maybe I missed you."

Kieran didn't move. Just watched her. Every inch of her. Like he was cataloging something sacred. She didn't ask questions.

The second the words left his mouth—"Turn around. Hands on the wall."—she moved. Her palms flattened against the cool plaster, her back straightening with an elegant kind of defiance. He stepped in close, the air thick between them, humid with everything unsaid.

"Spread."

Her legs shifted, just enough. Her breath hitched. She was already dripping for him, desperate, shameless, and she hadn't even felt his mouth yet.

Kieran gathered her hair in one hand, not neat, not gentle—just enough to make her gasp as he yanked her head back. Her spine arched like a bow, her ass pressed against him, her breath coming hard. He tipped his head down to kiss her—deep and possessive, his teeth catching her bottom lip, his tongue tasting the sharp edge of her need. She moaned into his mouth, desperate, already falling apart.

He dropped to his knees behind her, tugging at her waistband, pulling the slacks down slow, savoring the reveal. Her panties were soaked, clinging to her like a second skin. He slid them down too, baring her completely. Then he breathed her in.

She smelled clean—like expensive soap, skin warmed by friction and sweat, and something uniquely hers. Subtle. Addictive. He closed his eyes, inhaled deep, and it hit him low in the gut like a drug. He didn't touch her at first. Just watched her squirm. Watched the way she shifted her weight from foot to foot like she couldn't decide if she wanted to run or beg.

Then his mouth was on her—tongue slow and deliberate, tracing her folds, teasing her clit with maddening patience. She melted. Her hips jerked back toward him, greedy. He gripped her thighs, thumbs digging in as he worked her with lips and tongue, bringing her up, up—until she was panting, fists clenched against the wall, muscles drawn tight like a wire about to snap.

And then—he stopped. Nothing. No warning. Just cold air and silence where his mouth used to be. Her scream ripped through the stairwell, raw and furious, somewhere between rage and begging.

He stood, slow and smug, wiping his mouth with the back of his hand. His voice was low, dangerous.

"That's what you get."

She spun, eyes glassy and murderous.

"I swear to god, I'm changing the locks."

He was already walking away, grabbing his jacket that hung from the stair rail. Didn't even break stride.

"Not if I beat you there first. I'm already clocked out."

And he's gone—leaving her wet, furious, and still aching for more.

MORGAN STORMED INTO THE HOUSE, heels in one hand, fury in the other. The sun was still out. She came home at a reasonable time these days. The dogs were out in the yard.

She smelled it before she saw him.

Butter. Garlic. Cast iron.

The kitchen lights were low, but the sizzle was unmistakable.

He was at the stove. Dressed in all black loungewear, barefoot, smug as sin. Turning a perfect ribeye in a cast iron pan like he hadn't just sent her into a stairwell spiral.

She dropped her shoes loud on the tile. Slammed the front door for emphasis. He didn't flinch.

"Smells good," she snapped.

"Medium rare. Ribeye. Dry-aged," he said, over his shoulder.

"Okay, I'm still mad at you."

Kieran didn't rise to the bait. Just flipped the steak with one hand, cool as ever.

"I heard you've been skipping meals again."

She froze.

He turned slightly, enough to glance at her over his shoulder. "You thought hiring me would be cute? Now I've got people reporting to me when you pull that shit while I'm in the sky."

"Who?"

Morgan was already doing the calculus of betrayal in her mind and drawing up suspects.

He grinned. They both knew he was never going to give up his source.

"You know we talked about this."

His voice dropped—low, controlled, with just enough edge to make her pulse jump. "And what happens when you do that."

She crossed her arms.

"You're really going to lecture me after that stunt you pulled?"

He finally looked at her—slow, deliberate, heat in his eyes.

"I'm not lecturing," he said. "I'm promising."

She didn't say anything. She didn't have to.

"You want to mouth off over dispatch and think I won't handle it later?" he continued, voice like silk over steel. "Fine. But don't act surprised when I make you feel it after dinner."

The threat knocked the air from her lungs. She didn't speak. Just moved—slow, deliberate. Stood behind him and wrapped her arms around his waist.

"I'm sorry," she said, mock-contrite. "I just got...a little nostalgic. From when we first met. You landed that CRJ real nice just to seduce me."

He blinked once. Then laughed—low, surprised.

"Shit. I forgot I did that."

"You forgot?" Flat. Dangerous.

He scratched the back of his neck, sheepish.

"Well. Ok. I remember mid-flare. You were on Row Eight. Arms crossed like you were already judging me. I thought, 'I'm gonna make her feel it in her spine.'"

Her smile bloomed against his back, slow and wicked. "And you did."

He turned around, closing the space between them, wrapping her in his arms.

"I love you, Morgan. Always have."

Her breath hitched. "I know. Love you, too."

"Dinner first," he murmured, brushing her cheek with his knuckles. "Then punishment. Then bed."

She tilted her chin.

"And after that?"

"Then we fly," he said. Quiet. Certain. Like a promise they'd earned the hard way.

ABOUT THE AUTHOR

Kim Serrano writes fierce romances about powerful women, stubborn love interests, and the high-stakes worlds they crash into. When not working, Kim can usually be found making aggressive to-do lists, side-eyeing corporate nonsense, and finding new ways to romanticize survival. BURN RATE is their debut novel.

ALSO BY KIM SERRANO

Hold Control

Pressure Breach

www.ingramcontent.com/pod-product-compliance
Lightning Source LLC
Chambersburg PA
CBHW050512110726
47899CB00005B/1432